Deception

by

Ola Wegner

Deception

Email address: **OlaWegner@gmail.com**

to my mum
mojej mamie

Chapter One

Mr. John Brooke stepped outside the moderately sized country manor and turned his head upward to look at the façade of the building one more time. Overall, the house was well preserved, and only in places giving the impression of squalor and neglect. It needed repairs and refreshing for sure, but it was nothing which a couple thousand pounds could not easily aid. He turned in the direction of the gardens and park. They would need some attention as well; having not been tended to for so long, they had gone wild. Who once could have thought that he, of all people, would become an estate owner one day? He shrugged his arms inadvertently, tapping his elegant top hat against his leg. Twenty years ago, he was almost starving on the streets of London.

His eyes swept over his newly acquired possessions, and strange indescribable sensation gripped his chest when he spotted the figure of a young woman walking briskly across the front lawn. Soon, her walk changed into a light run, till she reached the large tree with low branches at the edge of the park. Judging by her attire, she had to be a gentlewoman. However, if that was the case, if she was the daughter, sister or wife of one of his new neighbours, what she was doing here, alone and unescorted? Brooke's eyebrows shot upright on seeing that the lady in question started to disrobe herself. Without much thought, he moved forward to have a better view. She stood with her back to him, so he could see only that she was petite and had dark hair elegantly pinned at the top of her head. Having unbuttoned her spencer, she placed it carefully on the grass together with her bonnet, in which she had tucked her gloves.

Brooke stopped at a distance from her so as not to be noticed. He eyed her belongings resting on the ground, and her simple, but fashionably made dress. She had to be a gentleman's daughter for sure, or perhaps a relative of a well-to-do tradesman. On the other hand, as far as he was informed of the ways of the world, it was not a common thing for a well bred young lady to behave in such an unusual manner. His eyes widened briefly when she supported her back comfortably against the tree trunk, her legs slightly apart and began removing her shoes. Instinctively, he moved behind a nearby tree and peeked at her, his eyes involuntarily glued to her slim smooth legs as she was sliding the gauzy stockings off them. She put her shoes and stockings neatly next to the rest of her things. Next she straightened herself, took hold of one the lower branches, placing one dainty foot on it, and began quite swiftly climbing up the tree.

Only when her light green dress disappeared completely between the branches did Brooke move from his spot. He walked slowly to the tree, being very careful not to make a sound by stepping on a twig. Already under the tree, and after a few moments of inspecting her abandoned belongings, he cleared his throat soundly.

A soft gasp came from the crown of the three and the branches moved.

"May I ask what are you doing on my tree, madam?"

There was a moment of silence before a strong, pleasant feminine voice was heard. "Your tree? This estate is uninhabited."

Brooke looked up, trying to catch sight of the lady. "Not any more, madam. I purchased it only last week. Do you want to view the act of ownership for proof?"

The crackling sounds came from the tree, suggesting that she was climbing down. "No sir, it is not necessary for me to see your documents of ownership. Pray forgive me, sir. It was not my intention to trespass on your estate, sir. Since I understood, the manor and park have been uninhabited until now. I would never dare to enter the grounds knowing I am not welcome."

"I have not said you are not welcome. But pray, it is a bit unconventional to speak to your feet dangling from the branch." He spoke amusedly, viewing with appreciation the delicate pink soles of her small feet hanging from one of the lower branches on which she had temporarily seated herself. "I will turn around so you may preserve your modesty while descending the tree and replacing your shoes."

He turned with his back to the tree, and soon heard the leaves rustling, and then a sound thud on the ground. A few more moments passed when she spoke.

"You may turn around, sir."

Brooke did as he was told, and his eyes rested on her. She was simply charming; young too, she could not be more than twenty years old. She could not have been considered classically beautiful, but surely she was very pretty. Her eyes were the first thing he noticed; large and dark, with long thick eyelashes, almost too big on her thin face. They were the finest eyes, reflecting intelligence and kindness. They were almost black, but not quite with a touch of violet which sparkled. He could not decide on their true colour in this light. She was perhaps a bit too slight for his taste, her figure reminding him more of a little boy than a grown woman. Even though her breasts were rather small, they were pert and perky, placed high on her chest.

"Welcome to my estate, madam." He bowed deeply. "Let me introduce myself. I am John Brooke. I presently live in London, however I have decided to buy an estate in the country, but still near town."

The girl dropped a perfect, well practiced curtesy, which only assured him she was a gentlewoman. "Miss Elizabeth Bennet of Longbourn." She looked straight into his eyes.

He bowed his head again. "It is a pleasure to make your acquaintance. Longbourn, is it not an estate just four miles from Purvis Lodge?"

"Yes, indeed sir. It belongs to my father." she answered evenly.

He felt her bright eyes upon him; she was assessing him as well. "I see. And pray, if I may ask, what is so unusual in this tree that you decided to climb it?"

The lady cocked her dark, finely drawn brow. "Perhaps you have not noticed it yet, sir, but Purvis Lodge is placed on a slight rise of the ground. There is a breathtaking view over the whole countryside from the top of the trees in your park, and this one in particular is very comfortable and safe to climb. You should try one day, sir." She smiled impishly, her eyes sparkling. "It is worth the effort of climbing. I assure you."

Brooke smiled back at her. She did not seem intimidated by the whole, rather awkward situation. "I trust your word, madam, on this. Even though I have not climbed trees for well over twenty years now, I believe; so I cannot be sure if I would manage such a feat again."

Her smile grew bigger, her eyebrows raised as if in a challenge."I think that climbing trees is one of those accomplishments when once learned, cannot be forgotten."

Brooke chuckled. He didn't remember ever having this kind of conversation with a woman. She was simply adorable. "I believe you are quite right, madam."

Slowly, her smile vanished, and a more serious expression dawned on her face. "I am afraid that it is high time for me to return home, sir. I apologize once again for my unannounced visit."

"Tis been a pleasure." He bowed again. "You are invited to climb any of the trees here which you find convenient, whenever you wish." He did his best to give his voice the air of seriousness.

"Thank you, sir. That is most kind of you." she replied in the same tone, but with her eyes smiling at him, before she curtseyed again.

He stood for a long time on his spot, observing her as she was walking away from him.

***

Mr. Thomas Bennet was having a peaceful time in the shelter of his library. A book in one hand, a glass of red wine in the other; this was surely in his estimation the best possible way to spend the early afternoon. His sanctuary was placed in the corner of the house; one of the floor length windows showed the front of the house, while the other prospect overlooked the gardens which were located directly behind the house.

He glanced out to see his two elder daughters, Jane and Elizabeth, walking gracefully, arm in arm between the rose bushes, picking blooms and laying them in their baskets. Mr. Bennet smiled indulgently as pride swelled in his chest. He could not be more proud of his two eldest. Elizabeth was so intelligent and witty, he had never met any other woman who could compare with such a brilliant mind. As for Jane, she was not only beautiful and serene, truly resembling an angel with her blonde hair and the bluest of eyes, but as well sensible, perfectly well mannered and the kindest soul.

Mr. Bennet turned his eyes to the other window and his heart quailed nervously. His wife and two youngest daughters, Kitty and Lydia, were moving at great speed in the direction of the front entrance. His wife looked seriously agitated with something she must have heard in Meryton at her sister, Mrs. Phillips'. She had been deprived of the latest news for the last several days, as heavy rains keeping her home.

Very soon, there was a clamour coming from the foyer, harshly breaking the previous peace.

"Mr. Bennet!" The door to the library was flung wide open with a loud bang, and his breathless wife stood in it together with Lydia and Kitty. "Such news!"

Mr. Bennet involuntary cringed, dipping more firmly into his armchair, raising the newspaper protectively in front of himself.

"My dear, dear, Mr. Bennet!" His wife exclaimed again, dropping on the nearby chair. "You simply cannot imagine what I have heard from Mrs. Phillips!" Mrs. Bennet clasped her hands together, the dreamy expression in her eyes. "Such a fine opportunity for our girls! Such happiness for our whole family!"

Abruptly, she stood up from her place, snapped the newspaper from his hands and threw it on the floor. "Netherfield had been let at last by a young wealthy unmarried gentleman from the north of the country. His name is Bingley and,"

"He has at least five thousand pounds a year!" Lydia interrupted her mother, standing at her father's other side.

"But that is not all." Mrs. Bennet announced all thrilled. "Another gentleman, a very rich one too, a childless widower, hear me well, Mr. Bennet, a childless widower from London, bought Purvis Lodge!"

She started pacing in front of her husband. "Such an opportunity for our girls, is it not?"

Mr. Bennet shrugged. "Why should it concern them?"

"Oh, Mr. Bennet! How could you tease me so! You know very well what I mean! They should marry at least one of our girls!"

"Both of them should marry one of our daughters?" Mr. Bennet asked dryly.

Mrs. Bennet rolled her eyes exasperatedly. "Of course not! But one of them simply must marry Jane. And perhaps we could succeed in marrying Lizzy as well, on condition that she restrains herself from showing off how smart she is and how many books she has read."

"What about us, Mama?" Kitty rushed to her from her place.

"Yes, what about us?" Lydia supported her immediately. "We may be the youngest, but it is so unfair that Lizzy should be married before us just because she is the second eldest. The older gentleman can go to Jane, as he is almost as old as Papa, but the younger one, Mr. Bingley, should marry one of us."

"Yes, why should he not marry one of us?" Kitty cried, emboldened by her sister's earlier speech.

Mrs. Bennet patted Lydia's cheek affectionately and squeezed Kitty's hand. "Do not worry yourself, my dears, you are so very young, you have still time; but you are perfectly right about Jane. I think that the gentleman who bought Purvis Lodge, Mr. Brooke, that is his name, should go to Jane. He is slightly older, six and thirty, I was told, but so very rich." She leaned into her husband confidentially, her eyes going round, and mouthed slowly, lingering on each syllable. "He is worth at least fifteen thousand pounds a year." She giggled excitedly, rolling her eyes and sighing wistfully. "Fifteen thousand pounds! Mrs. Leighton's son-in-law is nothing to him." She pursed her lips with contempt.

Mr. Bennet stared at his wife, a panic stricken expression on his face. He was simply terrified. Nothing in the world would stop her now from accosting their new neighbours. Perhaps he should consider closeting himself at home for the next months?

"What is more, I was ensured by my sister, Mrs. Phillips, that he is childless." Mrs. Bennet continued with energy. "Just think, Mr. Bennet, a childless, rich, mature man. He must be in need of an heir to pass on his vast fortune. And why else would he choose to move to the country? To look for a healthy country wife to bear him strong sons, of course."

"I do not like to hear of my girls being considered as breeding livestock." Mr. Bennet remarked, taking his newspaper back from the floor and carefully straightening it.

However, his wife seemed to entirely ignore his last words. "You must visit both of them, Mr. Bingley and Mr. Brooke. They will all attend the Meryton Assembly next week. There we will introduce them to our girls."

Mr. Bennet focused his attention on his newspaper, carefully avoiding looking at his wife. "I have no intention to call on either of them."

Three quarters of an hour later, after going through a hysteric feat of great volume and rare intensity by his wife, Mr. Bennet was mounting his stallion, dressed in his best Sunday church clothes. With quiet resignation and passive acceptance, he directed himself to Netherfield first.

***

That evening, the two eldest Bennet sisters were cuddled together on the bed in Jane's bedroom. As it was their nightly custom since they had been little girls, they shared their thoughts, observations, sometimes secrets and discussed the events of the day.

"Oh, Lizzy, I still cannot think peacefully about what happened to you this morning." Jane gave her younger sister a worried look.

Elizabeth placed a calming hand on Jane's arm. "Dearest, nothing of consequence has happened. I am safe and sound. Mr. Brooke behaved like a perfect gentleman."

"Lizzy, he is a stranger to us. We do not know him at all. We cannot be sure what to expect from him." Jane spoke fretfully.

"I cannot believe you are saying such a thing, Jane." Elizabeth tilted her head to the side with a smile. "You always speak so well of everybody."

Jane's smooth forehead creased. "Lizzy, be serious. We do not speak of a situation when you are introduced to an unknown gentleman at a ball, or at some tea party, in the presence of your family and acquaintances." Jane looked seriously into her sister's eyes. "You were all alone there with him, and something not only improper but as well unwanted might have happened. And what if he had turned out not to be a gentleman?"

Elizabeth sighed guiltily and lowered her eyes to the lacy counterpane. "I did not think..."

"Lizzy, I must agree with Mama on this." Jane's voice, though still kind, sounded now more strict and decided. "You should not walk alone so far away. Something may happen to you next time. Promise me, for my peace of mind, that you will be more cautious in the future."

"I promise." Elizabeth murmured.

"And Lizzy, there is another thing." Jane raised herself higher on the pillows. "Your meeting with Mr. Brooke was most compromising; you must see this. He saw you climbing the tree and most surely removing your spencer, shoes and stockings before that. You know very well that no man should see you like this, except your husband perhaps one day. You are not ten years old any more, sister. I know you never impose yourself on men, and always behave like a lady, but such escapades like this morning can easily put a blemish on your reputation. If this reaches any of our acquaintances, there will be scandal, Lizzy."

Elizabeth bit her lower lip apprehensively. "I do not foresee any reason why Mr. Brooke should inform anyone else about this."

Jane looked thoughtfully at her sister. "If he is a gentleman, as you perceive him to be, and a discreet person, he will stay silent on the subject; but as we do not know him, we cannot be sure of this. Papa called on him today, but he was absent. Consequently we cannot fathom whether he would or would not mention anything to Papa about your meeting."

"Do you think he would?" Elizabeth asked worriedly.

"I do not know, but we cannot exclude such possibility." Jane pointed out reasonably.

Elizabeth sighed wearily. "Everything will resolve itself at the Meryton Assembly, I presume. Mama said that according to Aunt Phillips, Mr. Brooke will be attending it."

***

Elizabeth sat in front of her vanity, the maid she shared with her sisters putting the last touches on her coiffure, putting tiny yellow satin flowers into her chocolate curls. For the last few days, an unpleasant sensation of worry and guilt had made itself home somewhere deep in her chest. Especially today, before the evening of the assembly, she felt unusually unsure of herself and somehow fretful. Such sensations were not common for her. She did not like to succumb to such feelings. She much preferred to be her own optimistic and feisty, decided self. Few people could hurt her, and even fewer people offered opinions she valued and took to heart; but her sister, Jane, was surely one of such people. If Jane thought her behaviour was reproachable, there was certainly much truth to it.

She was quiet through the entire short drive to Meryton. Earlier that day, she even thought to excuse herself from attending this evening. However, eventually, she decided it to be pointless. Mr. Brooke was their close neighbour. It was unavoidable for her to meet him, if not in a matter of days, surely in the course of the next fortnight. From what she heard of him, he was a serious, mature man. Hopefully he had found her simply a silly country chit, not worth his attention. Consequently, he would not take the trouble to spread the story of their first meeting. When talking to him briefly by that unfortunate tree, she noticed him to be intelligent and possessing a sense of humour, which she was convinced, allowed him to react rather leniently to her immature behaviour. He could have very well put her into the carriage and brought her on her father's doorstep for trespassing on his grounds and climbing his trees uninvited.

She felt Jane taking her gloved hand and squeezing it lightly. Her sister smiled at her kindly, as if saying that all would be well. Elizabeth smiled back, feeling immediately built up in her spirits.

When the Bennets entered the Assembly Rooms in Meryton, it was still early, and none of the much expected guests had appeared yet. Elizabeth and Jane went to talk with their mutual friend, Charlotte Lucas. Elizabeth glanced from time to time towards the entrance, expecting, or rather dreading to see the tall, well built figure of Mr. Brooke.

Soon the new guests entered, but they were the residents from Netherfield. As Charlotte informed her and Jane, the handsome blond man was Mr. Bingley, and the tall man behind him was his best friend, Mr. Darcy. There were also two elegant ladies, the older one supported on the arm of rather corpulent gentleman. They were Mr. Bingley's sisters and the husband of the older one, Mr. Hurst.

Elizabeth's gaze, like the attention of the others, rested on the newcomers. She found Mr. Bingley genuinely pleasant, the kind of person one tends to like from the first moments of acquaintance. Miss Bingley struck Elizabeth as pretentious, and over-elaborately dressed. As for Mr. and Mrs. Hurst, it was hard to say anything binding about them.

However, it was Mr. Bingley's friend, Mr. Darcy, who caught her immediate attention. His tall, fit frame, handsome, manly features, dark looks; all these made her heart beat faster, and she felt a light blush creeping up her face. Instantly, she became angry with herself for her uncontrolled reaction to this unknown gentleman. She was confused. Such sensations were a novelty for her, as she had never reacted quite like this to any man in the past. Consequently, she took great care not to look in the direction of the handsome man from Derbyshire, as Charlotte whispered into her ear.

She was so preoccupied with her musings over Mr. Darcy, that she noticed her uncle Phillips approaching with Mr. Brooke only when they stood directly before them. She glanced at Jane nervously, and her sister replied with the tiniest of smiles and a reassuring look.

"Ladies, may I introduce you to our new neighbour, Mr. Brooke." Mr. Phillips spoke gallantly. Brooke bowed deeply, and Elizabeth felt his eyes on her. She met his eyes for only a short moment before lowering her gaze to the floor as her uncle went through introductions.

"As far as I know, you have already met, Miss Lucas?"

"I have had the pleasure." Brooke bowed politely in front of Charlotte.

"And here are my nieces, Miss Bennet and Miss Elizabeth Bennet." Mr. Phillips extended his hand to the Bennet girls.

"It is a pleasure to make your acquaintance, ladies." Brooke spoke earnestly, as first Jane and then Elizabeth curtseyed.

"We are neighbours, I believe." he enquired politely. "Your father's estate is called Longbourn, am I right?"

"Perfectly right, sir." Jane answered, glancing sideways at her still flustered sister.

"It must be less than five miles from Purvis Lodge?" Brooke seemed to direct his last question specifically to Elizabeth.

"Four exactly." Elizabeth said, looking up at him at last.

"Ah, yes, four indeed." Brooke smiled pleasantly. "I thank you, Miss Elizabeth, for clarification."

"How do you find Hertfordshire so far, Mr. Brooke?" Jane decided to take the burden of carrying the conversation, as clearly her usually very talkative younger sister had not composed herself enough yet to fully participate in it.

Elizabeth sighed inwardly with relief. It was rather obvious that Mr. Brooke had no intention of mentioning their unfortunate first meeting. She managed a narrow escape this time. No more tree climbing in the future, she promised herself. Jane was perfectly right on this. Even though the activity was enjoyable, it was still not worth the later possible apprehension and worry.

Chapter Two

"Come on, Darcy, I must have you dance." Mr. Bingley cried, standing close to his friend.

The taller man gave him a dispiriting look and spoke in an impatient, haughty voice. "I have no intention of dancing."

However, Mr. Bingley did not seem either offended or discouraged with the visible lack of enthusiasm on the other man's part. "Darcy, you cannot stand here all alone, the entire evening in this stupid manner. Come, you must dance, there are so many agreeable ladies here."

Darcy's eyes wandered over the room, a scowl upon his face. "You exaggerate, Bingley." He remarked coldly. "You danced with the only pretty woman here."

Mr. Bingley's face broke into a wide smile, brightening his pleasant countenance even more. "Darcy, she is the most bewitching creature I have ever met. But look, look!" He hushed, pointing with his blonde head in the direction of Elizabeth. "There is one of her sisters over there. She is very pretty too, and I dare say, very agreeable."

Darcy very reluctantly turned his head, and his eyes swept over the second Miss Bennet, who was sitting on the chair nearby. "Tolerable by local standards perhaps, but certainly not attractive enough to tempt me." He pursed his lips and added impatiently. "Bingley, I am in not humour to entertain ladies slighted by other men. You are wasting your time on me. Return to your lady and enjoy her smiles."

Mr. Bingley walked from his grumpy friend, leaving him on his own. Perhaps he was not aware that their conversation had been overheard, not only by the lady in question herself, but by the gentleman standing close to the chair she was sitting on as well.

Brooke eyed Darcy, who did not move from his place where he was left by his friend. He looked at Miss Bennet with concern. She had to have heard everything. Poor girl, to overhear something like this. What a fool Darcy was; a rich and spoiled kid, who most likely had everything delivered to him on a silver tray since the day he had been born. Was he blind; or just too much engrossed in himself to notice how attractive and unique the girl was? Brooke watched as Miss Bennet rose from her place and walked to Miss Lucas. She leaned closer to her friend and whispered something, glancing at Darcy at the same time. Soon both ladies started laughing animatedly, covering their mouths with gloved hands.

Brooke smiled to himself. Good for her. He more expected her to lose her wits and excuse herself to home earlier after such a blow to her vanity. Most women in her situation would do just that, he believed. She had uncommon courage; he had to admit it. He could only imagine that it was not particularly enjoyable for a young lady to hear she was not good enough for a rich, handsome man with position in the world. Darcy's blunder would cost him dearly, even if that ninny was not yet aware of it. The man had lost her good opinion forever; she would never look at him in any other way than as the most disagreeable man.

Brooke observed as Miss Lucas' younger brother walked to Elizabeth, clearly asking her to dance with him. He would gladly have asked her himself, but he was not sure enough of his dancing skills. He had never taken any dance lessons, such a thing had been simply impossible and even silly in his youth. Although he had had the opportunity to observe many dances in the last few years, he would not risk fumbling, embarrassing himself and his partner. It was a pity he could not dance with her, to feel her walking closely past and around him, touching her hand, feeling her warmth and scent, looking closely into those fine eyes. The girl had a fire in her; he was curious how she would do in bed. She was a maiden, and despite her free spirit she seemed to be well guarded and sheltered by her parents. And he was sure; never having been even kissed properly. She was not the type he had had much to do with in the past, and for certain, his late wife had been far from being a pure maiden. He usually did not fancy inexperience in the bedroom, unlike some of his acquaintances with the fixation over deflowering young virgins; the whole rather ridiculous notion of being the first. He liked active lovers, women who knew what to do in bed. However, he also knew he would have nothing against making Miss Elizabeth Bennet more knowledgeable in the art of lovemaking.

***

Elizabeth was walking briskly through the fields and meadows, taking the shortest shortcut from Longbourn to Netherfield. Yesterday morning, her sister Jane had received an invitation from Mr. Bingley's sisters to dine with them. Her mother refused her the carriage and simply insisted she go on horseback, despite the rain. Mrs. Bennet hoped Jane would get wet, and consequently would have to stay at Netherfield overnight, gaining the excellent opportunity to see more of Mr. Bingley. As a result, the notice had come this morning, that Jane had developed a serious cold. Elizabeth was angry with her mother for her scheming; and ignoring her protests, she departed to Netherfield on foot first thing after the early breakfast.

Elizabeth enjoyed taking long walks, as it was her way to rethink everything what was currently happening in her life. It was no different this morning as she hurried through muddy fields, hedges and fences to her sister.

First of all, with relief, she came to the conclusion that the possibility of the truth about her unconventional very first meeting with Mr. Brooke would leak to the public had diminished completely. News and gossip spread with the admirable speed in Meryton, and if no one had mentioned the matter for the last three weeks, it meant her tree climbing remained known only to her and Mr. Brooke. When she had met him at the Lucases last week, he had spoken with her shortly, focusing on general topics, without even the slightest reference to their first meeting.

Elizabeth was grateful for this, and put forth her best effort to be nice to Mr. Brooke. She noticed, however, that he seemed to be a bit reluctant, or as her intuition told her, perhaps a bit shy in recommending himself to his new neighbours. She did her best to engage him into conversation with other people. Even though he was pleasant enough, he spoke little, and more often chose the role of being a mere observer, rather than active participant in the discussion.

Elizabeth could not help wondering why he was so cautious. She did not doubt his intelligence and sensibility, still he stayed aside, keeping his distance. Wanting to understand him better, she eagerly listened to everything concerning him at her Aunt Philips' house, or when visiting Lucas Lodge. She had not learned much, apart from the fact that many people had been hired at Purvis Lodge, bringing the house and grounds to a proper order.

Elizabeth's mother and her friends tried very hard to evaluate whether Mr. Brooke was perhaps considering entering Holy Matrimony again, but to their great dismay, they could not figure much about his intentions in this direction. He was being watched closely, but he did not seem to pay any special attention to any lady. True, he had been seen speaking twice with two eldest Miss Bennets and once with Charlotte Lucas, but being at the same time in the company of her younger brother. No matter how much Lady Lucas and Mrs. Bennet wished for the most affluent man in the neighbourhood to show an interest in one of their daughters, they honestly could not determine his preferences. Moreover, Mr. Brooke did not dance at all with anyone. It was suspected that his wife's demise was a recent one, and he could still be in mourning.

Elizabeth's mind then moved on to the other two gentlemen, Mr. Bingley and Mr. Darcy. To her great delight, Mr. Bingley seemed to be very attentive to Jane. Elizabeth thought very highly of her sister, considering her the most beautiful person in the world, not only in looks, but in character and disposition as well. Elizabeth loved Jane fiercely, and she prayed for her beloved sister to meet a man who would deserve her. She felt that Mr. Bingley could be that man, the one who would make her sister happy. She knew that Jane liked him, and was on a straight way to falling in love with him.

As for his best friend, Mr. Darcy, her feelings were quite the opposite. She could not even understand how it was possible that such a man could have become friends with such a charming, kind and solicitous person as Mr. Bingley. Elizabeth was much affected by Mr. Darcy's remarks about her more than she would have admitted even to herself. The audacity of the man! She believed her opinion about him was definitely grounded, and she had no intention of changing it in the future. Mr. Darcy was prideful, rude and arrogant, showing no consideration for the feelings of others. It did not help that he was so dashingly handsome. Elizabeth was most vexed with herself because of her violent reaction to the man. Based on what she had read from her father's library, it was clear that what she felt for him was purely a physical attraction. She could not really understand why her heart started beating faster and her palms started to sweat every single time she saw him. She certainly did not like him, or even respect him.

He unsettled her. She ignored him the best she could, being conscious not to even look in his direction when they were in the same room. However, it turned out to be a task extremely hard to accomplish, as the man seemed to develop the propensity to stubbornly stare at her every time they were in the same room together. His blank stares only made her more furious, because she knew very well the reason for this peculiar occupation of his. He was looking at her to find some more blemishes in her. Every time Elizabeth caught his dark eyes on her, she wanted to do one thing; simply stick her tongue out at him. Unfortunately, she was not ten years old any more, as Jane had reasonably pointed out, and such behavior was not allowed anymore (and for certain it had not been welcomed by her mother when she was a child).

Elizabeth climbed swiftly over the last fence, ran lightly a few yards forward, and turning to the right on the path leading to the manor, she ran into Mr. Darcy himself. Bumping into his tall frame, she felt that he immediately steadied her, placing one of his hands on the crook of her arm and the other lightly on her waist.

She felt the blood running to her face. How could she have not noticed him? She knew very well how this happened. Elizabeth had poor sight, similar to her sister Mary, which only tended to deteriorate due to all the reading she did on the daily bases. But as her younger sister wore her glasses with pride, fancying it gave her a certain intellectual air, Elizabeth put them on her shapely nose only as the absolute last resort; not that the glasses were that necessary in her case. She could see everything within a short distance very well, and more importantly, she could read and write without them. Her vision was blurred only when looking at more distant points; no wonder she had not noticed him earlier. Moreover, when lost deep in her thoughts like a moment ago, she had the propensity to temporarily cut herself entirely from reality, being oblivious to what was happening around her.

"Are you all right, Miss Bennet?" His deep warm baritone rang into her ears, banged into her head, warmly fluttered through her chest and quivered down her stomach. She looked up at Mr. Darcy. He stared intently into her face. His hands did not leave her arm or waist for a long moment. She flashed him an angry look and backed away from him abruptly.

"I am perfectly all right, sir. Forgive me for having walked into you." Elizabeth spoke, trying at least to give her voice a pleasant note. But when she saw that he seemed to smile at her, she narrowed her eyes and cried brusquely. "Pray, believe me, it was not my intention! I was lost deep in my thoughts, and I was not looking where I was going." He still appeared to be smirking at her. "I did not notice you, sir." She stated firmly.

"I understand." He did not cease his staring, but his eyes lowered from her face down her body. She flushed even more and squared her feet apprehensively. He was looking at her muddy skirt and petticoats for sure. She almost gritted her teeth.

"I came to enquire on the health of my sister."

He cocked his bushy brow. "On foot?"

She rolled her eyes. "As you can see."

She noticed him pinching his lips as if trying very hard not to laugh. She almost seethed. She wanted to punch him. "Will you take me to her?" she stated more firmly as a command rather than asked and spirited quickly past him in the direction of the manor, walking the fastest she could. After a few moments, she glanced sideways and saw him just behind her. Being aware of his eyes at the back of her head, she accelerated her pace. Having her bonnet removed just after leaving home (when her mother could not see her from the windows any more) she was perfectly aware that her hair was simply a mess now. Her most ardent wish at that moment was to get rid of his company.

***

Elizabeth arrived at Netherfield with Mr. Darcy following almost on her heel. She ignored the pointed looks given to her muddy petticoats by Miss Bingley and Mrs. Hurst and followed the servant upstairs to where Jane was located in one of the guests chambers. To Elizabeth's great worry, Jane had a fever and a sore throat, feeling weak and dizzy because of a heavy headache. She knew very well that Jane had been perfectly all right only yesterday, and that her sister's present state was solely the result of travelling horseback completely exposed to the rain. Elizabeth was more than angry with her mother for her scheming, for putting Jane's health into jeopardy; though she was aware it was not Christian to resent one's own mother.

Mr. Bingley turned out to be most kind as a host. He sent for the doctor at once and proposed for her to install herself in the room next to Jane's, which only made Elizabeth like and respect him even more. Elizabeth could not be happier seeing how concerned Mr. Bingley was about her sister's well-being, and how intently he listened to her reports on Jane's present state. She felt that he was on a good way to start truly care for Jane.

For the three days which Elizabeth spent at Netherfield, nursing Jane, her main endeavour was to avoid Mr. Darcy and Mr. Bingley's sisters as much as possible. She could congratulate herself on not spending more that three hours a day downstairs, including the meals. She did not care in the slightest what Miss Bingley and Mrs. Hurst thought of her behaviour. As for Mr. Darcy, the situation was more complicated. The man interchangeably ignored her, not speaking with her at all (which was more than fine with her), or engaged her into conversations, which at the end easily balanced on the verge of a quarrel.

Unfortunately, her disturbing reactions to his close presence, his voice, his tall figure, did not cease in the least. She questioned herself what was happening with her. Once when she was looking through Miss Bingley's music sheets and he came behind her asking her whether she fancied to dance a reel with him (honestly what he was thinking to ask her?), she felt hot again and had to fight the almost irresistible urge to lean into his tall strong frame. It was most unsettling, and she found herself being rude to him again. She knew tall men, much taller than her; she was the smallest of all her sisters, being her mother's height, so most men of her acquaintance towered over her. However, she never wanted to snuggle into any of them. Why was he affecting her so much? She did not even like him; she loathed him. Yes, that was right, she loathed him.

Prolonged coughing was heard from the adjacent room. Elizabeth rose abruptly, lit the candle on the bedside table and checked her personal pocket watch, which she once yet, as a little girl, had received as a gift from her grandmother Bennet. It was nearly one o'clock. The coughing repeated itself, and Elizabeth got up without hesitation, and looked for her slippers, abandoned next to the bed. She wrapped a soft woolen shawl around herself, took a candle and walked to the door. The corridor was pitch dark, and she lifted the candle high, locating Jane's door.

She was reaching for the doorknob, when the sounds of someone's heavy steps came to her, sending shivers down her spine. At once the scene from a gothic novel she had been reading earlier that evening stood behind her eyes, when a heroine encountered the ghost of a tragically deceased poet in the hall of her uncle's castle. Elizabeth more than once in the past had resented her vivid imagination, which made her crawl into Jane's bed in the middle night after late evening ghost stories. Jane tried to convince her that they were just novels, and if her reaction to them was so violent, she should simply cease reading them. But Elizabeth could never resist the temptation of a new novel, which her father always ordered for her together with his own books from London.

And now she was alone in a dark, cold, unfamiliar corridor, in the middle of the night, and someone or perhaps something was climbing the last steps of the staircase, just a few feet from the place where she stood. She knew she should enter her sister's room this instant and lock the door, but she stayed unmoving, her hand stilled on the doorknob. Raising her eyes, she saw the tall figure in a white shirt, illuminated by one single candle. The individual lifted the candle up, giving itself, in Elizabeth's view at least, a demonic appearance. She saw dark holes of eyes, a stubbly chin and wildly rumpled hair. She did the same as the heroine in the novel; she screamed.

"Are you all right?" Someone's hand was firmly placed on her arm, but it was warm, not icy cold. It was big and warm. "Miss Bennet? Are you all right?"

She opened her eyes, and relief washed over her. It was Mr. Darcy, not a ghost, only Mr. Darcy. She did not feel like the smartest person in the world at the very moment.

"Are you all right?" he repeated himself, leaning towards her. Elizabeth wrinkled her nose. Was that brandy?

"I am fine." she said at last.

"You screamed." He leaned even closer, and the smell of alcohol, mingled with some other scent, perhaps sweat and something spicy hit her again.

"You scared me, sir. I heard Jane coughing, so I decided to check on her, and I was to just about to open the door to her bedroom when I heard something climbing the staircase, and then I saw…"

"Something?" Darcy interrupted her, a deep laugh rumbling in his voice. "You did not think me to be a ghost, did you?"

"Of course not!" Elizabeth denied vehemently. "I thought that some stranger entered the house."

Darcy supported himself comfortably with his shoulder against the door frame. "A stranger?" He grinned, admirable dimples gracing his cheeks, his eyes like dark velvet slits sparkling at her. "Stranger you say… I do not think so, Miss Lizzy. You know… I would say you thought me a ghost after all. You see, my younger sister likes reading ghost stories, and let us say I am rather familiar with the possible reaction of a young sensitive lady to them." He was leaning very closely now, whispering into her ear. "I saw Bingley lending you one earlier today."

Elizabeth felt shivers running through her entire body. He had to be a bit in his cups, calling her 'Miss Lizzy." She felt dizzy from his nearness and his scent. The dark curly hair peeking from his opened shirt did not help her to keep her wits intact either. She closed her eyes, focusing hard on composing herself. At last she straightened herself to her full height, though still barely reaching his shoulder, narrowed her eyes at him, and pressed her lips together in a thin line.

"Good night." she huffed, walking stiffly past him with all the dignity she could muster. She opened the door and closed it soundly just in front of his still smiling face.

Chapter Three

The day was cold, even for the middle of November, and cloudy, though it was not raining. Elizabeth was on the way to Meryton with her two youngest sisters. Jane had been convinced to stay home to prevent the possibility of her recent illness renewing itself, as the two eldest Bennet sisters had returned from Netherfield only the day before.

Elizabeth would have gladly stayed home with Jane, despite the fact that their mother had been in a rather unpleasant disposition since their arrival. In Mrs. Bennet's understanding, they had returned home much too early, wasting the opportunity to stay under Mr. Bingley's roof a day, or perhaps even two days longer. The main reason Elizabeth had decided to join her younger sisters today was that her father expected the delivery of books he had ordered from London. Mr. Bennet asked Elizabeth whether she could check at the bookshop to find out if they had arrived.

Since the regiment of militia had come to Meryton a few weeks before, Lydia and Kitty made it the most crucial and absolutely essential point of every day to walk to Meryton, hoping for the chance to meet the officers, or at least to hear some news concerning them at their Aunt Philips's home. Today, Elizabeth was walking lifelessly, slightly behind her sisters, who kept a good pace, clearly being in high spirits, evidenced by the lively giggling coming from them every few moments.

Elizabeth had little doubt what the source for such merriment was. She did not condemn entirely her younger sisters' excitement over the militia stationing in the neighbourhood; she herself anticipated making some new acquaintances among the officers and their wives. She wrapped her warm velvet cape more securely around herself and looked up at the grey skies. Her mood reflected today's weather very well indeed. She could not forget about her meeting with Mr. Darcy two days prior in the corridor at Netherfield. The shame burned in her still; she felt she behaved as the silliest goose in the entire kingdom. She was telling herself over and over again that she should not bother herself in the least about Mr. Darcy's opinion about her, and what he could have thought about her.

The worst, however, was that the morning after the incident in the hall, Mr. Darcy did not speak a single word to her; even his staring stopped. Simply, he completely ignored her, as if she had not been in the same room with him, at the same breakfast table, at all. And even though his earlier stares, and his constant contradiction of her ideas and opinions, made her angry and unsettled her, his complete indifference to her person was incomparably worse. The fact that he had ignored her, to the point of averting his eyes when looking in her direction, somehow hurt her, leaving a pain in her chest she did not want to admit. She could not help but wonder whether he remembered their meeting at all. She doubted he was so drunk as to have no memory of the previous night. On the other hand, what did she expect him to say to her? What happened was, after all, most awkward and inappropriate.

Enough of Mr. Darcy, she ordered herself for at least the tenth time since her return from Netherfield. She should be content, and feel truly blessed that such a disagreeable and arrogant man wanted to have nothing to do with her.

Elizabeth was so lost in her thoughts that she did not notice they had reached Meryton, and Kitty was asking her whether she would come directly with her and Lydia to Aunt Philips's. Elizabeth answered she would first step in the bookshop and join them later. The three sisters parted, and soon Elizabeth was entering the bookshop. The owner, Mr. Blake, had her father's delivery already prepared, asking her to check only whether the order was as Mr. Bennet had placed it. Elizabeth looked through the books and asked to have them wrapped in paper.

She was leaving the shop when she heard a man's voice calling her name.

"Miss Bennet!"

She turned in the direction of the voice and smiled, seeing their new neighbour. "Mr. Brooke." She curtseyed politely. "I am surprised to see you. We have not heard of you lately."

The man stopped in front of her and bowed, removing his top hat. "I have been in London."

Elizabeth smiled archly at him. "Bored with the country life already, are you?"

Mr. Brooke shook his head. "No, not at all. On the contrary, I must say, I feel that life in the country suits me very well indeed, but my business called me to town."

"I see. Pray forgive me; it was thoughtless of me to forget you are a man of occupation." Elizabeth spoke earnestly.

Mr. Brooke smiled, speaking gently. "No harm done. I called on your father three days ago, but you were not at home, I understood."

"Yes, I was at Netherfield, nursing my sister, Jane. She dined with Mr. Bingley's sisters a few days ago, and developed a bad cold on her way, causing her to need to stay there a few days."

"It is admirable you decided to take care of her."

"I do not consider it as something admirable to aid someone you care about, especially a member of your closest family. I would rather think it to be most natural."

"Natural you say…" Mr. Brooke spoke in a detached, as if absent voice. "You are perfectly right, I am sure. It is just my perspective may be different as I have no family at all."

"No one at all?" Elizabeth asked softly, his admission involuntarily touching her heart.

Mr. Brooke settled his eyes on some point above her head. "No, my parents died when I was a lad, and my elder sister passed away so long time ago, I hardly remember her at all. My wife and I had not children; so after she died a few years ago, I was left all alone." He ended his speech looking at his shoes. Elizabeth could sense his uneasiness. She felt for him, poor man, all alone in the world.

"I am sorry to hear it." she spoke kindly. "You, sir, leave me all ashamed of myself. How many times I have resented having four sisters, even though I love my family dearly."

Mr. Brooke looked at her at last, meeting her concerned eyes. "Is that not too heavy for you, Miss Bennet?" He pointed to her package. "Perhaps I could assist you?"

"No, thank you. These are only a few books for my father. The have just arrived from London and are not really heavy." Elizabeth smiled reassuringly. "I am on my way to my aunt, Mrs. Philips's to join my younger sisters there."

"Let me at least carry your books to Mrs. Philips's." he insisted, and Elizabeth allowed her package to be taken from her and took the man's proffered arm. Mr. Brooke made their way through the muddy main street on the short distance to the Philipses' house. Elizabeth noticed he made an effort to choose the driest path, as she managed to spare her shoes and skirts.

"During my last visit, I noticed that your father possessed an impressive library." Mr. Brooke spoke again when they reached their destination.

"Yes, books are my father's true passion, I believe. He is a great reader."

"So are you, I hear."

Elizabeth shook her head with a smile. "I would not call myself such. I simply enjoy reading"

"I see." he said and then paused as if gathering his thoughts.

Elizabeth waited patiently for what he wanted to tell her. At length he started hesitantly. "Miss Bennet, there is something I would wish to ask you, a favour." He looked at her searchingly. "But only on the condition I am not too daring…"

"You know, Mr. Brooke, I owe you." Elizabeth spoke bashfully. "I should have done it earlier, to thank you, I mean. However, there was no opportunity and I did not know how to start."

His brows creased. "Thank me?"

"You must know what I mean." Elizabeth sighed softly. "You were so gracious and did not mention to anybody about my wild and unladylike behaviour that afternoon when we met the first time. I am most grateful for this, sir. I dread to think how my mother would react if she learned about this."

Mr. Brooke shrugged his arms. "It did not even cross my mind to tell anyone about it. I saw no reason."

Elizabeth gave him a rueful smile and shook her head. "I truly do not know how such situations happen to me all the time."

"You are simply young, Miss Bennet, and possess high spirits. Therefore, there is nothing unusual in your behaviour." He spoke calmly, and Elizabeth could detect the understanding or perhaps forbearing in his voice.

"You are very kind; but what about the favour you mentioned earlier?"

"Yes…" He cleared his throat. "I know your secret now, and only this makes me brave enough to share mine. It is a shameful thing for me to admit it, but you see, I have no formal education. I was orphaned young, had to struggle with life's hardships, and in my youth had no time or opportunity to go to any school. I feel myself lacking in this aspect. Now I have more time, and can afford to buy books, but have no idea where to start. Would you help me with this Miss Bennet? Would you recommend a basic reading list in such fields as history, botany and literature; something comprehensible enough and appropriate for a beginner?"

Elizabeth beamed. "That would be my pleasure, sir." she ensured him enthusiastically. "I shall draw the list yet today."

"Thank you." Mr. Brooke spoke with what Elizabeth thought was perhaps relief.

At length Elizabeth added thoughtfully. "But, sir, I am not entirely sure whether I am the best person to help you on such a matter. Perhaps you could find someone more competent."

"I think you will suit very well, Miss Bennet." he spoke, and in such a tone that Elizabeth felt suddenly uneasy in his company.

She remained silent for a moment, her brow creased, before speaking again. "Sir, there is only one thing I must ask you." She bit her lower lip. "You see, I think it would be the best to keep our agreement only between us. Meryton is a small town, and gossip is often the sole source of entertainment here. I am afraid that some people may come to some untrue conclusions about us, knowing of our understanding, even on such an innocent matter as books." Elizabeth searched the man's face, making sure he understood her meaning. "It would be far better if no one was to learns about this." she stressed and then added quickly. "But of course, we can discuss the books you complete later on."

Mr. Brooke held her eyes for a moment before speaking easily."I think I understand your point, Miss Bennet."

"I am glad." Elizabeth replied, feeling relieved. "Pray, believe me, it is difficult enough for me to speak about this with you; but I truly believe it would be for the best. I shall have the list prepared next time we see each other, which I think should be a tea party at my Aunt Philips's next week. I will give the list to you discreetly. There will be many people, I doubt anyone should notice anything."

"That would be very good, Miss Bennet. I thank you." Mr. Brooke bowed deeply and then replaced his top hat. Elizabeth curtseyed politely, relieved that he clearly understood her meaning, and took her books from him. She watched as he walked away from her for a moment before turning to her aunt's house.

"Miss Bennet!" She heard Mr. Brooke's voice once again, calling from in front of the entrance door. She turned around. Mr. Brooke stood face to face with her, due to the fact that Elizabeth was on the second step. Consequently, their eyes were at the same level.

"Yes." She enquired politely, her eyes searching his face.

He started to speak hastily. "I think I perfectly understand your caution on the matter we have just discussed, and even admire it, and I am determined to respect your wish. Nevertheless, pray let me assure you, Miss Bennet, I would have nothing against anyone suggesting that there is something more to our agreement. Contrary to some people's opinions, I find you incomparably more than tolerable."

Elizabeth's eyes widened at these words, and her mouth opened and closed as if she wanted to say something more. Mr. Brooke bowed deeply again, and spoke quickly. "Forgive me if I have said too much, Miss Bennet." And he was gone.

Elizabeth stood on her spot motionlessly, till the door behind her back opened, and she was almost forcefully pulled inside by her aunt.

"Oh, Lizzy!" The older woman cried excitedly, still in the hall, just when the servant closed the entrance door. "What were you doing there so long with Mr. Brooke? What was he speaking to you?"

Elizabeth came to terms with herself enough to answer evenly, her voice calm. "Nothing of consequence, Aunt. He was asking me questions about books."

"Books?"

"Yes, he saw me leaving the bookshop. He wants to start his own library at Purvis Lodge, I believe."

"Lizzy, this man is worth at least fifteen thousand pounds a year. If you could catch him…"

"Aunt." Elizabeth interrupted her firmly. "Mr. Brooke spoke to me about ordering books from London. Only books. There is nothing more to it."

"But he spoke with you, Lizzy, with you!" her Aunt insisted. "The subject of your conversation is not that important. I tell you that you may have the chance to take his fancy, if you play it well of course." Mrs. Philips patted her niece's rosy cheek. "You are smart girl after all. You can do it. It is high time for you to use your mind for something more substantial than books."

Elizabeth sighed heavily in exasperation, barely restraining herself from rolling her eyes. She removed her cape, bonnet, and gloves, leaving the items to the waiting maid, and followed her aunt upstairs, where the drawing room was situated.

Lydia and Kitty were sitting by the fire, warming their feet.

"Lizzy, you shall drink some hot tea. Such an unpleasant weather we are having today." Mrs. Philips put her hand to Elizabeth's nose. "You are cold, my dear. Kitty, Lydia, make a place for your sister next to the fire."

The girls left their occupation by the mantelpiece without protest, which allowed Elizabeth to take her place there. She stretched her legs with a sigh, and held her hands closer to the fire.

"So, Lizzy, your sisters told me earlier that this cousin of yours, Mr. Collins, who is to inherit Longbourn will come to visit you." Mrs. Philips enquired from the small side table where she was preparing tea for her.

"Yes, Aunt." Elizabeth replied eagerly, relieved that her Aunt clearly did not intend to further pursue the subject of Mr. Brooke and his possible interest in her any more. "We can expect him tomorrow, at four o'clock."

"I wonder what sort of man he is." Mrs. Philips handed Elizabeth her cup. "He cannot be entirely bad as he is a clergyman, after all. But one can never know."

"The letter he wrote to our father sounded quite polite, I believe, but I am not sure whether our cousin is a sensible man."

"Well, we shall see, shall we not? Remember to bring him next week to my party."

"I will tell him about your invitation, Aunt."

Mrs. Philips leaned closer to her niece and searched her face. "You look flushed, Lizzy." She touched Elizabeth's forehead. "Are you not feverish, perhaps? You could have caught a cold from Jane."

"No, Aunt. I am fine, truly; perhaps a little tired." She straightened herself in her comfortable armchair and smiled. "The tea has warmed me up, that is all."

***

"Oh, Lizzy! Mr. Brooke really said that to you?" Jane cried animatedly. The sisters were in Jane's bedroom, talking as usual before retiring to sleep.

"Yes, he did. You can imagine my astonishment."

Jane sat comfortably on the bed next to her sister, her feet curled under her. "Lizzy, he must have some intentions toward you. I cannot explain his behaviour otherwise."

"You think so?" Elizabeth looked worriedly into her sister's eyes.

"Yes. He told you such intimate things about himself, about his past. One does not talk about such private issues with just anybody, Lizzy. Perhaps he wants you to learn more about him?"

"When you put it that way, Jane, I cannot but agree with you." Elizabeth bit her lip worriedly.

"What is more, he stayed silent on the subject of your first meeting. If he plans to court you, it is natural he does not want any blemish on your reputation."

"Perhaps we misunderstand him, Jane. There must be some other explanation."

Jane shook her head slowly. "I cannot imagine what could it be, Lizzy. He plainly said that he would have nothing against people thinking he was courting you. Moreover, why he would mention that he was lonely, without family and having no children?"

Elizabeth closed her eyes and dropped on the pillows, hiding her face in one of them. "Oh, Jane." she mumbled. "I am afraid to think how Mama will act when she finds out about this, or sees Mr. Brooke paying attention to me."

Jane rubbed her sister's back. "Mama is not that bad. She means well. She only worries about our future. We have no dowry, the estate is entailed and…"

Elizabeth sat up abruptly. "Yes, but it is different when she matchmakes you with a man you like."

"You do not like Mr. Brooke?"

"Oh, Jane, how can you even ask? I do respect him, he is a sensible man, but I have no feelings for him, certainly not like you for Mr. Bingley."

Jane blushed prettily. "Why do you think that I have feelings for Mr. Bingley?"

Elizabeth rolled her eyes, smiled, shook her head and pulled gently at her sister's long blond braid. Jane only flushed more, smiled back and hid her face in her palms.

"I like him too. He will be good for you. You will be happy with him."

"You think he will want me?"

"Jane, dearest, of course he will, and I am sure he already does. You are the sweetest, the most beautiful woman he has ever met. He would be not in his right mind to let you slip away from him."

"I hope so, Lizzy. I do hope he likes me." Jane spoke softly, yet shyly. "But let us return to Mr. Brooke. What do you think about him? You are sure you cannot…"

"He is sooo old." Elizabeth made a face, her eyes going round. "He could be our father."

"You exaggerate. He is six and thirty, younger than Uncle Gardiner."

"I know, but still… I just cannot imagine him to be someone more. I see him more like one of our father's or Sir William's acquaintances. I simply cannot see him in another light. That is simply… unthinkable. He does not affect me…" Elizabeth started, but paused and averted her eyes uneasily.

"You mean he does no affect you the way Mr. Darcy does?" Jane enquired gently.

Elizabeth felt herself turning brightly red, and she did not know where to look. At length she murmured uneasily. "How do you know?"

"Because I know you, Lizzy." Jane cupped Elizabeth's flushed cheek. "Dearest sister, at last you met a man who was able to pique your interest, which is quite a feat I believe." She spoke amusedly and added warmly. "You like Mr. Darcy."

"I do not!" Elizabeth cried fiercely. "I loath him."

Jane smiled, biting her lower lip. "Lizzy, I heard your conversation with Mr. Darcy by the door to my bedroom at Netherfield. It was not my intention to listen, but I woke up when you screamed."

Elizabeth did not comment on this; a distressed, embarrassed expression appeared on her face, so Jane added softly. "I've seen the way he looks at you. He is not indifferent to you either."

Elizabeth lifted her suddenly sad eyes. "But he is, Jane, he is." She shook her head slowly. "He said so himself. I was not good enough for him. It will be best for me not to think about him at all, to forget about him."

Chapter Four

Mrs. Thomas Bennet was a woman with a mission in her life; marrying off her five daughters. The arrival of three eligible wealthy single men into neighbourhood had understandably put her into state of utter frenzy and readiness; her mind occupied constantly with the possible splendid matches for her girls. Like a General before the decisive battle, she did the reconnaissance of the opposite side, re-evaluated her own assets and began the first manoeuvres.

At the early stage, indisputably, the top place on the list of priorities was occupied by Mr. Brooke and his fifteen thousand pounds a year, estate in the country and house in town. Mr. Darcy, with his ten thousand pounds, huge estate in Derbyshire and house in town, seized the second place, but only for a very short period of time. Offending any of her daughters, even the one she herself liked the least, was in Mrs. Bennet's eyes a capital offence. Hearing that *her* daughter was found to be not handsome enough to dance with, hurt Mrs. Bennet's personal pride and vanity. The Bennet girls had always been considered the jewels of the county after all. No one dared to argue the obvious fact. As the disagreeable Mr. Darcy was crossed out from the second location, Mr. Bingley with his five thousand a year naturally took his place.

Very soon, however, Mr. Bingley, though the least affluent of all three men, pushed himself into the position of the favourite. Though, Mr. Brooke would have been undoubtedly a better catch for Jane, his lack of any visible interest together with the frequent absences from parties and gatherings, always explained with urgent business in town, put him involuntarily in the shadows.

For the time being, Mrs. Bennet decided to invest her energy into bringing Jane and Mr. Bingley closer together. It was certainly not prudent to overlook such an amiable young man's infatuation of her beautiful daughter. Five thousand a year was neither Mr. Darcy's ten nor Mr. Brooke's fifteen, but it was still a very attractive perspective to look upon. Sending Jane to Netherfield with a strong possibility if catching cold was a masterful move on which Mrs. Bennet could only congratulate herself. As for Mr. Brooke, she did not give up her hopes on him in the least. She simply decided to wait and observe how things would develop themselves on their own in his case.

When the letter came from Mr. Bennet's cousin, Mr. Collins, to whom Longbourn was most unfairly entailed, announcing his visit, Mrs. Bennet had to quite understandably include him in her plans as well. Mr. Collins, when compared to the other three gentlemen in terms of his situation in life, was truly nothing. He was the parson of Lady Catherine de Bourgh, at the village of Hunsford, which neighboured her estate, Rosings Park, in Kent. From descriptions given by Mr. Collins, she seemed to be a truly grand and wealthy lady; one who could offer a lot to people loyal to her. Mrs. Bennet agreed that though Mr. Collins was neither particularly entertaining nor attractive, he certainly possessed other valid qualities. He already had a comfortable income, and marrying one of her daughters to him would ensure Mrs. Bennet a safe home at Longbourn till her very last days, in case she would live longer than her husband. There was no doubt that the choice for Mr Collin's wife should fall of course on Elizabeth, as Mrs. Bennet doubted the girl would make a better match anyway with her wild manners, headstrongness and peculiar interests.

Mrs. Bennet made it immediately clear to Mr.Collins that Jane was practically spoken for, delicately turning his attention to her second daughter, Elizabeth. Mr. Collins followed the clue immediately, gluing himself to Elizabeth's side and showering her with compliments. Mrs. Bennet, on her part, promoted the courtship, seating him by Elizabeth's side at every meal, and encouraging, or rather ordering her to show him the gardens, the park, or whatever spot around the village he desired to see.

Sticking to this policy, on the third day after Mr. Collins' arrival, when the weather at last seemed to improve itself, Mrs. Bennet arranged a trip to Meryton for Mr. Collins, to show him the town. Elizabeth was to be his guide, and it was decided that Jane had recovered enough and would accompany them as well. It was, after all, quite possible to encounter Mr. Bingley on the way to town or in Meryton itself. Lydia and Kitty, hearing about these plans, insisted on going as well, understandably hoping for the chance of meeting officers. Mary had no desire to meet anyone, but her mother decided she should go as well, insisting she was in drastic need of fresh air and exercise.

This decided, shortly after breakfast, all five Bennet sisters plus Mr. Collins set off to Meryton. Kitty and Lydia walked first, followed by Elizabeth with Mr. Collins close at her side, and later Jane and Mary.

Mr. Collins took an effort to stay next to Elizabeth the entire way to Meryton, making it a most unpleasant experience instead of her usual enjoyable walk. He walked by her side, very closely indeed, frequently rubbing his arm against hers. Moreover, he leaned into her face every time he spoke to her, and often stared into her face at the same time, licking his plump red lips.

More than once during the walk, Elizabeth felt simply dizzy. However, it was quite a different type of light-headedness than the one she had experienced when being close to Mr. Darcy. Mr. Darcy's scent was manly, spicy and intoxicating, but at the same time clean and heavenly; nice to breathe. That could not be said about Mr. Collins. He looked, and worse, smelled greasy. Elizabeth could not help but wonder when the last time was that he had taken a bath and brushed his teeth. However, absolutely the worst thing to bear was the perfume Mr. Collins had doused upon himself. Elizabeth was now absolutely certain that there could have been nothing worse than the unwashed male body in the combination with cheap perfume.

On entering the town of Meryton, Lydia and Kitty scanned the area for even the smallest trace of a red coat. Having noticed

Captain Denny, they rushed to him instantly, so only their red capes fluttered after them in the air.

Elizabeth, being literally sick to her stomach as a result of the close proximity to Mr. Collins, came between Mary and Jane and led them decidedly to the nearest shopping window, taking a sudden interest in the bonnets. In this way, the abandoned Mr. Collins was left with little choice other than to occupy the place behind the sisters.

Soon the Bennets girls' attention was drawn by a gentleman's voice clearly calling one of them.

"Miss Bennet, what a fortunate meeting." They turned in unison from the window display to see Mr. Bingley dismounting his horse, a genuinely happy expression on his face.

"We were on the way to Longbourn to call on you and enquire after your health, Miss Bennet." Mr. Bingley approached Jane hastily, smiling at her, his eyes taking into every detail of her serene form, his whole countenance as if beaming at the sight of her.

Jane smiled, blushed and averted her eyes shyly.

"Are you well, Miss Bennet? Are you fully recovered?" Mr. Bingley enquired earnestly, trying to meet her eyes.

"Yes, Mr. Bingley." Jane looked up at him, smiling, her colour still high. "I thank you. I am very well indeed. I believe you had not the opportunity to know our cousin, Mr. Collins?"

When Jane was introducing Mr. Collins to Mr. Bingley, and Mr. Bingley on his part was basking in the whole presence, blushes, smiles and blue eyes of his angel, Elizabeth's attention was definitely occupied elsewhere. She had promptly taken notice of Mr. Darcy on a big black horse; and now felt now familiar sensations in her stomach, as if dozens of butterflies were fluttering inside her. She averted her eyes, being very careful to look at Jane and Mr. Bingley. However, she was perfectly aware of *him* dismounting his horse and walking slowly to their group. She knew he came to stand almost in front of her, and to her great displeasure, she felt the blush creeping up her face. At length, being painfully conscious of his stubborn stare, she removed her eyes from the space somewhere between Jane and Mr. Bingley and met his gaze. It did not help. It was as if he was drawing her to him with his eyes. She forced herself to look away, and asked Mr. Bingley about the earlier discussed plans concerning a ball at Netherfield.

Then Lydia ran to them, and curtseying quickly to the gentlemen, pulled at Elizabeth's sleeve. "Come, Lizzy, come Jane and Mary. We met Denny when going to Aunt Philips' and he introduced us to the new officer, Mr. Wickham. Come, you must meet him, he is absolutely dashing." The girl squeaked excitedly.

"Lydia, we are talking with Mr. Bingley now." Elizabeth scolded the girl gently in a lowered voice.

"That is all right, Miss Lydia, I think it is high time for us to go." Mr. Bingley spoke easily and bowed his head deeply in front of Jane. "It has been pleasure to see you, Miss Bennet, in such an improved state." He then looked at all the Bennet sisters and spoke. "You should expect the invitations to the ball in a few days. I do count on your presence, ladies, and you too, Mr. Collins."

Jane started to thank Mr. Bingley on behalf on the whole family, and Elizabeth couldn't resist the temptation to glance once again at Mr. Darcy. The look at his face literally gave her shivers. He looked more than unpleasant; his face bore a scowl, it seemed a combination of anger, fury, hatred and something else she could not depict. He was not looking at her, or at anyone in their company, his eyes were set over her head. Elizabeth turned around slightly and followed his gaze, curious of the reason for this sudden change on his countenance. Mr. Darcy was clearly looking at the small group standing on the other side of the street. It consisted of her sister Kitty, Mr. Denny, and a young pleasant looking tall man with a gentleman's bearing about himself, who had to be the Mr. Wickham whom Lydia had mentioned.

***

John Brooke could not help feeling disappointed. He arrived to the Philipses quite early, hoping for the opportunity to talk with her privately. The Bennets came early too, but it was impossible for him to approach her as that cousin of hers, Mr. Collins, did not abandon her side for one single moment. Was he courting her? The man seemed to be rather ridiculous to say the least. Brooke could not imagine that Elizabeth accepted his advances. At last, Elizabeth managed to maneuver him to a card table, and then he expected she would sit nearby to give him the opportunity to talk to him. However, she chose the company of a young, handsome officer, to whom he had been earlier introduced, a Mr.Wickham. They were talking in the corner, or rather the man was talking and she was listening attentively to him. Most assuredly, she must have forgotten about their conversation and her promise of a reading list.

"Mr. Brooke, here you are." Mr. Bennet came behind his back unexpectedly, interrupting his observation of Elizabeth talking with the new officer.

"Mr. Bennet." Brooke bowed seriously and shook the other man's hand.

"You know, Mr. Brooke, that you are the main reason for my attendance tonight." Mr. Bennet spoke dryly.

The tone of the elder man's voice instantly suggested to Brooke that this conversation would be rather far from the usual drawing room chit chat. "You are responsible for the fact that I had to leave the quiet warm library tonight, dress myself up, and make my presence here."

Mr. Bennet reached into the inner pocket of his coat. "Here you are. My daughter, Elizabeth, asked me to attend and hand you this."

Brooke took the elegantly folded card wordlessly. He opened it to see it was indeed, in a tight, neat hand, a long list of books.

"Your reading list, I believe?" Mr. Bennet raised his brow in the same manner Brooke had observed on Elizabeth's face more than once.

"I thank you, sir." Brooke only murmured. For all his age and experience, he felt suddenly unsure and unequal in Elizabeth's father's presence.

"So you decided to ask my daughter to advise you on your reading education?" Mr. Bennet stated rather than asked, not looking in his direction. "Singular, I would say. Will you not agree?"

"Sir, I can assure you my intentions towards Miss Elizabeth have been, and still are, nothing other than entirely honourable." Brooke spoke hastily.

"I see." Mr. Bennet took the glass of wine from the passing servant. "I cannot say I am rejoiced to hear this." He proclaimed after taking a sip.

"Mr. Bennet, I think that I do understand your concerns as a father; but I am a serious man, and I am perfectly able to support a family." Brooke spoke nervously. He had not perceived such a turn of the conversation. Mr. Bennet's eyes were wandering all over the room, not meeting the other man's gaze directly, which only made Brooke more uneasy. Elizabeth's father seemed to act as if he had been speaking of some inconsequential, indifferent matter, not about his favourite daughter's possible future.

"I have not said this against you, Mr. Brooke." Mr. Bennet spoke after a while. "I may not know you very well, but you seem to have more sense than most of my acquaintances. But you see, Elizabeth is my beloved little girl. Consequently, it is extremely hard for me to accept the fact that she will one day be taken from me by some man, that she will put this man first before me."

"Is it not a natural course of life, Mr. Bennet?"

"You will understand me one day when having a daughter." Mr. Bennet turned to his companion at last, looking straight into his face now. "Mr. Brooke, it is not my intention to do anything which could promote her leaving my home any time soon and getting married to any man. Unless of course…"

Brooke's eyes narrowed. "Unless?"

"Unless she wants to have you. You understand what my meaning is? Unless she will be determined to be bound to you. But I can tell you even now, the chances are small for that." Mr. Bennet pronounced flatly, looking pointedly across the room at Elizabeth laughing animatedly at something Mr. Wickham was telling her, her eyes sparkling, her cheeks flushed.

"Perhaps you should set your eyes on someone closer your age." Mr. Bennet spoke before nodding his head slightly and walking away to talk with Sir William Lucas.

***

"That was a very pleasant evening, was it not, Lizzy?" Jane asked, unpinning her long hair while sitting in front of her vanity.

"Yes, that is true." Elizabeth arranged herself on her sister's bed, her knees hugged to her chest, her chin supported on them. "It is only a shame Mr. Bingley did not attend."

"I wonder why, Aunt Philips ensured me he received the invitation." Jane met her younger sister's gaze in the mirror.

"I think it is all his sisters', and of course, Mr. Darcy's doing" Elizabeth spoke confidently. "They all think us to be inferior to them."

"Lizzy, I am sure it is not like that. Perhaps they had some other reason not to attend, or a prior engagement." Jane spoke gently.

Elizabeth scrambled out of bed and walked to her sister's side. "Oh, Jane you are too good. You always think so well of everyone." She took the hair brush and started combing through Jane's thick long hair. "Have you forgotten what Mr. Darcy said about me? I am sure that is his opinion about our entire family, relation and acquaintances. As for Mr. Bingley's sisters, you cannot deny that Miss Bingley clearly hopes to become Mrs. Darcy in the future. She tries so very hard to engage his attention, fawning over him all the time and agreeing with everything he says. Consequently, she will support him in everything."

"I found Caroline quite pleasant and amiable, Lizzy."

"I think she is amiable only when she wants to be, when she see some advantage for herself in it. And I feel that Mr. Darcy is not a good man at all. I cannot believe him to be friends with Mr. Bingley." Elizabeth wanted to say she was afraid Mr. Darcy could influence his friend to discourage him in his attentions to Jane, but she stayed silent, not wanting to upset her.

"Lizzy, I agree Mr. Darcy is rather reserved, and perhaps a bit too prideful, and he should certainly guard his tongue more; but it is perhaps too little to consider him a bad man." Jane admonished gently.

"Jane you will change your opinion upon hearing what Mr. Wickham told me about Mr. Darcy."

"Mr. Wickham?" Jane looked up at Elizabeth. "The officer you talked to for so long?"

"Yes, Jane. Apparently he knows Mr. Darcy very well, and I think Mr. Wickham is the main reason why Mr. Darcy did not attend tonight."

"How can that be?" Jane turned on the stool, her eyes wide and curious.

Elizabeth took the chair and sat in front of her sister. "Mr. Wickham told me that his father was a steward at Pemberley, Mr. Darcy's family estate, when Mr. Darcy's father was alive. Clearly the old Mr. Darcy was very fond of Mr. Wickham. He was Mr. Wickham's godfather. He sent him to school and promised a living in the future, a parsonage at the village of Kympton. But after his father's premature death, Mr. Darcy, probably jealous of the affection the old Mr. Darcy had for Mr. Wickham, flatly refused the long promised living, consequently reducing Mr. Wickham to near poverty and making him seek his luck in professions other than the church."

Jane stayed silent for a while after her sister finished her tale. At last she spoke, her delicate eyebrows creased. "Lizzy, I am not entirely sure about this history Mr. Wickham told you. I doubt Mr. Bingley could be friends with such a man, the man who would have been able to deliberately defy his late father's wish, ruining someone else's future through his actions. There is something wrong in this." Jane shook her head. "I think we need more proof to give faith into Mr. Wickham's story about Mr. Darcy."

"I have all the proof I need." Elizabeth spoke confidently. "I saw the way Mr. Darcy looked at Mr. Wickham in Meryton. Jane there was such a vengeance in his eyes."

Jane turned her head to the side, a thoughtful expression on her face. "But Lizzy, is it not strange that Mr. Wickham told you all this in the first place? Why did he do that? I think it is unusual at least to inform on the subject one's misfortunes a complete stranger."

"Perhaps he needs some sympathy, somebody who would listen to him?"

Jane looked up at her sister's searchingly. "Mr. Wickham is a very attractive man, is he not? Good looks and engaging manners, that is a rare combination, I dare say. He paid a lot attention to you, Lizzy; it must have been a pleasant feeling."

"Well, it was a pleasant feeling indeed." Elizabeth admitted reluctantly but with a small smile playing on her lips.

"What about Mr. Darcy?" Jane enquired tentatively.

"What about him?" Elizabeth spoke brusquely, shrugging her arms dismissively.

"Lizzy, I am not blind. I saw the way he looked at you, and you at him, the other day when we met the gentlemen from Netherfield in Meryton.'

Elizabeth stood up abruptly and started pacing the floor in front of her sister. "Oh, Jane! I am so displeased with myself for the way I react to him every time I see him." She threw her hands up in an exasperated gesture. "I cannot understand the feelings he evokes in me, I cannot understand myself. I do not like him, I do not want to like him! I do not want to care what he thinks of me, or if he thinks at all. I simply must bury this inside myself. Thankfully after what I was told about him from Mr. Wickham, I think it will not be difficult at all."

Jane walked over to Elizabeth and being considerably taller, drew her to herself, placing her sister's head on her shoulder. "Lizzy, just promise me to be cautious and keep your eyes wide open when it comes to both Mr. Wickham and Mr. Darcy. I do not want you to be hurt, dear sister."

Chapter Five

Elizabeth stared critically at her own reflection in the vanity mirror. Not all of her youngest sister's ideas were bad after all. Lydia had found the hairstyle in a magazine borrowed from Aunt Philips, insisting that Elizabeth should arrange her hair this way for the upcoming ball at Netherfield. Elizabeth glanced at herself once again. She had to admit she looked truly pretty. Additionally, her face did not seem so thin in the new coiffure.

Standing up, she walked to the floor length mirror. She turned around, checking whether her dress looked well; but everything seemed to fit perfectly. If only she had more of a womanly figure! Lydia and Kitty, though much younger than she, already had more womanly shapes. Elizabeth was afraid that she would always stay like this, with a body of a ten year old lad. Her mother had said many times that she would probably gain a fuller figure only after giving birth. Hopefully the new dress she was to wear today for the first time was stitched under the bosom in such a way to create the impression they were fuller than they really were.

"Lizzy! Lizzy!" Mrs. Bennet's high pitched voice was heard from downstairs.

Elizabeth grabbed her gloves and an elegant ivory cape, leaving her room hastily.

"I am coming, Mama." She cried, running down the stairs.

"We are only waiting for you, Lizzy." Mrs. Bennet scolded her. "Do you want us to be late? Do you, do you?"

"I am sorry, Mama. I have lost the sense of time."

Mrs. Bennet only rolled her eyes, replying nothing to Elizabeth's last words. She directed herself to the library to fetch her husband, who though already dressed for the evening, decided to cave himself there till all his women folk were ready to go.

Elizabeth exchanged the amused look with Jane, seeing her parents leaving the library a moment later, or rather, to be precise, her mother dragging her father out of it.

"Do I really have to attend tonight?" Mr. Bennet asked meekly with the expression of a martyrdom on his face.

"Of course you have to attend!" His wife hissed sharply, smoothing the lapels of his black evening coat. "This is perhaps the most important evening in the life of at least one of your daughters. What if Mr. Bingley decides to propose to Jane? You have to be there to give your consent."

Mrs. Bennet left her husband's attire in peace and walked over to examine the appearance of her daughters, standing in a line next to the staircase.

Mr. Bennet walked to Elizabeth. "You look very lovely, my dear."

"Thank you, Papa." Elizabeth smiled. "You look very handsome yourself."

Mr. Bennet waved his hand dismissively at the compliment. "I am only afraid that I will not be the only man tonight to notice how charming you are." he said somewhat sadly, his voice resigned.

"Papa…" Elizabeth started to speak, but stopped as the only too familiar of late, truly unique smell came to envelop her. Mr. Collins was just behind her, leaning over her shoulder.

"Fair cousin, Elizabeth, you look extremely charming tonight." Mr. Collins gave her a half smile and waggled his bushy eyebrows in what Elizabeth presumed was intended to be a seductive manner. "You are like a spring day on this cold November evening, like a little lark which lightens our vision with its bright feathers, like the Grecian goddess who stepped down on this mortal vale of tears to enlighten our existence." Mr. Collins spoke, almost forcibly taking her cape from her and putting it on her.

"I thank you, Mr. Collins." Elizabeth murmured, concentrating on breathing through her mouth, instead of her nose. She was sure her cousin had used some new scent today, but at the same time, clearly neglecting the bath. It was a blessing she had eaten little today, or she would be afraid of it returning. Mr. Collins stepped toward her decidedly again, flashing an inviting smile. Elizabeth stared at the parson's teeth, seeing there clearly, a trace of vegetable from their early, light dinner.

"Let me help you to put those gloves on your lovely, little hands." Mr. Collins snatched her gloves from her hand, and grabbing one of her hands, bent his head, sucking his wet lips to the top of her palm. Feeling an unpleasant wetness on her skin, she stopped her eyes on the top of Mr. Collins bent head, noticing the emerging bald spot for the first time.

"I think that is quite enough, Mr. Collins." Elizabeth heard her father's voice behind her, and saw Mr. Collins was gently, but decidedly, pushed away from her by Mr. Bennet.

"My daughter is perfectly capable of putting her own gloves." Mr. Bennet said sharply, handing Elizabeth her gloves after retrieving them from the parson.

Elizabeth thanked her father wordlessly with her eyes for his assistance, and walked hastily to Jane's side. Having finished putting her gloves on, she thought whether she more anticipated or perhaps dreaded this evening. The fact that she had promised to dance the first two dances with Mr. Collins definitely deflated her spirits. She only hoped he would keep her distance from her, otherwise she could faint simply by inhaling his aromas. Although her cousin praised himself on his dancing skills, and especially on the lightness of foot, Elizabeth seriously doubted his accomplishment in the area. His usual heavy walk and the propensity of bumping into the furniture made it difficult to imagine him as a good dancer.

Fortunately, after the torture of the first two dances, she would be free to dance with someone much more amiable, like Mr. Wickham for instance. Since the evening at the Philipses' she had met him twice, and each time, he was all charm and politeness. Elizabeth had enjoyed his attentions. It was definitely an uplifting feeling that he seemed to find her company more agreeable than her younger sisters' or even Jane's. Moreover, he did not ignore her like a certain gentleman did, but always looked for the immediate place by her side, often sharing his life's stories with her. Mr. Wickham had talked to her extensively about Derbyshire and the vast Pemberley estate where he had grown up. He had not acknowledged it directly, but she easily guessed that his father had been much more than just a steward there. The old Mr. Wickham seemed to have all but run the estate by himself, being the one responsible for its grandness and richness. Elizabeth perceived as well, that Mr. Wickham had hoped in the past to continue his father's life work, which of course turned out to be quite impossible, due to a certain person's selfish actions and petty-mindedness.

As for Mr. Darcy himself, Elizabeth firmly decided not to pay even the slightest attention to the man. She would ignore him and do her best to put an end to this irritating infatuation she seemed to somehow have developed for the man.

With their arrival at Netherfield, Elizabeth and Jane squeezed their hands and exchanged excited looks. Soon Jane was engaged by Mr. Bingley, who seemed to only be waiting for her to arrive, standing in anticipation near the entrance to the main ballroom. Elizabeth left Jane with Mr. Bingley and walked into the crowded room, standing on her tiptoes and narrowing her eyes to see better through the sea of people. Bringing her eyeglasses today was understandably out of question, but having a few inches more height would sometimes be very helpful. She did a little hop in attempt to see over the head of Colonel Forster's wife, who had adorned her head with three feathers tonight.

"Looking for someone, Miss Bennet?" The male voice behind her asked. Mr. Darcy of course; she did not have to even turn around to know it was him. She would have probably recognized the deep, slightly throaty baritone anywhere, not to mention the shivers which ran up and down her spine clearly indicating his presence.

"Mr. Darcy." She turned around, greeting him coolly, without a smile.

He stared at her as usual, and she raised her brow at him in a challenge. And he… Elizabeth took a closer look at his face, yes, he smiled, shaking his head a bit at her.

"You look very lovely tonight, Miss Bennet." He spoke at last, and Elizabeth's breath was taken away by his warm tone. He leaned slightly into her, and the volume of his voice dropped considerably, so she could barely hear him. "Beautiful, I would say."

Elizabeth narrowed her eyes at him, and without giving a second thought to what she was to say, in a moment, the words came out. "Beautiful you say, but only by the local standards, I am sure." Darcy eyes widened and he flushed. Elizabeth enjoyed herself for a long moment, observing his dumbfounded embarrassed expression. He was closing and opening his mouth interchangeably as if trying to say something.

"Would you not agree, Mr. Darcy?" she said harshly; and not waiting for his reply added hastily. "Excuse me, Mr. Darcy, but I see my friend Miss Lucas."

She left him alone and did not glance back at him at all until she reached Charlotte.

"Lizzy!" Charlotte kissed her cheek and clasped her hands into hers. "What did you say to Mr. Darcy?" She whispered into her ear. "He looks almost devastated standing all alone on the exact spot where you left him."

"He does?" Elizabeth turned her head slightly and glanced with the corner of her eye at the tall man.

"Yes, Lizzy. Like an abandoned puppy."

Elizabeth laughed shortly. "Oh, Charlotte. A puppy? Please." She rolled her eyes.

"What happened?"

Elizabeth shrugged her shoulders. "Nothing, I just delicately let him know what I think of him."

Charlotte furrowed her forehead and spoke earnestly. "Elizabeth, be reasonable. It does not happen everyday that a man with wealth, position in the world and intelligence pays attention to you."

Elizabeth only lifted her chin higher in reply to her friend's words and changed the subject. "Have you seen Mr. Wickham?"

"Mr. Wickham is not here today." Charlotte spoke confidentially, leaning into her. "I spoke with Mr. Denny earlier, and he told me Mr. Wickham could not attend tonight as he was detained by some urgent business in town."

"Urgent business in town!" Elizabeth cried, narrowing her eyes and tightening her lips. "I cannot believe it, Charlotte. I am sure it is all Mr. Darcy's doing. He must have convinced Mr. Bingley not to invite Mr. Wickham at all."

"Lizzy, that cannot be true." Charlotte whispered with energy. "Mr. Bingley invited all the officers after all. Moreover, I do not think you should give so much faith to that woeful story which Mr. Wickham delivered to us. Mr. Darcy is a respectable man with position in the world, and the whole story may very well look differently from his point of view. Perhaps Mr. Wickham tried in some way to abuse his father's friendship with the old Mr. Darcy."

"Charlotte, how can you say this?" Elizabeth cried with a force. "There was truth in Mr. Wickham's words, in his every expression. I think that..." She wanted to say it was surely all entirely Mr. Darcy's fault, but Charlotte grabbed her hand almost painfully, squeezing it. "Elizabeth, you must see reason. Do not be so obstinate! By ignoring Mr. Darcy, you may lose the best match that may ever happen to you."

Elizabeth wanted to retort hotly to her friend's words, but she saw Mr. Collins approaching them.

"Are you hiding from me, my dearest cousin?" Mr. Collins asked with a pout on his too full lips, standing in front of the ladies.

"No, of course not." Elizabeth spoke tiredly, taking an involuntary small step back. "Mr. Collins, may I introduce you to my dear friend, Miss Charlotte Lucas. Charlotte, this is my cousin, Mr. Collins."

The parson bowed deeply. "A pleasure to make your acquaintance, madam. I see that Hertfordshire should be acclaimed the garden of England, taking into consideration the number of beauties which this county has nurtured in its womb."

Elizabeth looked curiously at her friend, checking how she would bear Mr. Collins' nonsense, but Charlotte merely smiled and curtseyed politely.

"Fair cousin." Mr. Collins turned to Elizabeth, rudely leaning into her face. "I believe the first dance will start in a short time. You do remember your promise of the first two dances?"

"Of course, Mr. Collins. How could I have forgotten?" Elizabeth spoke with resignation, taking the professed arm, trying desperately at the same time to keep her distance from the man.

Two dances with Mr. Collins was strictly speaking, a nightmare. He mistook the steps and figures far too many times, almost trotting over the other couples with his heavy bulk. He held her hand much too long, squeezing it almost painfully. At the end of the second dance, Elizabeth was tired and humiliated, as a woman could only be with such an ungraceful partner. Furthermore, she felt sick to her stomach because of her cousin's scent, being almost on the verge of returning what she had eaten earlier at home. Lastly, she suffered from a considerable pain in her left foot. Mr. Collins had stepped on it with the force of his two hundred and fifty pounds of weight at least, she was sure.

The moment the music ended, she excused herself from her cousin's company under the pretence of refreshing herself. She remembered well from her previous visit that the library was situated close to the ballroom, but she rejected the possibility of going there as some gentlemen likely occupied the room while their wives and daughters danced. Fortunately, she remembered that just a few steps from the library was a small music room where she could rest undisturbed by anyone.

She quietly removed herself from the ballroom, trying not to catch anyone's attention. Ignoring the persistent pain in her foot, she managed to reach her destination. Thankfully, the door was not locked. She entered and sat on the small sofa with a relieved sigh. She still felt hot and dizzy even though the room was cold, as the fire was dying. Raising herself up with an effort she walked a few steps to open the widow. That was better, the fresh cool night air. She returned to the sofa and unlaced the ribbons of her left shoe. She could see through the gauzy stocking she wore, that her foot was swollen. Oh that odious Mr. Collins! How was she to dance now?

Suddenly the door cracked open and she startled in place, her hand coming to her chest.

"Miss Bennet?" The dark head appeared in the door frame.

"Mr. Darcy, what are you doing here? You should not be here, sir." Elizabeth spoke surprised, frowning. However, the man was clearly not paying attention to her words. He closed the door after himself, and the next moment he was kneeling in front of her, taking her uncovered foot in his big hands.

"Mr. Darcy!" she protested, trying to take her foot away.

"Allow me." His warm hands stopped her foot gently but firmly. "I know something about this. My sister sprained her ankle seriously a few years ago. It renews itself from time to time; every time she missteps." Saying this, he was gently probing her foot.

"It is not broken, just seriously bruised, I believe." he said gently after a moment, his hand still lightly massaging her foot. "You will probably have some heavy bruising here tomorrow. That cousin of yours should not be permitted on the dance floor." he added angrily, and then his tone softened. "You could have had one of your bones broken; you are so delicate."

Elizabeth flushed and stayed silent. She was getting warmer and dizzier with each passing moment. His eyes were staring into hers, and she could smell him and feel his warmth, his hand absently stroking her foot which still rested in his hands.

At last she reluctantly broke the eye contact with him. "Mr. Darcy, I thank you for your assistance, but I am much better now." She snatched her foot from his grip and began putting her now too tight shoe on her already considerably swollen foot.

When she stood up and hissed in pain, accidently supporting her weight on her injured foot, Mr. Darcy was beside her instantly, taking a firm hold of her arm. "You cannot go back there. Let me arrange to place you in one of the guest rooms upstairs and call the doctor to make sure that nothing is broken." She felt his arm coming around her waist. "I will carry you. You cannot move on you own."

Elizabeth almost surrendered to the temptation of leaning into the strong frame of the man beside her, but then she remembered her mother. If any of this reached her, there would have been no mercy. Her mother would do everything in her power to make Mr. Darcy marry her. She dreaded to think how her mother would act. She turned into his arms slowly to see his face, still supporting her weight on his arm.

"Mr. Darcy, I thank you for your kindness, but you must understand we cannot possibly be seen leaving this room together. Someone may observe us, and it would put both of us in a very awkward situation." She spoke earnestly, staring into his face, checking whether he took her meaning.

He looked at her for a moment, his expression clouded before the understanding of her words seemed to dawn on him. "I see, Miss Bennet." He bowed his head seriously with visible respect. "I can only admire your integrity."

Elizabeth felt pleased with his words of praise, and the look of admiration in his dark eyes, but she only said, "Mr. Darcy, I simply want to avoid putting both of us in a difficult position."

Darcy stepped a bit closer and spoke worriedly. "Still, you should not walk on your own."

"Mr. Darcy, I will manage." She smiled bravely. "I saw the settee nearby in the corridor. I will hobble there somehow, and later ask someone to fetch my father. He will take care of me, as I am rather sure I will not be able to dance any more tonight."

"I am sorry to hear that, and I am even sorrier that you have been hurt." He spoke earnestly. "I had hoped to dance with you." He looked almost shy saying the last words.

She blushed involuntarily, her heart beating faster. "You had?"

He leaned into her, as if wanting to say something, indescribable emotions crossing his face, when there were heard loud voices outside.

"I had better leave now. Someone might have noticed my absence." she said quickly. She supported herself heavily on his solid frame, and he helped her to walk to the door. "I will ask you, sir, to stay here a few moments more, so no one shall think we were together in this room."

"Of course." Darcy said, opening the door for her, but in such a way that he could not be visible by anyone outside.

"I thank you." she whispered, and closed the door after herself quietly.

She had barely walked, or rather hobbled a few steps outside the music room when she saw Mr. Brooke. He stood by the entrance to the library, as if waiting for someone.

"Miss Bennet." He rushed to her side. "Are you all right?"

Elizabeth looked up at him, surprised. "Yes, I am well, perhaps not entirely well, but sir what are you…?" She wanted to ask what he had been doing here, and what his questions had meant, but he interrupted her. "Miss Bennet, are you all right? Has someone offended you?"

Elizabeth glanced at the man confused. "Offended me?"

"Yes, I was afraid that someone might have upset you." He looked into her face closely.

"Sir, I am afraid I do not understand your meaning."

"I saw Mr. Darcy entering the music room earlier."

Elizabeth flushed and bit her lip worriedly. "Mr. Brooke, pray believe me, I did not invite him. I hurt my foot during the dance and I wanted to rest somewhere. I thought about the music room, thinking I would be undisturbed there, but Mr. Darcy entered after me and…"

"Did he hurt you?" He interrupted her again.

Elizabeth creased her brows and spoke slowly, trying to guess the reason for all these strange enquiries. "No, he offered his help, he was very kind."

Mr. Brooke let a deep sigh. "Thank God."

"I do not understand."

"Miss Bennet, I must tell you something." Mr. Brooke led her to the settee near the library door, speaking quickly in a hushed tone. "I do not want you to be hurt in any way by Mr. Darcy."

"By Mr. Darcy? But he had never…"

"I have seen the way he looks at you, and I am afraid he bears intentions towards you which are not entirely honourable. I know for sure he is not the man a young woman like you should trust. He keeps a mistress in London, and I know for sure that a few years ago he seduced a young girl and abandoned her pregnant with his child. There is no time to go into details of this now, but I know about it because the girl's late father was once my partner in business. Mr. Darcy refused to marry her because of her lack of connections and substantial dowry, I believe."

Elizabeth shook her head, her eyes wide. "I cannot believe that. It is horrible."

"Yes, I know, it is hard to believe. Miss Bennet, I am telling you this sad story only because I want you safe and unhurt. I would never forgive myself if you were to be his next conquest."

"I thank you, Mr. Brooke." Elizabeth spoke slowly. "I shall be careful. I am simply… speechless and astonished."

"I can well believe that."

Elizabeth was silent for a long moment, the thoughts running through her mind with great speed before she spoke at last. "Mr. Brooke, could I ask you a favour? Would you be so kind to fetch my father? I am afraid the swelling in my foot makes me unable to participate in the ball."

"Of course, Miss Bennet. I saw you father in the library with the other gentlemen. I shall fetch him directly. But you must stay here and not move. You should not put weight on your foot."

She watched with unfocused eyes as Mr. Brooke walked away from her and entered the library. After what Mr. Wickham had told her about Mr. Darcy, Mr. Brooke's revelations should not surprise her in the least. But still, she could not give faith to them. She could not believe that Mr. Darcy might have had an intention of seducing her or imposing himself on her in any way. Back in the music room, his behaviour had been all that tender and kind. He had seemed to be genuinely concerned for her.

"Lizzy, my dear, what happened?" Her father's worried voice brought her back to reality. She looked up to see her father standing over her, Mr. Brooke and Mr. Bingley behind him.

"Nothing serious, Papa, I simply mistepped during dancing, and now it hurts when I walk."

Mr. Bennet stroked her head gently. "I will take you home."

"I shall order your carriage immediately." Mr. Bingley proposed, his voice full of concern. "The maid will fetch Miss Elizabeth's coat, and perhaps she would like to rest in my study till the carriage is ready. There is a comfortable couch there, and the fire should be still up."

"I thank you, Mr. Bingley. That is very kind of you." Mr. Bennet spoke distractedly, not looking at the younger man, only at his daughter.

Elizabeth smiled at Mr. Bingley, and tried to stand up on her own, but when she sighed quietly and frowned, her face in pain, her father took a firm hold of her arm.

"You cannot walk, child."

"No, Father, I will manage." Elizabeth assured him, but Mr. Bennet was already bending, taking her into his arms.

"Father, I am too heavy. What about your back?" she protested.

"I am not so old yet, daughter." He pretended offence, carrying her to the study down the corridor, pointed out by Mr. Bingley, who walked first in front of them. "I can carry such a slight thing like you. Besides you do not weigh much more than when I carried you last time, when you fell off the tree in the park at Longbourn. Do you remember?"

Elizabeth blushed in mortification, knowing that Mr. Bingley and Mr. Brooke heard her father's words; though Mr. Brooke should not be surprised in the least, taking into consideration their first meeting.

When she turned her head slightly, looking over her father's arm, she saw Mr. Darcy standing by the door to the music room, looking at her. His expression seemed to reflect only worry and genuine concern; but Elizabeth averted her eyes quickly from him. She was confused. She did not know what to think about any of this at all.

Chapter Six

Elizabeth rolled to the other side of her bed and glanced outside the window, her eyes meeting grey skies. It was nearly eight o'clock in the morning, but she did not fancy getting up yet. She hurt, and it was not due to her injured foot, which did not bother her at all when she did not move it, like now. She felt a pain inside her somewhere between her stomach and chest, and the squeeze in her throat. Facing the truth was not a pleasant thing, but she could not deny her feelings any more. She had obviously managed somehow to fall in love with a man she had known for just two months, and who, according to many, was not only rude, arrogant and unsociable, but also unfeeling, selfish and cruel.

Elizabeth knew that gentlemen had children outside wedlock. It was something quietly accepted by the society. She had a prime example of such a situation example in her own family. A few years ago, Elizabeth had accidentally overheard a conversation between her parents; one that she should not have heard. Her mother was talking with her father about her sister in law, Mrs. Gardiner. To be precise, Mrs. Bennet was talking to her father, as Mr. Bennet was not participating as usual. Elizabeth had been shocked to learn that Mrs. Gardiner, her beloved aunt, was in truth a natural daughter of some young reckless aristocrat and a governess. Her mother had died in childbirth, and she had been raised by her aunt, her mother's sister, being well provided for by her grandfather, the earl, in a quiet little town in Derbyshire. Her mother had not managed to say much more, because her father interrupted her, demanding she not speak about it. However, it was enough information for Elizabeth. She perceived that Mrs.

Gardiner's family had chosen such a distant county to keep the child far away from London's society, perhaps wanting to prevent more gossip. Elizabeth was well aware that her aunt had been even given a substantial dowry, which together with what Uncle Gardiner had received from his own father, enabled him to start a very profitable business.

The history of Aunt Madeline was very sad, of course. She had never met her parents, even thought it was possible that her father was still living somewhere. But at least her father's family had not rejected her entirely, they had considered her future, ensured she had been safe and well cared for. Elizabeth always admired how accomplished Aunt Gardiner was. She stared at the picture hanging on the opposite wall, showing the view from Oakham Mount. It had been painted years ago, when Mrs. Gardiner visited them for the summer, pregnant with her first child. Uncle had been very busy in London then, his company developing rapidly at that time.

The doctor had recommended Aunt Madeline stay for the period of pregnancy in the country, with better food and fresh air. Elizabeth remembered well that Uncle Gardiner had asked her and Jane to take care of his wife during his absence. Two little girls, had walked with their aunt every day to Oakham Mount, helping her to carry the easels, paints and brushes.

Aunt Madeline did not draw much nowadays, with several little ones to care for, but Elizabeth was aware now of something she had not noticed as a child. Mrs. Gardiner must have been professionally trained in her youth, not only in drawing, but also playing the pianoforte and speaking French and Italian. Such accomplishments were perhaps common among ladies in London, but not so much for a girl living in a small town in the north of country. Her aunt's excellent education was the best proof that her family had not forgotten about her. Despite the fact that she was an illegitimate child, and her father had not given her his name, she had been always looked after.

Could the same be said about Mr. Darcy's child living somewhere? Elizabeth felt a squeeze in her heart; poor little thing, not knowing its father. Or perhaps Mr. Darcy visited the child from time to time? But if that was the case, how difficult for his future wife it would be to accept the fact that there was another woman and her child in her husband's life. This always would be his child, and that woman its mother. What would a future Mrs. Darcy feel, knowing he was visiting them? How would she cope being put in such a situation? *A future Mrs. Darcy, what are you thinking of, Elizabeth Bennet?* she scolded herself in her thoughts. She reminded herself what Mr. Brooke had said. Mr. Darcy had refused to marry the child's mother as she had no dowry to speak of and poor connections. *You have no dowry as well, and though you are gentleman's daughter, there are no connections to speak of.*

She glanced at the clock on the mantelpiece. Almost nine, but the house was still quiet. For sure everyone was still fast asleep after last night's ball. She soon heard muffled noises from the room next to hers; Jane was clearly up. Should she tell Jane about everything she had learned yesterday? After a moment of hesitation, she opted not to. She somehow felt strongly against speaking about the whole matter with anyone, even with her beloved sister; it all felt too painful and too personal.

There was always a chance that Mr. Brooke was wrong, that somehow it was a case of mistaken identity. Perhaps Mr. Brooke was misinformed, and the whole affair concerned Mr. Darcy's cousin, or some other man with a similar surname? She would have to ask Mr. Brooke about the details when the first occasion arose to speak with him without witnesses. And there was also what Mr. Wickham said about Mr. Darcy to consider, which seemed to be entirely consistent with Mr. Brooke's words. The image of a rich, selfish, spoilt man, playing on his own pleasures and desires, emerged from the relations of both men about Mr. Darcy's character.

But still she could not believe it. She felt deep in her heart Mr. Darcy was not like that. He was perhaps unsociable, moody, conceited, proud and most certainly, he should not have said that she was not handsome enough for him to dance with. However, since that ill spoken comment, he had been rather nice to her; delicate and tender. It had been she who had been rude to him.

And last night he had complimented her looks, as if wanting to apologize for what he had said before. Charlotte was right on this, he looked a bit like a puppy when she had made him aware that she had overheard his comments at Meryton Assembly. Moreover, considering his behaviour in the music room, she could not believe that he was a rake. She had been alone there with him, unable to escape him had he tried to impose himself on her. Even if her foot had not been injured, and she had been in state to move freely on her own, he was obviously too strong for her to protect herself. He had done nothing of the kind. The only liberty he took was when examining her foot, but she sensed he had been much too worried for her at that time to think about the propriety issues of seeing her unclothed leg. He had neither tried to touch her in an improper manner, nor kiss her. He had done nothing which would have suggested he was a rake. Even when they had met in the hall at Netherfield, when she had thought him a ghost, his behaviour had been more playful than rakish.

Elizabeth sat on the bed abruptly, a thought crossed her mind. *Or perhaps you are already so much infatuated with him you cannot see his real self? Like in a novel when a heroine is so much in love with a man she refuses to see his faults.*

A soft knock at the door brought her back to reality. "Lizzy, are you asleep?" Jane's quiet voice was heard and her blond head appeared in a doorway.

"No, Jane. I have not been asleep for a while." Elizabeth smiled at her sister. Jane looked lovely as always, her complexion glowing, though she probably had gone to bed no earlier than at two or three o'clock in the morning.

"I thought we could have some coffee together, sister." Jane placed a tray on the bedside table. "How is your ankle?"

Elizabeth rose from the bed and impulsively hugged her sister. "Oh, Janie, what would I do without you?"

"Lizzy, it is really nothing." Jane scolded her gently, laughing softly. "Let me go, or I will drop the pot and ruin the carpet."

Elizabeth removed her hands from her sister and supported her back against the headboard. Jane poured the coffee into the cup, adding two sugars and a healthy amount of milk, and handed it to

Elizabeth. Both sisters, like their father, preferred to take a strong coffee in the morning instead of tea.

"Now tell me why I heard of you being unwell from Mr. Bingley only when you were already on your way home?" Jane asked, looking pointedly at Elizabeth.

"I asked father and Mr. Bingley not to inform you earlier. I knew you would insist on accompanying me, and it was not my intention to ruin your evening."

"But Lizzy, what happened with your foot? I did not notice anything happen to you."

"Of course you did not notice, you were too busy gazing into Mr. Bingley's eyes." Elizabeth teased, smiling happily at her blushing sister.

"Lizzy, be serious." Jane huffed and approached the bed, lifting the covers aside. "Oh, Lizzy dear, it does not look well." She touched lightly the bluish- violet skin of Elizabeth's foot.

"It does not hurt." Elizabeth ensured quickly. "Though I have not tried yet to stand on it since yesterday."

Jane shook her head worriedly. "Lizzy, the doctor must see this. We cannot be sure that nothing is broken. Before retiring last night, Father told me he had arranged for Doctor Trenton to visit us early this afternoon, to see your foot."

"I do not think that is it necessary; it is just a bruise, and will diminish in time." Elizabeth glanced at the clock. "But Jane, it is already after ten o' clock. If the doctor is to come, I must make myself more presentable soon. When we have finished coffee, will you help me with washing and dressing."

"Of course I will." Jane ensured her, covering Elizabeth's leg gently with the blankets. "But sister, you did not tell me how it happened." Jane pulled herself a chair closer to Elizabeth and sat on it holding her cup.

Elizabeth took a sip of her coffee before speaking. "Oh, Jane, it was Mr. Collins. You must have noticed the way he mistook the steps and figures constantly. You were dancing in the same set with Mr. Bingley. And at one moment he stomped on my foot with his entire weight, and you know how heavy he must be."

"That is horrible." Jane gasped. "Did he apologize at least? Did he assist you somehow?"

"No, Jane, he did not. He pretended as if nothing wrong happened."

Jane's delicately drawn eyebrows creased. "He did not mention you at all later, nor did he ask about you."

Elizabeth shrugged her shoulders. "Perhaps he really did not think himself doing anything wrong."

Jane reached for her sister's hand. "But why did you not tell me about this?"

"Oh, Jane I was so mortified with this entire situation. There is nothing worse during a ball than to get injured due to you partner's clumsiness. It was not my intention to make a spectacle out of myself. It did not hurt so much at first; I was just dizzy and hot so I removed myself from the ballroom into the corridor next to the library. There I noticed my foot was beginning to swell. I saw Mr. Brooke and Mr. … Mr. Darcy and asked them to fetch our father from the library." Elizabeth hesitated when mentioning Mr. Darcy. She decided not to say anything about their meeting in the music room for the time being.

"Did you inform Papa about what Mr. Collins had done?"

"No, I just said I had simply misstepped during the dance, and he did not ask more. Furthermore, your Mr. Bingley was there, and Mr. Brooke as well, and I was too embarrassed to explain the whole situation in front of them."

"Lizzy, how many times must I tell you that he is not my Mr. Bingley?" Jane tried to sound angry, but there was a smile caving in her blue eyes.

"Not yours? Truly? And pray tell me, how many times did he dance with you yesterday? Ten?"

"No, not ten. Only four." Jane murmured bashfully.

"Only four, you say." Elizabeth grinned at her, cocking her eyebrow. "If that is so, I see he neglected you shockingly."

Jane shook her head smilingly, and standing, took the empty cup from her sister's hands. "You said something about washing and dressing?"

Half an hour later, Elizabeth, already dressed in one of her morning gowns, was sitting in front of her vanity, her sister pinning up her thick hair.

"Lizzy." Jane murmured, concentrating her attentions on securing long silver pin in her sister's heavy tresses. "You must tell Papa about what Mr. Collins did. If you will not do so, I shall. Perhaps after hearing this, Papa will remove Mr. Collins from our home."

Elizabeth turned abruptly, looking up at her sister's calm face with astonishment. "Jane! I cannot believe you said such a thing. It is so unlike you. You always speak so well about everyone."

Jane turned Elizabeth's head back to its previous position, securing the last pin. "I stop being nice when someone hurts one of my sisters." she said firmly. "No, it is done."

Elizabeth stood up from the stool slowly. Jane helped her to wobble to the sofa without putting pressure on her injured foot.

"Now, tell me, how was the ball after I left? I want to know everything." Elizabeth spoke, settling herself comfortably, her foot arranged on the cushioned chair, which Jane had placed strategically opposite the sofa. She reached over and took a plate with chocolate cookies Jane had brought with the coffee.

"Oh, Lizzy I would wish to say that all went well, but I cannot." Elizabeth noticed her sister blush in embarrassment, the distressed expression on her pretty face. "After father left with you, Mama and our sisters, especially Lydia, they…." Jane stopped uneasily.

"Completely and utterly embarrassed us in front of the whole neighbourhood." Elizabeth finished calmly. "Tell me, dearest. I want to know the worst."

Jane sighed miserably before speaking. "First, Mary started to play the pianoforte." Elizabeth cringed involuntarily. "I know her intentions are the good, but I do not think that an opera aria is the best choice with her voice."

"But that is not all, is it?" Elizabeth bit another cookie.

Jane covered her face with her hands, murmuring. "Lydia… she somehow managed to take off Captain Denny's sword. She was running around the ballroom with it, crying she was the sultan's captive and she would protect her virtue with it."

Elizabeth's mouth dropped wide open. "No." she breathed.

"Yes." Jane nodded her head sadly. "But the worst of all was Mama. She… Lizzy, I thought I would die of shame. She said at the top of her voice in front of all these people that she expected Mr. Bingley to propose to me any moment, and what changes she would advise me to introduce at Netherfield." Jane met Elizabeth's gaze with her own now teary eyes. "Lizzy, he heard everything. What must he think about me now?" Two large tears ran down Jane's smooth cheeks.

Elizabeth's arms went instantly around her sister. "He thinks nothing wrong dearest." She pulled the handkerchief out of the pocket of her dress and dabbed Jane's wet cheeks. "He knows you are not like this. He has feelings for you, and I am sure they are strong enough to overlook certain, let us just say, idiosyncrasies of our family."

"I hope so." Jane managed a small smile.

At that moment, the door to the room opened abruptly with a loud bang, making both sisters jump in place. Mrs. Bennet stood in the opening, still in her nightclothes, her hair sticking wildly in all directions.

"Heavens to be thankful, you are dressed." she exclaimed. "Go quickly downstairs, they are here!"

"Who?" the sisters cried in unison.

"Mr. Bingley, of course! He brought Doctor Trenton with himself to examine your foot, Lizzy. And he brought Mr. Darcy as well, though I cannot understand what for."

They stared at their mother, neither speaking nor moving. "What are you doing, looking like this at me? Both of you, go downstairs!" Mrs. Bennet ordered, but seeing no visible movement from her daughters cried more firmly. "Now!"

"Mama, Lizzy cannot walk." Jane interjected.

"So you Jane, you must go immediately to the drawing room. I am sure Mr. Bingley has come to propose to you."

"But Mama…" Jane tried to protest, but her mother was already pulling her by the hand to the door.

"Lizzy, you stay here. The doctor will come too see you soon." Mrs. Bennet exclaimed, shutting the door after herself and Jane.

Elizabeth stared numbly at the door. There was only one thought tumbling through her head at that moment: he was here.

Chapter Seven

Jane opened the door to the drawing room to see three gentlemen there. Doctor Trenton was seated comfortably in the armchair, Mr. Bingley stood leisurely, supporting himself against the mantelpiece, and Mr. Darcy was pacing the length of the room in a rather restless manner.

The attention of the men was directed immediately to her the moment she entered.

"Miss Bennet!" Mr. Bingley spoke first with feeling, approaching her instantly. "I cannot express how sorry I am for the accident which happened to Miss Elizabeth under my roof."

Jane smiled at the concerned, sincere face of the man in front of her. "It was not your fault at all, Mr. Bingley, not in the least. You did everything you could to see to my sister's comfort yesterday; she told me so her herself. We thank you for that."

"Well, Miss Bennet." Doctor Trenton rose slowly from his place and walked to Jane. "What did this adventurous sister of yours get herself into this time? Has she fallen from the tree again? Or perhaps she jumped into the pond?"

Jane blushed instantly at the older man's words. Mr. Bingley and Mr. Darcy might have thought that Elizabeth was some wild creature from such a description. "It was not her fault this time, Doctor…" Jane hesitated whether to divulge all which had happened yesterday in front of the gentlemen. "It was a mere accident while dancing, but I am afraid that her foot is not in the best condition. You see, she cannot stand on it at all, and there is some heavy bruising on her skin."

Doctor just raised his grey bushy brow. "Well, we shall see, shall we?" He gathered his bag, and directed himself to the door. Jane made a move to follow him, but he stopped her.

"I can find my way." Doctor patted Jane's hand. "You have guests to entertain." He looked at the younger men with an amused expression in his eyes, and closed the door after himself quietly.

Jane turned to the gentleman and gave them her most engaging smile. Mr. Bingley beamed back at her, while Mr. Darcy looked at her seriously, his forehead furrowed, his expression sullen.

"I thank you for bringing Doctor Trenton." she said at last in the direction of both men.

"Oh, that is nothing, Miss Bennet. At least this we could do." Mr. Bingley exclaimed while Mr. Darcy said still nothing.

Jane sat, indicating to the gentlemen to take a seat as well. "Would you care for a cup of tea?"

Mr. Bingley looked at Darcy for a moment and shook his head. "No, we thank you, Miss Bennet. We would wish to wait for the doctor's return to make sure your sister is well."

"Yes, of course." Jane said, looking slightly dumbfounded at the gentlemen. Mr. Darcy had not said a word so far. It seemed as if his friend was here to speak for him. She started to understand why the tall gentleman evoked such mixed and contradictory emotions in her younger sister.

There was a long moment of awkward silence, interrupted to Jane's relief, by the arrival of her father.

"Mr. Bingley, Mr. Darcy." Mr. Bennet shook the younger men's hands. "I did not expect you so very soon in the morning after such a late night last evening."

"We have been concerned for Miss Elizabeth's welfare." Darcy spoke at last.

Jane noticed her father to stiffen, and look sharply at Mr. Darcy. "I see." was all Mr. Bennet said.

Jane's eyes moved from Mr. Darcy to her father, and she noticed that Mr. Bingley's gaze followed the same route.

"I am so sorry that such an unfortunate accident happened to Miss Elizabeth under my roof, Mr. Bennet." Mr. Bingley said, drawing the attention of Mr. Bennet at last.

"Do not fret yourself so much, my friend." Mr. Bennet smiled at the other man. "There was no fault of yours for certain, and you did everything to see to my daughter's comfort."

"We are truly very grateful Mr. Bingley." Jane added shyly, lowering her eyes. Bingley grinned happily at her, causing Mr. Bennet to roll his eyes. Mr. Darcy, noticing the older man's reaction, lowered his eyes to the floor, but something resembling a tiny smile seemed to play in the corner of his lips.

Nothing more was said, because the door opened abruptly, and Mrs. Bennet stood there, with Mr. Collins following closely at her heel.

"My dear, dear Mr. Bingley." Mrs. Bennet opened her arms wide and approached the young man hastily, almost trotting down her husband and eldest daughter in the meantime. "Such a joy to greet you here, sir. You must forgive me for not welcoming you first, but I had to see to some things." She put her hand to her lacy cap as if checking whether it was in place. "If you understand what I mean."

Mr. Bingley took a small step back. "Perfectly so, madam. We should apologize for calling so early, but we were concerned for Miss Elizabeth's state."

Mrs. Bennet waved her hand dismissively. "I am sure she will be quite all right. The doctor is with her." She looked at the nearby small side table. "Jane, child, why have you not offered refreshments to our guests?" She hissed in the direction of her daughter.

"I have, Mama, but they refused." Jane spoke softly.

Mrs. Bennet started trying to convince Mr. Bingley that he was surely in need of the cup of strong tea so early in the morning, after all, when the door opened again and Doctor Trenton entered.

Before he managed to close the door after himself, Jane was at his side asking about Elizabeth's condition.

"All is well, Miss Bennet." The doctor smiled reassuringly. "It does look rather bad, but thankfully no bones are broken. She should not put the weight on that foot for the next two weeks, at least. I can only imagine how hard it will be to detain her at home for such a long time."

"I will see to it, Doctor." Jane said in a firm voice.

"I must only say that I was very much surprised when I saw the condition of Miss Elizabeth's foot." Doctor continued. "When you told me that she had had an accident while dancing, I thought her ankle was simply twisted. But it looks as if someone or something put too much pressure on it. When I interrogated her on the subject, she admitted that the gentleman she was dancing with stepped on it. That man should not be allowed into the ballroom in the first place. He could seriously hurt his next partner."

"Jane, do you know with whom Elizabeth was dancing the last dance before her foot was injured." Mr. Bennet asked sharply.

All eyes were directed at Jane. She looked at her father, then glanced quickly at Mr. Collins, whose complexion turned instantly pale. After a moment, she lifted her face higher and said in a steady voice.

"Elizabeth said that it had happened during the dance with Mr. Collins. She did not manage to dance with anybody else last night, Papa."

"Oh, Jane, that is not true, you know that." Mrs. Bennet cried energetically, winking at Jane and shaking her head at her at the same time. "Our dear Mr. Collins could not possibly do anything like that. Elizabeth must be mistaken." she stressed.

"I am afraid she is not, Mama." Jane spoke calmly.

"I think that she simply stepped on her own foot, and is now trying to blame someone else for her condition." Mrs. Bennet said with great conviction.

"Mama, how can you say so?" Jane cried in outrage at her mother's insensibility.

"Oh... but she is all right after all." Mrs. Bennet cried impatiently. "Doctor Trenton said so himself." she added dismissively.

"Bingley, Doctor Trenton, I think it is high time for us to go." Mr. Darcy said unexpectedly, in a stern voice with an unreadable expression on his face.

"But Darcy..." Mr. Bingley started to speak, but his friend was already walking briskly towards the door, without so much as a curt bow in the direction of Mr. Bennet and Jane.

"Darcy… wait." Mr. Bingley cried again after the man, who had already disappeared into the corridor leading towards the main foyer.

"Forgive me, madam." Mr. Bingley bowed in front of Mr. Bennet. "I am afraid we have to go. We are happy to hear that Miss Elizabeth is faring better." He said, dropping another bow in front of Jane and Mr. Bennet, and then quickly following his friend.

"Miss Bennet, remember to keep your sister from any walking for the next two weeks." Doctor Trenton said only, collecting his things calmly and disappearing through the doorway as well.

***

At the same time, Elizabeth was settled comfortably in her room, curiosity burning in her about what was happening downstairs. She was sitting in the armchair by the window, her foot supported on the cushioned ottoman. She thought she heard raised voices from below, so she lifted herself from her place and wobbled a few steps to the window. First she saw Mr. Darcy walking hurriedly out of the house and climbing into the awaiting carriage without a second glance back. Soon Mr. Bingley ran out of the house, exclaiming something after his friend. At last, Doctor Trenton walked out calmly, and with the help of the servant, got into the carriage as well. The door closed and the carriage drove away.

Elizabeth returned slowly to her place, wondering what could have happened downstairs to put Mr. Darcy into such an agitated state. Before she had managed to reach any conclusions, there was a knock at the door. It was her father.

"How are you, my dear?" Mr. Bennet approached her.

"I am fine Papa." Elizabeth smiled.

Mr. Bennet moved a chair and then sat down beside her. He raised the hem of her gown, taking a long look at her bruised foot. "Does it hurt?" he asked, his expression clouded.

"No, Papa. Only when I step on it." Elizabeth assured him, still smiling.

Mr. Bennet sighed, lifted from his place and titled her chin. "Why did you not tell me last night it was Mr. Collins who did this to you?"

"Father, I could hardly do so in front of Mr. Bingley and Mr. Brooke." Elizabeth spoke uneasily. "Moreover, you cannot imagine how embarrassing it is to confess such a thing in front of strangers. It was not my intention to draw anyone's attention."

"You will not have to bear that man's company any more, my dear." Mr. Bennet said, reaching his hand to stroke her head. "I promise."

"But Papa…" Elizabeth started, but her father was already walking out of the room.

In the next half hour, Elizabeth could hear that her mother and father were arguing. At last, the door to her room opened wide, the much like in the drawing room that morning, her mother filled the entryway.

"Lizzy, Lizzy, you must tell your father you will marry Mr. Collins!" Mrs. Bennet demanded, her chest heaving, her complexion flushed as if from great exertion.

Elizabeth stared at her mother, her mouth slightly agape. "I do not understand."

Mrs. Bennet dropped on the chair beside her and started to speak very quickly. "Mr. Collins told me only last evening that he was decided to propose to you, Lizzy. But now your father has told him such horrible things. He has nearly thrown him out of Longbourn. Oh, my poor nerves!" Mrs. Bennet fanned herself with her handkerchief. "And when I mentioned to him that Mr. Collins is graciously willing to ask for your hand in marriage and rescue all of us from destitution after his death, your father…" Mrs. Bennet took a deep breath as if to calm herself only to exclaim almost hysterically. "He refused his consent. Can you imagine that? Mr. Bennet does not care for us at all." Mrs. Bennet waved her hands in apprehension. "At all." She added as she continued to cry out.

Elizabeth stayed silent, too astounded by all she had heard from her mother in the last couple of minutes to formulate a coherent reply.

"Now, Lizzy you must go downstairs and tell Mr. Collins you are ready to accept him."

"I cannot do that, Mama." Elizabeth said without much thought.

"I will help you walk downstairs, Lizzy." Mrs. Bennet offered readily, obviously thinking that her daughter's words referred to her injured foot and her inability to walk. "We must hurry, because Mr. Collins is already packing his belongings. He is threatening to move to Lucas Lodge. Can you imagine such a thing? He says that Sir William has invited him for a prolonged stay at Lucas Lodge. Oh, I always knew that Lady Lucas was a cunning woman. She has been waiting to snatch away Mr. Collins from us for her own daughters."

"Mama, I will not go anywhere." Elizabeth straightened herself in her place. "I will not try to convince Mr. Collins to stay because I have no desire to accept his proposals."

Mrs. Bennet blinked a few times. "Lizzy, child, you cannot be serious."

"I am perfectly serious, Mama." Elizabeth answered steadily.

"But child, you cannot overlook your own good fortune in Mr. Collins' proposal. You will have this home after you father's death, and you will ensure the safe future for all of us, for me and your sisters."

"Mama, I am aware of our situation, but I cannot marry Mr. Collins."

"And why not?" Mrs. Bennet's voice started to sound irritated. "Could you please enlighten me?"

"Mama, it is simply that I do not love him."

"Love him?" Mrs. Bennet cried mockingly. "You think that love is what marriage is about? Let me tell you, it is not the matter of love, but finding a respectable place for a woman in life, ensuring yourself a safe future. What has love to do with that?" She shrugged her shoulders.

"Mama, it is not even so much the matter of my lack of feelings towards Mr. Collins. I might have perhaps given second thoughts to his offer were he a man of some sense and education. I simply know I will never be able to like him or respect him. He is not my equal as far as interests and intelligence are concerned."

"So what if he is stupid?" Mrs. Bennet cried incredulously. "That is even better that he is so. He will be more easily controlled. Were you as smart as everyone thinks you are, you would understand this."

"It is not what I want in a marriage. I want a partnership."

Mrs. Bennet stared at her second daughter, mouth wide agape, for a long moment. "This is all you father's fault. All those books he encouraged you to read! And this is the result. A bluestocking upstart under my roof! Oh, my poor nerves!"

"Mama, please put yourself in my position." Elizabeth caught her mother's hand, and looked pleadingly into the older woman's face. "I simply cannot marry him. Not him." She paused as if looking for the right words. "I find him repulsive." She added quietly at last.

Mrs. Bennet's previously harsh and unyielding expression suddenly softened. "Daughter, I imagine you must have heard some tales concerning a marriage bed, but it is not that bad; I assure you." She gave Elizabeth's hand a squeeze. "I think that Mr. Collins will not be too demanding. It will be enough for you to welcome him into your bed once a month. I promise to teach you how to avoid the occurrence as much as possible. And after you will have given him a son, perhaps you will be in the right to lock him out completely in this respect. You will have children to take care of, and I am sure there are enough country girls in Kent to find to appease you husband's needs in this respect."

Elizabeth looked in sheer disgust at her mother saying the last words, but said nothing.

Mrs. Bennet leaned towards her and whispered into her ear. "If everything goes well, it will be enough to let him come to your bed no more than a few times. That's all. You see, I got pregnant with Jane just the first night."

Elizabeth did not look at her mother, but turned her head to the window. "No, Mother. I will not do it. I will never marry Mr. Collins."

There was a moment of silence before Mrs. Bennet spoke again. "As you wish, you ungrateful girl. But be aware that you are losing your only chance to catch a husband. Who will want such an impertinent, headstrong girl, without dowry or even looks?" Mrs. Bennet voice sounded cold and cruel. "But do not come to me for support you when your father's time comes." She added before leaving the room.

***

The next few days, Longbourn was as quiet as ever. Both Mr. Bennet and Mrs. Bennet closed themselves in their rooms, leaving them rarely. Elizabeth was happy to stay in her room with her books, in fear of encountering her mother. She had no desire to be carried downstairs for the time being. She wrote a very long letter to her beloved Aunt, Mrs. Gardiner, pouring her heart into it. Her foot changed colours daily, and the week after the ball, it took on the shade of an unattractive yellow. Her father visited her every morning, asking about her health, but never starting the subject of Mr. Collins. Her mother had not visited her even once since the day when their cousin moved to Lucas Lodge. Elizabeth told herself that she did not care.

More than once, her thoughts returned to Mr. Darcy and the reasons for which he had come to Longbourn the day after the ball. She thought over and over again about what Mr. Brooke had said to her about Mr. Darcy, trying to grasp the meaning of it all. She knew from Jane that Mr. Brooke had called and asked about her. She was so engrossed in her thoughts that only after a few days, did she notice that Jane, who kept her company theses days, was in a strange mood herself.

"You are sad, Janie. Has something happened?" Elizabeth enquired gently one day when her sister brought her breakfast.

Jane was silent for a long moment before answering while preparing Elizabeth's tea. "You would learn about it from other people, so perhaps it is better to know it from me." Jane made a pause and added in a slightly trembling voice. "Mr. Bingley has left Netherfield."

"When?"

Jane avoided her eyes carefully. "The same day they visited here."

"Perhaps they had some urgent business in town." Elizabeth suggested, attempting to give her voice a light tone.

But her sister shook her head. "I thought the same, but Hill said that servants from Netherfield where ordered to pack all the things and close the manor for the winter. And only yesterday I received a letter from Caroline Bingley." Jane took out a folded card from a pocket on her apron and handed it to Elizabeth.

Elizabeth opened it and scanned the elegant note quickly. "That cannot be…" She raised her confused eyes to her sister.

"But it is. Caroline writes very clearly that they intend to stay the entire winter in town." Jane spoke, her voice only bearing the resemblance of calmness. She lowered her eyes, let a soft sigh and added quietly. "From what she writes, it seems that Mr. Bingley is about to be engaged to Miss Darcy. I heard her to be such an accomplished and lovely young lady, with the excellent connections and a large dowry. It is no wonder that Miss Bingley desires such a young lady as Miss Darcy for her sister-in-law."

"Oh, Janie." Elizabeth breathed, feeling her heart breaking for her beloved sister.

Jane tried a smile, but it ended in a short, muffled sob. "Oh, Lizzy." She lifted up her tear-filled blue eyes toward her sister. "I had thought that he really cared for me." She broke down with a quiet cry, supporting her head on Elizabeth's arm.

Cradling her weeping sister to herself, Elizabeth wanted to say something, but she stayed silent. She wanted to assure Jane that Mr. Bingley loved only her, and that it was surely only his sisters' doing to separate them. However, her only coherent thought was that with the disappearance of Mr. Bingley from her Jane's life, Mr. Darcy disappeared from hers.

Chapter Eight

"You look so shocked, Lizzy." Charlotte Lucas said, looking at her friend carefully, both of them sitting in the drawing room at Lucas Lodge.

"No, Charlotte, perhaps I am a bit surprised with such a course of action." Elizabeth said slowly, her eye resting on Mr. Collins and Sir William as they were moving across the room. "When Jane told me that you accepted Mr. Collins' proposal, I could hardly believe it."

Charlotte stared perceptively at Elizabeth's confused expression and spoke calmly. "I know it may seem odd that Mr. Collins proposed to me merely a fortnight after he had asked for your hand. However, you must understand that he is determined to find a suitable wife before the end of the year. His patroness, Lady Catherine de Bourgh, expects this of him."

Elizabeth reached out her hand and placed it on Charlotte's palm reassuringly. "Pray, believe me, Charlotte, I am happy for you; on condition that you are satisfied with your marriage to Mr. Collins."

Charlotte smiled contentedly. "Indeed I am very well pleased, my friend. It is the fulfilment of all my wishes in life, to marry a respectable man, with adequate fortune. Mr. Collins has a position in the world, and his prospects for the future are very promising. Moreover, what cannot be overlooked in my situation, he does not ask for a dowry."

"Yes, that is all true." Elizabeth said hesitantly, staring at her lap. "But Charlotte, do you like Mr. Collins?"

Charlotte laughed merrily, shaking her head. "Oh, Lizzy! I wish you could see your expression at this very moment. You look positively terrified. You speak about my betrothed s if he was some strange, alien creature."

Elizabeth blushed instantly and murmured. "Forgive me, It was not my intention to offend your betrothed."

However, Charlotte did not seem to take the offence. "I know very well what you are thinking, Lizzy. I know you, and I am well aware of those ideas of romantic love you believe in. Pray, believe me, that I am very well satisfied with my present situation. And Mr. Collins is not that bad, and when I eventually order him a good bath, he will become a very pleasant company in every respect."

Elizabeth's eyes widened and she stared at her friend for a moment, before erupting in an animated laughter. Charlotte joined her, which soon brought Mr. Collins to her side, asking for the source of such an amusement.

Charlotte winked at Elizabeth before turning to him. "We have recalled our adventures when we were little girls, Mr. Collins. I will be missing Eliza after leaving Herefordshire for my new home in Kent. I thought that perhaps she could pay us a visit later next year."

"That is a most excellent idea, my dear!" Mr. Collins exclaimed, rubbing his hands together. "Most excellent idea! Lady Catherine would be well pleased to meet one of my fair cousins. And you, Cousin Elizabeth, I think you will be happy to have the opportunity to meet in person such a noble lady as my patroness."

"I am sure of that, Mr. Collins." Elizabeth answered, concentrating very hard to keep a straight face. "Meeting Lady Catherine de Bourgh must be the most unforgettable experience for anyone, there is no doubt of it."

"My father and my younger sister are to come to Hunsford in March. You could join them, Eliza." Charlotte said, with a pleading look in her grey eyes.

Elizabeth looked from her friend to Mr. Collins, and spoke cautiously. "It is my fervent wish to visit you in you new home, Charlotte, but I will have to first talk with my father. I cannot give you a certain reply now."

"Of course, Eliza, I understand that you have to discuss it with your father. But you would go together with my father, so I cannot imagine that Mr. Bennet could have any objection against such a trip."

"I expect you are right, Charlotte." Elizabeth agreed with a kind of reluctance, clearly not entirely convinced about the idea. "My father will undoubtedly allow me to go."

"Then it is settled." Charlotte squeezed Elizabeth's hand, at the same time placing her other palm on Mr. Collins' arm. "We shall await you early in the spring. I have heard so much about the beauties of Kent, I know you will like it."

"I am sure I will." Elizabeth smiled at her friend, while carefully avoiding looking at her betrothed. "Once again, let me thank you for you kind invitation."

***

Soon Elizabeth excused herself from the company at Lucas Lodge, refusing even to take tea with Charlotte and Lady Lucas. She could not stay there longer and calmly observe Charlotte allowing that man to attend her, kiss her hand, pay her those nonsensical compliments. The worst was that her poor friend had to pretend that she was delighted with Mr. Collins' attentions.

It was the very first day Jane had allowed her to venture outside the house for a short walk. Her foot had healed very well, and the bruising diminished almost completely. She longed to go out, as being kept at home had never affected her spirits in a positive way. Visiting Charlotte had seemed to be a very good idea when she had woken up earlier in the morning. She certainly had not expected that such shocking news would be awaiting her at Lucas Lodge. She wondered whether her mother had already learned about Charlotte's engagement to Mr. Collins. Probably yes, because on leaving Longbourn this morning, Elizabeth had caught a glimpse of Aunt Philips approaching the manor hastily.

Before entering her home, Elizabeth took a deep breath, preparing herself to hear her mother's hysterics about Lucases throwing them out of Longbourn, and about her selfishness and ungratefulness as a daughter, for the rest of the day.

Already in the foyer, Elizabeth heard voices coming from the drawing room, indicating that perhaps they had guessed. Hill, together with a maid, came from the back of the house, carrying trays with refreshments.

"Oh, Miss Elizabeth." Hill approached her quickly. "We have guests. Mr. Brooke has called. He has been asking after you."

"He has?" Elizabeth handed the housekeeper her bonnet and gloves.

"Yes, he has." Hill reached for Elizabeth's coat and looked critically at her hair. "I heard Mr. Brooke saying that he would wait till you return home from your walk. Mistress asked to tell you to go directly to the drawing room the moment you are back."

Elizabeth raised her brow. "She did?"

"Yes, Miss Elizabeth." Hill seemed to be appraising her gown now. "That dress must do, there is no time to put on your new muslin. Mr. Brooke is waiting."

Elizabeth looked in confusion at the housekeeper. She had an odd feeling that something unusual was happening here. Hill went ahead, and opened the door to the drawing room for her.

"Ah, Lizzy, dear child, here you are!" her mother exclaimed, nearly jumping from her place at her sight, rushing to her. "We have been worried about you." Mrs. Bennet took her by the arm and led her to the sofa, sitting her between herself and Mr. Brooke. "You should not walk so far, so early after the accident you suffered at the ball, from that odious Mr. Collins."

Elizabeth stared in utter shock at her mother. Had someone charmed her? She was so astonished that she barely registered that Mr. Brooke stood up from his place and bowed deeply in front of her.

"I am fine, Mama." Elizabeth found her voice at last. "I visited Charlotte. It is a short walk to Lucas Lodge."

"And how is she?" Mrs. Bennet asked in a voice of false kindness. "I guess Lady Lucas is delighted to have caught Mr. Collins for her daughter."

"I think that both Charlotte and her family are well pleased with the engagement."

Mrs. Bennet pursed her lips. "And they should be, nothing better could happen to them. Charlotte is so plain."

"Mama!" Elizabeth cried angrily.

"Shush, my dear." Mrs. Bennet patted Elizabeth's hand. "I know that Charlotte is your friend, but neither she nor her sister can match my daughters as far as beauty and accomplishments are concerned. It is well known here that Jane is said to be the jewel of the county, and you, Lizzy dear, more than once I heard you named the most accomplished and intelligent young lady in this part of England."

Elizabeth's eyes widened and she stared at her mother, her mouth half open. "Mama…" She whispered. Her eyes went to Jane, who only shook her head slightly at her, her expression tense, as if she had wanted to say something to her with her eyes only.

"I see that you are well recovered, Miss Bennet." Elizabeth heard Mr. Brooke's voice, which made her move her eyes from her sister, to the man beside her.

"Yes, I thank you, Mr. Brooke." Elizabeth focused on replying coherently to the gentleman. "I am happy to be able to walk again. I missed my daily rambles."

"Ah, yes." Mr. Brooke gave her a friendly smile. "You mother mentioned to me that you enjoy walking. I have not seen the park and the gardens here at Longbourn. Would it be too much, Miss Bennet, to ask you to show them to me? Not today, of course, you have walked enough, but tomorrow perhaps. Would tomorrow morning be convenient?"

Before Elizabeth managed to answer, Mrs. Bennet clasped her hands together, exclaiming enthusiastically. "What a splendid idea it is, is it not? Is it not, Lizzy? I assure you, Mr. Brooke, that Elizabeth knows every nook and corner here. She will be more than happy to accompany you."

Elizabeth could not stop staring at her mother, till Mr. Brooke's voice drew her attention again. "Will that be all right, Miss Elizabeth?" The gentleman enquired politely.

"Yes, of course, Mr. Brooke." Elizabeth answered distractedly at last.

"I thank you, Miss Elizabeth." To Elizabeth's surprise Mr. Brooke stood up, took her hand and bowed deeply in front of her, squeezing her fingers gently.

"It is time for me to leave, I am afraid." he said, bowing in front of Jane and Mrs. Bennet. "I am sorry I could not see Mr. Bennet today."

"Oh, I am sure that my husband will be delighted to have a private conversation with you tomorrow." Mrs. Bennet winked meaningfully at Mr. Brooke. "But perhaps could you not stay a little longer? I believe you have no had opportunity yet to hear Elizabeth to play the pianoforte."

"Perhaps some other time, madam. I would be delighted to hear Miss Elizabeth play." Mr. Brooke bowed again in front of Elizabeth and directed himself to the door.

"I shall see you to the entrance, sir." Mrs. Bennet cried after him and fled from the room.

Jane and Elizabeth were left alone. It was Jane who spoke first, looking with concern at her younger sister. "Oh, Lizzy, dear."

Elizabeth blinked and shook her head, still astonished with her mother's behaviour. "Jane, am I dreaming? What is happening here?"

Jane moved from her place and sat by her side speaking quickly. "Mr. Brooke suggested he was ready to court you."

"But how?" Elizabeth's eyes widened. "When?"

"Before you came. Mama was talking to Mr. Brooke, telling him how ungrateful you were refusing Mr. Collins, especially now, when we have learned that Charlotte is engaged to him. Finally, Mr. Brooke said that she should be pleased that you had refused our cousin, as there was another man, as he put it, in this very house, who would be honoured to court you. Mama stayed silent for a moment or two before the understanding of Mr.

Brooke's words seemed to dawn on her, I believe, but later she became so very pleased and she started to…"

"Jane, Jane..." Elizabeth interrupted her, a frown on her face. "That cannot be. You must have misunderstood Mr. Brooke."

Jane shook her head slowly. "No, Lizzy. I think that this is exactly what he meant to say. He wants to court you. You heard yourself that he wanted to speak with Father."

"There has to be some misunderstanding to this." Elizabeth insisted, but before Jane managed to answer, Mrs. Bennet returned.

"Oh, my dearest child." She went straight to Elizabeth and hugged her in manner her daughter could scarcely recall since she had been a little girl. "Such a man! Such a man! My girl!" She rubbed Elizabeth's arms. "Such a man! Fifteen thousand a year! But why have you not said anything? You must have known for some time already that he admires you."

"Mama, pray believe me, I had no such suspicions. It is true that Mr. Brooke has always been very kind to me, but certainly not to the point to… He never said it outwardly. It must be some misunderstanding."

Mrs. Bennet continued her raptures, as if she was not listening to what her daughter was saying. "You sly little thing." She patted Elizabeth's cheek affectionately. "I knew that you were not so smart for nothing. But I never thought that you would be able to catch such a man. What carriages, what gowns, what pin money, fifteen thousand a year at least, a house in town and an estate in the country, fifteen thousand a year." Mrs. Bennet was murmuring to herself, like an enchantment, pacing the room.

"Mama, do not agitate yourself so much." Jane said softly.

However, Mrs. Bennet ignored her words and exclaimed with new energy. "I must go to Meryton this instant! It is such a shame that your father took the carriage today, but it is nothing. I shall walk. I have to tell my sister Philips about the news. Hill, Hill, bring my coat and fur hat!" She cried, running out of the room.

"Jane, we must stop her!" Elizabeth cried, panicked. "Before nightfall, half of the county will know about it."

"I think it is a bit too late for that, sister." Jane said softly, giving Elizabeth a compassionate look. "We cannot keep Mama home against her will, after all."

Elizabeth bit her lower lip and said nothing for a few moments. Next she stood up abruptly and walked to the window. Turning back to her sister, she asked. "Janie, how can I get out of this now?"

***

The next day, shortly after ten o'clock in the morning, Mr. Brooke was announced at Longbourn. The ladies of the house were gathered, as was their everyday custom, in the smaller parlour.

Elizabeth raised herself first, even before her mother, and met Mr. Brooke's gaze with a challenge in her eyes. Mrs. Bennet welcomed the guest effusively and proposed tea. However, Mr. Brooke had a different idea.

"I think that it will better for me to first talk with Mr. Bennet." Mr. Brooke said, looking at Elizabeth, who flashed him an angry look.

"I know for sure that Papa is busy now with his steward, sir." Elizabeth spoke, her voice decided and firm. "Perhaps you would wish to see the park and gardens first, as it was agreed yesterday." She did not even wait for him to answer, but left the room quickly.

"Certainly, Miss Elizabeth." Mr. Brooke agreed promptly, following her.

They were already outside the house, on the path leading to the park, still within the view from the windows, but far enough not to be heard but anyone, when Elizabeth looked up at the man beside her and spoke.

"Sir, would you be so kind and enlighten me on one matter? I was informed after you had left yesterday that you had clearly declared yourself as a suitor to my hand. You did that without my knowledge, not to mention my consent. How could you suggest such a thing to my family before first asking me first? Can you imagine into what an awkward and difficult position it has put me." Elizabeth paused to calm her breathing, and added, her voice breaking slightly through emotion. "I am asking you, sir, who gave you the right to do this?"

Brooke looked down at her, his expression serious. "Miss Bennet, please calm yourself." He made a move with his hand as if he had wanted to touch her, but eventually his arm dropped by his side. "It was not my intention to upset you."

Elizabeth stared at him, her features tense. "Sir, I have trusted your and you breached my trust."

"Miss Elizabeth," he stepped closer to her, leaning his head down, his voice deep. "You can always trust me. I do care about you. I do not want to harm you. As I said, what I did and said yesterday was neither intentional, nor previously planned."

"I thought you were my friend." Elizabeth cried, the pain clear in her voice and eyes.

"I am your friend." Mr. Brooke stressed, trying to catch her gaze. "Please let me explain what induced me to tell your mother of my admiration for you yesterday."

Elizabeth walked to the nearest bench, sat on it, and said, her chin high in the air. "I am listening, sir."

Chapter Nine

John Brooke looked down at the petite young woman sitting on the garden bench in front of him. Such spirit and defiance in such a small body. He had, perhaps, acted too hastily yesterday, he concluded. Now he had to repair the damage he had done, and gain her trust anew.

"Miss Bennet." He folded his hands behind his back and started pacing in front of her, glancing at her from time to time in order to emphasize his words. "What I did yesterday was entirely the result of my own impulsiveness, I dare say. You see, I called yesterday hoping to see with my own eyes that you are well recovered. When I was told that you were not home, but visiting friend, I decided to wait for you. Your mother and elder sister kept my company." He stopped, considering how to mention Mrs. Bennet's comments about Elizabeth in a most delicate way. "You mother made some remarks concerning your rejection of Mr. Collins' suit, stressing what unhappy consequences it would cause to your entire family. She was quite, I must say, ruthless in accession of your conduct. I reacted, perhaps too violently hearing this. Forgive me, but I found your mother's words unjustified and unfair towards you, Miss Bennet!" With the last words, he looked straight into Elizabeth's eyes.

Elizabeth stared at his face searchingly, her fine eyes narrowed, her forehead creased. "Mr. Brooke, you do not have to explain this to me." she said, her tone not showing the signs of softening. "I can imagine very well what my mother likely said about my rejection of Mr. Collins' suit. I have been hearing it for two weeks now."

"Miss Bennet, Miss Elizabeth." Brooke spoke softly, almost pleadingly, sitting on the bench beside her. "I felt I could not listen to it passively. I care about you, and I admire you. All I wanted was to protect you from those hurtful words. That was the only reason for which I suggested, utterly on the spur of the moment, that you could, madam, expect a much more advantageous proposal in the future. I made myself clear that your family might expect my interest in your person, and that my intentions towards you are entirely honourable. And I stand by what I said yesterday. I am ready to go to your father and ask for the honour of officially courting you, and eventually marrying you."

During his speech, Elizabeth lowered her eyes, and the gentleman beside her noticed with satisfaction, the blush coming on her lovely face. "Mr. Brooke, I can understand, I believe, that your intentions were honest." She said slowly after a considerable moment of silence. "If you wanted to protect me in your own way, as you say, I thank you for that. But, sir, I do not need either your pity or your protection." She looked straight into Brooke's eyes. "I have not given you the right."

Brooke's expression clouded. "It was not pity. It simply touches my heart when I hear, forgive me, that your own mother speaks in such terms about you. I cannot help it."

Elizabeth took a deep breath before speaking again in a well measured, even voice. "Mr. Brooke, it should not bother you. I thank you for your concern, but my affairs are not your business, sir. I do not want to be impolite and rude, but as I have already said, nobody has given you the right to act as my protector."

Brooke reached for the small gloved hand, and closed it gently into both of his. "But I want it to be my business. I want it to be my right." he stressed, trying to meet her dark eyes, which were stubbornly avoiding his gaze. "I want to protect you, keep you safe…"

"Mr. Brooke, I do not wish to hear any of this." Elizabeth stood up abruptly, removing her hand from his grip. "I hold you in a high esteem, sir, but as a friend." She looked up at him and stressed, "Only as a friend."

Brooke leaned towards her, his voice sounding pained, and perhaps even bitter. "Why do you say this, Miss Elizabeth? You think me unsuitable for yourself, perhaps not worldly enough, not educated enough?"

"No, Mr. Brooke." Elizabeth turned towards him, speaking more softly. "I do think highly of you. I respect your mind and sensibility, as well as many other of your admirable traits. I am also sure that you can make a woman perfectly happy and content; but I am not that woman."

"Why not?" He asked very quietly after a moment, carefully judging her expression.

Elizabeth averted her eyes. "I cannot explain it; but I know that I could never feel for you as wife should feel for husband."

He stepped closer . "You do not know me well enough, perhaps in time…"

"No, that is not possible." She shook her head decidedly and walked a few steps away. "But after what you said yesterday to my mother… Right after you left, she went to Meryton herself and informed my Aunt Philips about your visit and what you had said. Now the entire neighbourhood is aware of your intentions towards me." She brought her hands to her face. "What am I to do now? Everyone will expect us to…" She sighed worriedly and went silent.

"I understand you want to have nothing to do with me." Brooke murmured darkly, his eyes never leaving her small form. For a short moment he considered the possibility of using his current advantage and forcing her into an engagement. However, observing her distressed, pale face, he opted against it. She was so adamant in her refusal; clearly she had to imagine herself to feel something for Darcy. He could have her now; her father seemed to be unwilling to marry her off quickly, but Brooke believed that despite his silly pose, Mr. Bennet was not so foolish as to refuse a man of his means the hand of his daughter. As for Elizabeth, he wanted her willing, sweet and compliant when she would come into his house and bed as his wife. Forcing her into marriage now, he would likely end up with a hostile, moody, bitter and generally very unhappy lady by his side. It was not something he looked towards. Time was his ally. A few months of constant wooing and she would be his. He would play on her tender heart, and she would soon forget that snob from Derbyshire.

"No, I value your company but… now my father expects you would talk with him about me." Her soft voice brought his to reality.

"I see. Miss Elizabeth, it is my most desirable wish to ask your father for the right to court you, but of course I will not do anything against your wish." he said pleasantly, confident with his plan. "I will talk with your father privately and explain the whole misunderstanding to him. I will assure him I am more than ready to take full responsibility for my words and actions, at the same time informing him about your rejection of my intentions."

Elizabeth looked up at him, her eyes searching his. "Can I trust you on this, sir?"

Brooke bowed. "You can. You have my word. You must believe it was not my intention to put you in an awkward situation. I believe that if we ignore all the gossip and speculations, the entire matter will calm itself down in a few weeks. There will be other affairs to feed people's curiosity."

"I can only hope you are right, sir." Elizabeth said doubtfully, but visibly relieved. Brooke did not like that look of relief on her face, but for now, he could not do much about it. Patience was the key to her.

***

To Elizabeth's contentment, Mr. Brooke fulfilled his promise to talk to Mr. Bennet. When she visited her father in the library later that day, he even made fun of her, teasing her because of the staggering number of admirers wishing to marry her recently. Elizabeth laughed at her father's jesting, ensuring him she had no intention of accepting any offers of marriage in the nearest future. Mr. Bennet seemed to be pleased with her assertions, kissing her head and calling her his Lizzy girl.

Elizabeth felt a little guilty, remembering the look of raw disappointed on Mr. Brooke's face when she had made herself clear that she had seen no future for them. Mr. Brooke's attentions flattered her own pride, but she knew that her future could not be by his side. Despite his obvious interest in her, she felt nothing for him. However, just hearing the name of a certain gentleman from Derbyshire made her heart race. She convinced herself to bury the hope of meeting Mr. Darcy ever again, hoping that in the course of time she would forget him, and in the future, she would be more cautious when engaging her heart.

Her mother was clearly still convinced of Mr. Brooke's serious intentions towards her. It resulted in Mr. Bennet's unusually kind behaviour towards her. For the first time in her life Elizabeth found herself the recipient of her mother's tenderness and loving attentions. However, she was not fooled. Painful as it was, she knew that the only reason for Mrs. Bennet's kind words and embraces was that her mother thought she was bringing a rich suitor into the family.

Elizabeth awaited with anticipation for the arrival of the Gardiners for Christmas. They were to stay at Longbourn till the New Year, at least and Elizabeth could hardly wait for a chance of a sincere conversation with Aunt Gardiner. There was no one she could talk to about Mr. Darcy, as she and Jane had seemed to make a silent vow to avoid the subject of the two gentlemen from Netherfield.

It was the fourth day after the Gardiners' arrival when Aunt Madeline and Elizabeth at last found the opportunity to have a long desired conversation. The little Gardiners were left under the care of Jane, who was always full of ideas of how to organize their time and occupy their attention. Mrs. Bennet suffered from her nerves that day, resting in her room upstairs. Mary was diligently practicing the pianoforte while the youngest Bennet girls went to Meryton. The weather was surprisingly pleasant, sunny and unseasonably warm for late December. Consequently, Elizabeth and Mrs. Gardiner decided to take a long walk to Oakham Mount.

"So, Lizzy." Mrs. Gardiner said, sitting on the fallen log after her niece had told her in detail about all what had happened since the three gentlemen had arrived into neighbourhood. "To sum the matters up, your heart feels for Mr. Darcy, disregarding entirely

Mr. Brooke and Mr. Collins." Mrs. Gardiner laughed heartily, seeing Elizabeth's almost disgusted expression on mentioning Mr. Collins among the group of her admirers. "While Mr. Darcy is away with little hope of coming back soon." she continued. "Mr. Collins is to be married to your friend, Charlotte, in early January, and Mr. Brooke is ready to take a most serious commitment to you at any moment."

"It would seem you have the truth of it." Elizabeth agreed, nodding her head.

"But what is most important, you are worried about what Mr. Brooke told you about Mr. Darcy and his elicit affair, and his illegitimate child. Your heart tells you to trust Mr. Darcy, but Mr. Brooke's and Mr. Wickham's words suggest that he is not to be trusted by a young woman like you."

Elizabeth bit her lower lip. "Yes."

"Well, my dear." Mrs. Gardiner shook her head. "What a web we have here. Whoever wove it should have put some control over his imaginings for sure. Such creativity freely unleashed may prove to be dangerous."

Elizabeth frowned, pouting. "Aunt, please, it is a serious matter for me."

"I know, dear, and I am sorry. I know it gives you much of heartache." Mrs. Gardiner patted Elizabeth's hand in a compassionate gesture. "Let me tell you something which I think should raise your spirits a bit. Although I do not want to imply that Mr. Brooke told untruths about Mr. Darcy on purpose, I think that there is a possibility he might have mistaken him for some other young man from Mr. Darcy's social circles."

Elizabeth brightened immediately. "I thought the same!"

"I should think you did." Mrs. Gardiner smiled knowingly. "Elizabeth, I…" The older woman's expression turned suddenly more serious. "You are aware that I was brought up in Derbyshire, are you not?"

Elizabeth nodded her head. "Yes."

"I was acquainted with the Darcys." Mrs. Gardiner stood up and walked to the edge of the cliff, staring at the countryside spread beneath her. "Until I married your Uncle, I had lived in the small town, Lambton, situated just five miles from Pemberley, the Darcy family estate."

"And you know the family?" Elizabeth asked curiously.

"I had a pleasure of knowing Mr. Darcy's mother and his father as well." Mrs. Gardiner turned to Elizabeth. "I met Lady Anne a few times, and she was always very kind to me. She was a very understanding person, very forgiving of the faults and vices of others. Mr. Darcy's parents were the best, the most honourable people I have ever met in my life. Trust me on this, Lizzy. And although I left Derbyshire almost ten years ago, when Mr. Darcy was yet a boy, I never heard a bad word concerning him from anyone there. All seemed to believe he would follow admirably into his father's footsteps as landlord and master of such a grand estate. And even if it happened that he had a child out of wedlock, which is, as you must have heard, quite common for the gentlemen of his circle in general, I assure you the child is well taken care of. Darcy would never abandon his child."

Elizabeth looked searchingly at Mrs. Gardiner. "Aunt, forgive me, but you sound as if you knew Mr. Darcy's family very well."

Mrs. Gardiner stayed silent for a while to speak in a soft voice. "Because I knew them quite well." She raised her hand in the gesture of protest seeing Elizabeth's most curious expression. "But please, niece, do not ask more questions. Just trust me on this. The Darcys were good people, and I believe that your Mr. Darcy is a good man as well. As I said, we cannot entirely exclude the possibility that Mr. Darcy fathered a child, and for some reason did not marry, or more probably could not marry the mother, even though I find it rather hard to believe, knowing his father's..." Mrs. Gardiner paused, as if deciding how much to say. "I have reasons to believe that his father specifically warned his son against such liaisons. Old Mr. Darcy was a decent man, even if not perfect." Mrs. Gardiner stopped again, a strange unreadable expression on her face. "Which cannot be said about Mr. Wickham, for example." she added more cheerfully after a moment.

"Mr. Wickham?" Elizabeth cried in surprise. "You were acquainted with his family as well?"

"No, though I heard his father to be a decent man. However, his son was well known for his misbehaviours in the entire neighbourhood."

Elizabeth eyes sparkled with new interest. "What misbehaviours?"

"He did not live in a way that a young man should have lived. I know, for example, that just before I left, he was indebted to most of the merchants in Lambton. Moreover, there were also some gambling debts, from what I heard. And…" she hesitated for a moment before adding in a lowered voice. "tales that he tried to seduce every servant at Pemberley under the age of thirty."

Elizabeth gasped and shook her head in confusion. "Mr. Wickham? Who would have thought? He seems to be such a pleasant gentleman."

"I must say that I am relived to see him paying more attention to Miss King than to any of my nieces. Do not trust him, Elizabeth. I think he tends to omit the truth much too often, especially in the story I have heard him spread about Mr. Darcy!" Mrs. Gardiner huffed. "I am certain it is a falsehood. Mr. Darcy would never go against his father's wish; I am convinced of it. I think that Mr. Wickham simply refused to take that living and was given some handsome compensation instead. Besides, the thought of him being a curate at Kympton is simply ridiculous. He is as suited for the clergy as me for the Navy."

"Charlotte suggested almost the same, Aunt." Elizabeth remarked, remembering her friend's words from the ball at Netherfield. "She thought from the very beginning Mr. Wickham's story concerning Mr. Darcy to be unbelievable."

"Your friend is a very reasonable person. She knows the realities of life."

"And I do not?"

"You are still very young." Mrs. Gardiner cupped Elizabeth's cheek with a smile. "When you are closer my age, you will see many things in a different light."

There was a moment of silence before Mrs. Gardiner spoke first. "We should be going back, Lizzy. Little Edward is still too small to be left alone for a longer time."

Elizabeth glanced at the older woman's preoccupied expression, and she knew that her Aunts' thoughts were already with her children. Mrs. Gardiner was a most devoted mother and wife, and in that sense, she was a role model for Elizabeth, which she perhaps lacked in her own mother. Every time Elizabeth stayed in London with the Gardiners, she observed how much hard work Madeline Gardiner put every single day into raising her children into good, worthy people and creating a welcoming, warm home for her husband. She never pushed her children away from her, nor pretended to be ill, locking herself for the whole days away from her family in her rooms. She never ignored her children when they were sad or came to her with their own little worries, no matter how silly they might seem to be for an adult.

"As for Mr. Brooke." Mrs. Gardiner continued as they were walking down the hill. "I saw the way he looks at you. He wants you. He will not desist in pursuing you."

Elizabeth thought for a moment before she answered. "I do respect him. He flatters me and my own pride with his admiration. I like talking with him, but that is all. I do not desire anything more."

Mrs. Gardiner laughed. "But he desires much more from you, Elizabeth. You must tell him in no uncertain terms how you feel."

"But I have!" Elizabeth cried.

"Forgive me, my dear, but I observed you with him, and your behaviour tells him *maybe* and not *never.*"

"I enjoy his company." Elizabeth spoke in guilty voice, as if defending herself. "He is an intelligent man, and his opinions and his understanding of the world are refreshing. He talks with me about politics and current affairs. No other gentleman of my acquaintance, apart from Papa, of course, is willing to speak on such matters with a woman."

Mrs. Gardiner stopped abruptly and put her hands on Elizabeth shoulders, speaking firmly. "Elizabeth, Mr. Brooke is a mature, experienced man. He knows how to engage you, how to draw the attention of a young, intelligent, but still very innocent and naive woman like you. He knows exactly what he is doing, my dear. If you really do not wish to marry him, my advice is to keep your distance and stop any kind of flirting, no matter how innocent it may seem to be to you. Otherwise, you will end married to him before springtime comes. He does not understand, or rather refuses to understand, the small nuisances of drawing room chit chat, especially when it comes to you."

"Perhaps you are right. I have not thought about it in this way." Elizabeth murmured, her brows creased. "You do not hold Mr. Brooke in high esteem, do you, Aunt?"

"I have nothing against him. He is very rich, but he seems to be very determined in all aspects of his life, I dare say. Your uncle has never had any business connections with him, but he has heard that Mr. Brooke has the reputation of being very firm, and even ruthless, in dealings with his business partners." Mrs. Gardiner looked at her niece with genuine concern. "I want you simply to understand that he is not a man to trifle with."

"Thank you, Aunt. I shall give due consideration to your words." Elizabeth said earnestly.

Mrs. Gardiner smiled. "That is all I ask."

They were approaching Longbourn's park when they heard the happy children's cries. The two eldest, well bundled Gardiner children, the seven year old twins, Samuel and Lucy, were running around the park, clearly looking for something. The game was, however, immediately stopped the moment they spotted their mother and Elizabeth.

"Mama, Mama, Cousin Elizabeth, we are playing hide and seek with Cousin Jane!" They cried excitedly one through the other. "Cousins Jane is hiding now with Edward. You and Cousin Lizzy must help us to look for them. Come!"

"Of course we will!" Mrs. Gardiner smiled, gathering her children to herself. "But first there is one very important matter I need to finish discussing with Lizzy."

Elizabeth leaned confidentially and whispered something into Samuel's ear. The boy's face brightened, and taking his sister's hand, he pulled her with him, both of them running in the direction of the stables.

Mrs. Gardiner took Elizabeth's hand. "And what about Mr. Darcy?"

Elizabeth shrugged her shoulders and sighed. "I do not know."

"But you still like him, I reckon."

Elizabeth nodded her head.

"But you are afraid whether you would be able to accept Mr. Darcy as a suitor, knowing he may have a child with another woman."

Elizabeth's expression clouded. "Aunt, I will not have to deal with such a situation. I doubt I would see Mr. Darcy ever again."

"Oh, I would not be so sure of it, Elizabeth." Mrs. Gardiner smiled, her eyes twinkling. "I think that sometimes we should help the luck a little. I think that you and Jane should come back with us to London and spend some time there. You could call on Mr. Bingley's sister, perhaps. What do you think of such a plan?

"Oh, Aunt that would be wonderful!" Elizabeth spontaneously kissed Mrs. Gardiner's cheek. "Thank you!"

"We have found them!" They heard Samuel's voice and turned to see the twins running to them, with Jane walking behind them, carrying little Edward. The baby, on seeing his mother, started twisting in Jane's arms, extending his tiny hands towards Mrs. Gardiner.

"Jane!" Elizabeth ran to her sister. "Aunt invited us to stay with them in London. Do you know what that means? You will be able to call on Mr. Bingley's sisters!"

Jane blushed instantly, carefully handing the baby to his mother. However, Elizabeth could see that her sister was pleased with the news.

***

The next day, Mr. Gardiner got a letter from London, his business calling him back to town even before the New Year. He went alone the same day, while his wife and children were to join him in two days. Mrs. Gardiner revealed the plan of Jane and Lizzy accompanying her to London and staying there some time. Mrs. Bennet acclaimed the idea when it came to Jane, but rejected the thought of Elizabeth going as well. It was not to be borne for

Elizabeth to leave Longbourn when Mr. Brooke was here, so close to proposing.

To Elizabeth's disappointment, her father supported her mother this time. Mr. Bennet asked her to stay, explaining that he would not survive with her and Jane absent at the same time. Elizabeth took it to heart, considering as well that in a little over two months, she was scheduled to travel to Kent to visit Charlotte.

Two days before New Year, Jane went with Mrs. Gardiner and children to London. Every day Elizabeth anticipated a letterwith the news about Jane's meeting with Mr. Bingley, and perhaps even with his friend Mr. Darcy.

Chapter Ten

Elizabeth was sitting on the bench in the quiet corner of Longbourn garden, reading the last letter from Jane for perhaps the tenth time. The content of the letter was the source of great distress and true worry for her. Though her sister had been in London for five weeks already, she had not seen Mr. Bingley even once. Jane had called on Mrs. Hurst and Miss Bingley, only to hear that their brother had been extremely busy, clearly too busy to see her. Moreover, Jane informed her as well that she had been told by Mrs. Hurst that Mr. Darcy and his sister had decided to spend Christmas in Derbyshire, and they had been absent from London for the entire winter.

Elizabeth's worried eyes returned again to the last paragraph of her sister's letter.

... I must admit, Lizzy, that you were perfectly right in your observation of the true character of Miss Bingley and Mrs. Hurst. When I called at Mrs. Hurst's they talked to me as if their only wish was to end the visit as soon as possible. I had waited for over two weeks for them to return their visit to me, and when they came at last, they stayed for not more than a quarter of an hour. They barely spoke a word to Aunt Gardiner, as if ignoring her presence or perhaps finding her not suitable enough to be even civil with. Mrs. Hurst, as well, made me aware that they were all invited for the entire summer to visit at Pemberley, Mr. Darcy's estate in Derbyshire, as his special guests. Moreover, Caroline hinted in no uncertain terms that it was Mr. Darcy who insisted on their visit, as he wishes Mr. Bingley to become better acquainted with his

sister, Miss Georgiana Darcy. I am convinced now, Lizzy, that even if Mr. Bingley cared for me, if only a little in the past, he does not feel anything for me now at all. It is perhaps painful to acknowledge this, but I think it is truly better to do it now and cease feeding myself with the illusions in the future.

"May I ask what has brought such a poignant expression on such a lovely face?" Elizabeth lifted her distracted face on hearing the man's voice.

"Mr. Brooke, I have not expected to see you today." she said, folding her letters carefully, her eyes not meeting his face.

"I have come to call on your parents to invite them, you, of course, and all your sisters to a small dinner party I plan to throw next week at Purvis Lodge. I have come on horseback today, entering from the other side of the park, and when I saw you sitting here, I simply could not help myself but greet you.

Elizabeth smiled wanly, and stood up, her eyes catching the sight of a fine, black horse tied to the nearby tree.

"But perhaps I interrupted you on something important." Mr. Brooke eyed her carefully. "I do not wish to impose…"

Elizabeth shook her head. "No, I have been reading a letter from my sister, Jane, that is all. I was about to go back home before you came. It is getting cold." she adjusted her velvet cape around herself more securely.

"Shall we?" Mr. Brooke offered his arm, which she accepted with a polite smile.

They walked to Mr. Brooke's horse to untie him so it could follow them.

"We have not seen you for quite a while now." Elizabeth noted.

Brooke stopped instantly and leaned over, gazing into her eyes. "You have noticed." he spoke in a low voice, his other hand covering her small one resting on his arm.

There was a moment of hesitation on her part before she answered, lifting her calm eyes at him. "Yes, I have."

Mr. Brooke did not reply with words, but he took her other hand and brought it gently to his lips, kissing her gloved hand, his eyes not leaving her face, even for a short moment.

"I have been in London." he said when they resumed their walk.

"Really?" Elizabeth asked blankly, staring in the opposite direction.

"Yes. I had the pleasure of meeting there our mutual acquaintance and neighbour, Mr. Bingley."

Elizabeth stopped and turned abruptly to him. "You saw Mr. Bingley…" she whispered. "Did you talk to him?"

"Yes, we talked but shortly, and he invited me to call on him. When I did the other day, he enquired much about your parents and about your elder sister. Can you imagine that he had no idea whatsoever that Miss Bennet had been staying in London since New Year? Well over a month." He glanced at Elizabeth intently. "It is rather odd, will you not agree?"

Elizabeth stared at him, her expression tense. "I understand you made him aware of the fact of my sister's stay in London." she said breathlessly.

"Yes, I did." Mr. Brooke allowed himself a little smile, when her eyes were not directed at him. "Do you think that I should not have done it?"

"No, I mean yes, I am very glad that you did." she shook her head, staring at the frozen ground beneath her with a frown, before lifting her eyes to him again. "How did he react?"

"As I said, he was very much surprised to hear about it. He asked me whether I was aware where exactly she was staying. I said that all I knew was she was staying with Mr. and Mrs. Gardiner in Cheapside."

Elizabeth stood as if frozen in place, her mind still focused on what she had just been told.

"Miss Bennet, I think we should go inside." Mr. Brooke said, giving his horse to the stable hand as they neared the stables. "I do not want you to catch a cold." He touched her arm.

"Yes, of course." Elizabeth agreed, still distracted. She accepted the professed arm again, and they walked into the house.

The following day, Elizabeth received a new letter from her dearest sister. Jane wrote that quite surprisingly, Mr. Bingley had called on her at their uncle's house. He had heartily apologized for not calling earlier, but he had not been aware that she had come to London at all. If not for an accidental meeting of Mr. Brooke, he would not have been aware of the fact at all. The letter was short because Jane and Mrs. Gardiner had plans for a short shopping trip. Jane needed new gloves, as Mr. Bingley had invited all of them to his opera box the following week.

***

It was a broad daylight, in a spacious room, on the upstairs of the elegant home in the fashionable part of London. A tall, well built man was disrobing himself, throwing the items of his clothing dismissively on the nearest chair. A beautiful, raven haired woman was sitting on the bed, her naked form barely covered with the sheet.

When the man removed his last article of clothing, he walked to the edge of the bed and took hold of her abundant curls, moving her face to his groin.

She took him obediently into her mouth, pleasuring him till he stopped her. He then flipped her over on her stomach, pulling her shapely bottom high. He reached beneath her, palming her breasts roughly for a few moments. Next he started rubbing her purposively between her thighs. All too soon, he entered her swiftly from behind. The woman's eyes widened, she whimpered softly and swallowed hard.

After a few minutes, the man collapsed on her, and then rolled from her on one side of the large four poster bed.

"This is the last time you will see me." he said after a long moment.

She snuggled close to him. "You are not pleased with me?"

"I am pleased, but I plan to marry soon. I am not going to cheat on my wife. She is young and beautiful. I will not need a mistress anymore."

"But perhaps…" The woman reached her hand to stroke his chest. "In time you will change…" she said softly.

He stopped her hand wandering over his body. "No." he stood up and started dressing himself.

The woman got up as well and walked to him. "You met her in the country, did you not?"

"Yes, she is a real lady." the man said, not looking at the woman. "A gentleman's daughter, well bred, innocent, genteel and accomplished."

The woman's expression hardened. "Congratulations. You always get what you want."

"Yes, I do." he said, not paying any attention to his lover's now somehow bitter tone. "This house is in your name. You can stay here or sell it; I don't care. You will receive your monthly allowance for half a year yet."

He finished dressing and left the room.

***

Georgiana Darcy tiptoed to the door of her brother's study. Reaching for the doorknob, she opened it, trying not to make the slightest noise. She peered inside cautiously, but seeing her brother sleeping on the couch instead of working, she entered.

She walked to him quietly and smiled. The furniture he lay on was undoubtedly too short for him. His long legs stuck out at the other end of it. Once she had tried to convince him that perhaps he would need a bigger and more comfortable sofa in his study, knowing very well that he liked to nap there when his eyes got tired from reading his correspondence.

But he only huffed at her, informing her that he had a bed in his bedroom, and that was enough for him. He would have never admitted openly that he often took a nap in his study during the day. Georgiana gazed lovingly at his darling face. He looked tired and pale, and he had lost weight lately, and now was much too slim; always working too much, wearing himself down too much. She sighed. He would not listen to her when she told him he needed more rest.

With an affectionate smile, Georgiana took out the papers from his limp hand and put them neatly aside on the small side table. Next she retrieved the soft woolen blanket from one of the bottom drawers of the bookcase and covered him with it.

He murmured something and turned on his side, his hair falling over his eyes in the process. Georgiana reached with her hand to gently comb away the disobedient curls. She stilled in surprise, when he caught her hand, and kept it firmly to his chest.

"Elizabeth…" he murmured. " Do not go… Stay with me, my love."

Georgiana perched on the edge of the sofa beside him, letting him keep her hand, watching his blissful expression. Elizabeth again, a mysterious Miss Elizabeth Bennet. She was curious to meet her, to know her better. Georgiana shook her head at the thought of her brother being in love; it was so hard to imagine. She had never seen him pay any attention to any of the young ladies of their acquaintance. On the contrary, usually he seemed to use all in his power to escape from their attentions.

This Miss Elizabeth could not be as horrible as Miss Bingley described her if her brother clearly admired the lady. Miss Bingley, when Georgiana had seen her in London in December, made a few condescending remarks about Miss Elizabeth, her mother and four sisters. Georgiana, however, thought that it must be a very happy family indeed with five girls in it. She loved her brother, he was the best brother she could wish for, but there were matters she could not discuss with him. It would be different if she had a sister.

Fitzwilliam murmured something again and released her hand. Georgiana adjusted the blanket around his neck, put another log on the fire so he would not get cold and left the room quietly.

Later that day when they sat in the smaller, private drawing room, Georgiana carefully observed her brother while she was playing for him. Her fingers were moving swiftly over the keyboard, performing the complex composition, but her eyes were on her brother's absent expression.

"That was beautiful, sweetie." he said when she finished.

"I am happy you enjoyed it, brother." She walked to the sofa that he was sitting on, and took a seat beside him.

She smiled at him with her sweetest smile and was rewarded with a grin of his own, showing his dimples (she had always secretly thought that it was rather unfair that it was her brother who inherited such adorable dimples and not her).

"What is the matter, sister?" Darcy gazed at her perceptively. "Are you up to something?"

She gave him her most innocent expression, and shook her blond head. "No, everything is perfectly all right, it is just…" she started, as she let out a little sigh and peered at him through her eyelashes.

He was looking at her patiently.

"Have you had any news from Mr. Bingley lately?" she asked at last.

"Yes, I received a letter from him yesterday, but why you are asking?"

Georgiana lifted her eyebrows and spoke lightly. "Oh, some time ago I was reading the book about the geography of England, and there was a very interesting chapter there about Hertfordshire."

"Really?"

"Yes. And then I remembered that Mr. Bingley leased an estate there. Netherfield, was it not?"

"Yes, he did."

"And when we saw Mr. Bingley in London before Christmas, he talked with such an enthusiasm about Hertfordshire and the people he had met there. Do you know, perhaps, whether he intends to go back there?"

Darcy leaned back in his seat, and took a careful look at his sister, his expression not a bit perplexed. "As a matter of fact, he does, and soon, next week or so. I think he intends to stay there for some time, for the entire spring at least."

"Oh, perhaps you could visit him?" Goergiana cried, clasping her hands together. "You could take me with you, as I would like to see Hertfordshire very much indeed."

"You know that I am scheduled to visit Lady Catherine together with Colonel Fitzwilliam, and you are to stay with Lord and Lady Matlock during that time." Darcy reminded her.

"Yes, I know, but I would prefer to spend the time with you." she pouted. "I could go with you to Kent, and later we could perhaps visit Mr. Bingley in Hertfordshire."

"Georgiana, you have never wanted to visit Lady Catherine before." he looked at her with concern, taking her small hand into his. "Sweetie, you can tell..." he started gently. "Do you like Mr. Bingley?"

"Of course I like Mr. Bingley." Georgiana answered instantly. "He is you friend, and he is terribly kind."

"Yes, but I meant whether you like him in a different way..." Darcy gave his little sister an embarrassed look. "You know what I mean." he stressed.

Georgiana looked at him, greatly confused, before the understanding of his meaning dawned on her. "No, of course not, no!" she exclaimed without hesitation.

"But you want to visit him." Darcy persisted worriedly.

"Brother, that is truly a strange idea." she glared at him. "Mr. Bingley is simply Mr. Bingley. He is like Cousin Richard to me, like my other brother. Besides, I think he is quite taken with that Miss Bennet he met in Hertfordshire. I heard him telling you that she was an angel."

"Yes, he was quite taken with her." Darcy agreed slowly. "And from his last letter, I can guess that his intentions towards her are most serious."

"Will he marry her?" Georgiana asked, biting her lower lip.

"It is possible."

"Splendid!" Georgiana cried, all but jumping up in place. "You will attend the wedding, of course, as his best friend."

"Yes, I suppose so." Darcy said, greatly confused with the turn of the conversation. "Georgiana." he spoke earnestly. "Why are you asking me all these questions? I truly cannot fathom the reason for your sudden interest in Bingley and his affairs."

Georgiana took a deep breath and spoke with determination. "Correct me if I am wrong, but Mr. Bingley's Miss Bennet has a younger sister, Miss Elizabeth Bennet."

Darcy blinked in surprise. "Yes."

"I heard her to be very accomplished and witty. I understand she enjoys reading, long walks and lively conversation. She plays the pianoforte and sings with great feeling." Georgiana enumerated on her slim long fingers. "She has beautiful dark eyes and possesses a kind heart."

"How on earth do you know so much about her?" Darcy cried, astonished.

"From you, brother." Georgiana said softly.

Darcy opened his mouth, staring at his little sister. At last he spoke unbelievably. "Georgiana…?"

"We could go together to Hertfordshire after visiting in Kent." she said quickly, placing both of her hands on his arm. "I am sure Mr. Bingley will welcome us."

Darcy still stared at her, not commenting. His sister leaned to him. "I would very much like to meet her."

"Meet who?"

"Miss Elizabeth Bennet, of course." Georgiana said a bit impatiently, thinking that her very smart brother could be quite daft at times. "I imagine her to be very amiable."

Darcy stood up and walked to the fire place. "Georgiana, it is not as easy as you may think." he murmured.

She walked to him quietly and snuggled closely to his side, resting her head on his arm. "Why not? Miss Bingley said she was very horrible, and that is the best proof that she must be quite the opposite."

To Georgiana's satisfaction, her last comment brought a reluctant smile to her brother's face. She took his hand and lifted on her toes, gazing at him pleadingly with her big blue eyes.

"Georgiana Darcy, you are not ten any more, and this pleading expression does not work its charm on me." he said sternly, but there was a smile hiding in the corner of his eyes.

In response, she let a little sigh, pouted, and folding her hands together as in prayer, whispered. "Pretty please?"

"You are impossibly spoilt." Darcy said at last, shaking his head. "We will talk about it later." he added formally, kissing her on the cheek and leaving the room.

Georgiana Darcy smiled in triumph and rubbed her hands together. She knew she had won.

***

"Mama, Mama, we must go to Meryton, I need a new bonnet!" Lydia Bennet cried, approaching her mother, who seemed to be hiding behind a tree.

"Child, do not speak so loudly." Mrs. Bennet hissed, catching her youngest daughter's hand, and pulling both of them behind the large rose bush.

"But Mama..." Lydia started again, but Mrs. Bennet shushed her and pointed to the couple passing some twenty yards in front of them.

Lydia frowned and spoke quietly this time. "It is only Lizzy with Mr. Brooke." she said dismissively. "Mama, I want a bonnet made like the one Jane brought from London for Kitty. I cannot imagine why she did not bring me a similar one."

"Jane brought you very lovely gloves and new ribbons." Mrs. Bennet reminded her absently, her attention entirely focused on her second daughter talking with Mr. Brooke.

"But a new bonnet is much better than gloves." Lydia protested. "Kitty is so selfish, she refuses to exchange her bonnet for my gloves. That would be for the best, the bonnet suits me much better than her."

"Lydia, child, there are more important things now for me to deal with than your bonnets." Mrs. Bennet whispered impatiently. "Look." she pulled at her hand to make her look at the couple in front of them.

Lydia's eyes widened. "He's kneeling..." she gasped. "Do you think he is proposing?" she frowned, moving a bit forward. "I cannot hear a word from what he is speaking."

Mrs. Bennet bit her lower lip, her face all tense. "Good Lord, I beg you, do not let that girl do anything stupid." she muttered to herself.

"Yuck." Lydia stuck her tongue out in obvious disgust a moment later. "He has kissed her on the cheek."

Mrs. Bennet turned to her youngest daughter and hugged her. "At last!" she cried in a hushed tone, her eyes following Mr. Brooke and Elizabeth walking slowly back to the manor. "He has been taking ages, I almost thought him to be lost to us. Lydia, child, just imagine, fifteen thousand a year, Purvis Lodge and a house in town. We are truly blessed!"

Lydia shrugged her shoulders. "I am only happy that it is Lizzy marrying that old man and not me." she peered at her mother and added thoughtfully after a moment. "But you are right, Mama. It is a good match for Lizzy. Do you think Mr. Bingley will propose as well? He calls every day. Jane sits for an hour before the mirror every morning, as if she did not always look beautiful in any case."

"I think he will, Lydia. I think he will." Mrs. Bennet squeezed Lydia's rosy cheek.

Lydia smiled and asked pleasantly. "So if we are so fortunate, and Lizzy is to be so very rich, perhaps I could get a new bonnet after all?"

Chapter Eleven

The day was pleasantly warm, and Elizabeth Bennet was taking her everyday walk on the grounds surrounding Rosings Park. Since the day of her arrival, when she had the opportunity to admire the countryside through the carriage's window, she had taken a strong liking to the natural beauty of Kent. She especially fancied the wilder parts of the park, far away from the precisely manicured in the French style gardens situated in the closest vicinity of the manor. However, in the last few days, she had taken special care to keep her distance away from the great house and its surroundings, being well aware of the guests who had come to stay there.

For the duration of the last week, the inhabitants of Hunsford had not received the invitation to join Lady Catherine for dinner, or even for tea, even though it had been an established custom that the parson and his wife dined at Rosings every few days. Elizabeth rightly thought that her ladyship now had more attractive company to amuse herself in her nephews, Mr. Darcy and his cousin, Colonel Fitzwilliam, the younger son of the Lord of Matlock, as Mr. Collins had readily informed her. The lack of invitation was much to Elizabeth's satisfaction, who, contrary to her cousin, considered visits at Rosings to be neither highly pleasant, nor stimulating, and not in the least something to look forward to. She treated them as a duty she had to perform for Charlotte's sake.

There were many different reasons, Elizabeth Bennet was extremely glad to leave Longbourn for a few weeks to visit her friend, Charlotte, in her new home in Kent, even though she had definitely had mixed feelings about it when the invitation had been placed the previous autumn. Back then, spending several weeks in the company of Mr. Collins had not held that level of attraction for her. But when in the last days of February, the letter had come from Kent, renewing the invitation to spend the Easter at Hunsford in the warmest of tones, Elizabeth had found herself more than eager to accept it.

She craved some time away from her family and everyday life to be able to rethink and re-evaluate everything that had happened in the course of the last months. What she had not perceived, was that she would be compelled to meet Mr. Darcy there. Certainly she was aware of the fact that Mr. Darcy was related to Lady Catherine, however, the last thing she expected was for them to come to Kent exactly at the same time. Had she known about Mr. Darcy's intentions, she would have surely found some excuse not to come and stayed at home. The presence of the handsome gentleman from Derbyshire could only add to her current confusion about her life. How was she to make final the decision concerning her future with Mr. Brooke with Mr. Darcy separated just a lane apart from Hunsford.

Sitting on the fallen log, she propped her chin on one hand and stared at the green pastures below. Mr. Darcy was here, but it did not indicate anything, and she should not bother herself with him in the least, she chided herself. He had made himself perfectly clear that he had no serious intention towards her at all when leaving Hertfordshire so abruptly last autumn. Though Elizabeth felt deep in her heart that he had once liked her and felt attracted to her, it did not change the fact that he had chosen not to pursue her. She was sure that her old infatuation with him was gone as well, and she felt herself much more mature than last autumn. There was no true cause for her to fret and worry. She had made her decision, accepting John Brooke. In a few weeks, she would return home, and tell her father that she was unchanged in her decision to marry their neighbour, and then Mr. Bennet would give his consent to make the engagement public as he had promised. Mr. Darcy was nothing to her now, truly nothing.

The more Lizzy tried to reconcile her true feelings about John Brooke, she acknowledged that he had proved to be her true friend.

He had kept her company for the entire long winter, lifting her spirits, and eventually reuniting Jane and Mr. Bingley. It was something she was immensely grateful for. He was a good, intelligent and reasonable man, wealthy too, and attractive in his own way. Marrying him, she ensured the safe future for her family. She liked his company, she respected him, his obvious admiration for her flattered her own pride, and her decision to accept his proposal was right. Yes, the decision to accept him was the best she had ever made. She would find peace and happiness at the side of a man who respected and loved her. Closing her eyes for a moment, she shut the lushly green picture from in front her eyes, suddenly feeling terrified of the turn her life was about to take.

Elizabeth knew that something was very wrong; she felt it in her body and soul, especially when she was lying wide awake in the middle of the night. Some voice deep inside her was telling her that she should not have felt such a relief when her father had insisted on delaying the official announcement of the engagement till the time of her return from Kent, withdrawing his consent till she would be absolutely sure of the commitment she wanted to make. She felt as if was not ready to be married at all to anybody, and with every day of her stay at Hunsford, far away from Longbourn, and away from John Brooke, this conviction grew stronger.

Despite John's calm reaction to Mr. Bennet conditions, she was perfectly aware that he was less than pleased with her father's attitude towards his proposal. Elizabeth had wished to tell him that her heart was his, that her devotion for him was strong, deep and unbendable, and that these few weeks of separation meant nothing, as they had their entire life together. However, she had not dared to speak such assurances, even though she had been convinced he expected them and had every right to receive them from her. Most likely John must have felt her doubt and indecision, because the afternoon before her departure to Kent, he asked her for a few moments alone with her. As they took a turn around their usual spots along Longbourn, he had spoken little, but when they had reached the outskirts of the park, without any warming of sorts he pulled her into his arms, hiding them behind the large tree.

He had not forced her, giving her enough time to pull away from him when he had been leaning over her. But she had obeyed him; closed her eyes and titled her face, thinking she should start adjusting to him in this aspect; understandably as her husband he would do much more to her than a kiss. He was very gentle, and had not caused her any kind discomfort, but she had felt literally nothing. It had not even been unpleasant, she simply stood there stiffly, letting him press his lips to hers.

When he had pulled away, and she had met his gaze, his expression was strange, both worried and confused, if she had read it properly. She had given him a wan smile, averting her eyes, being perfectly aware that her reaction had been not something the man should expect from his future wife.

He had not commented on her reserve, but a moment later, she had felt herself drawn into his arms one more time. He held her very gently, as if she had been made of fine glass, and when she had sensed him leaning down for another kiss, she had closed her eyes, and imagined being in the darkened side room at Netherfield, the night of the ball, in the company of quite another gentleman.

When she had recollected herself, and broke the kiss, opening her eyes, she had seen John Brooke looming over her, his breathing laboured, eyes burning at her, face flushed. His arms had been wrapped firmly around her waist and back, keeping her so close to him that there had not even been the tiniest space between their bodies. Gazing into his eyes, she had frozen and paled abruptly, realizing that while kissing him, she had pictured herself to be in arms of Mr. Darcy.

Elizabeth could see how pleased John Brooke had been because of the way she had accepted his second kiss and embrace. Clearly, he had associated her earlier withdrawal and reserve with her maiden coyness or something of the kind, because he had only kissed her temple, tenderly asking forgiveness for his straightforwardness and frightening her.

The sound of someone's steps brought her back to reality. Turning around, she saw a young girl standing behind the log she had sat herself on. Standing up, she eyed the girl carefully. She was finely dressed, in a simple but very elegant dress, and could have been Lydia's or perhaps Kitty's age. How unusual. In a way, she looked strangely familiar to Elizabeth, even though she was sure they had never met before. But the shape of her eyes, her rounded face and straight, pale blond hair, yes... she looked so much like…

"Pray forgive me…." the girl started speaking, or rather stammering, drawing Elizabeth's attention away from her thoughts. "I am aware we have not been introduced, and it is rude of me to address you in the first place, but are you perhaps Miss Elizabeth Bennet?" she asked shyly.

Elizabeth's creased in confusion. "Yes, I am."

The girl's countenance brightened visibly and she spoke again, her voice much more animated. "I have heard so much about you." She smiled a bit unsurely. "My name is Georgiana Darcy."

Elizabeth's brows shot up. "Mr. Darcy's sister?"

The girl nodded. "It is such a pleasure to meet you at last, Miss Bennet." she spoke softly, still smiling. "I have heard so much about you from my brother. I must admit I decided to take a walk in hope of meeting you. I know about your love for long walks."

Elizabeth stared at the young girl in astonishment, not knowing how to respond. "I have heard much about you as well, Miss Darcy." she managed at last, not wanting to be rude, sensing that the young lady wanted to make friends with her.

The girl smiled, lowering her eyes to the ground, but saying nothing. She was visibly embarrassed. Elizabeth kept regarding her carefully… the way she titled her head… what a likeness… She had seen exactly the same movement so many times before when looking at her Aunt Madeline. Good gracious, was it possible that…? Elizabeth found it hard to believe such a possibility, but could it be true that her aunt, Madeline Gardiner, was related to Darcys themselves?

Elizabeth pushed those alarming thoughts aside, considering there would be time later to focus on them. "I have heard from Mr. Collins that the guests arrived at Rosings, but I have been only aware of Mr. Darcy's and his cousin Colonel Fitzwilliam's presence." she noted pleasantly.

Miss Darcy returned Elizabeth's warm gaze, speaking in soft musical voice, "It is not surprising, Miss Bennet, as usually my brother comes here alone every year to visit our aunt. I do not accompany him because I am busy with my studies in London. However, this time I asked him to bring me with him."

"Miss Darcy, would you care to join me?" Elizabeth asked, gesturing to a fallen log. The girl's smile grew bigger, and she sat next to Elizabeth.

"You mentioned your studies." Elizabeth enquired with smile. "Do they take a lot of your time?"

"Yes, quite." Miss Darcy said seriously, clasping her hands primly on her lap. "When I am not with my brother, I live with my companion, and I have several tutors, and see at least two every day, like my French and Italian tutor, then the music tutor, dance tutor, history and literature tutor, drawing and painting tutor." the girl counted on her slim fingers. "As well as the mathematics, and science tutors, as my brother thinks that lady deserves to have a broader view of the world than is usually expected in the society." she added.

Elizabeth's eyes widened in astonishment, and instantly her own youngest sisters came to her mind. It was impossible to imagine that Kitty and Lydia would have been able to bear such a regime, even for a few days. "You must have your entire days occupied." she noted with respect.

"Yes, but I do like it." Miss Darcy stressed. "My brother wants me to be a truly accomplished lady, and I am always happy to learn, to make him proud of me, but sometimes..." the girl paused, letting out a soft sigh. "I miss him." she said simply.

"I see." Elizabeth acknowledged softly, eying the younger girl. "You must feel lonely."

"Sometimes." Miss Darcy agreed quietly, but then added more cheerfully. "But I do understand that he is very busy, running the estate, and being involved with so many other important matters. My brother has many responsibilities, not just me. So many people depend on him for their wellbeing." meeting Elizabeth's somehow compassionate gaze, she spoke hastily. "He is the best brother one can possibly have."

Elizabeth's face spread in a reassuring smile. "Oh, I am sure of that. When I met your brother last autumn in Herefordshire, he mentioned you quite often to me, and to others as well, speaking very warmly about you each time, especially praising your skill on pianoforte."

Miss Darcy blushed in obvious pleasure. "I practice diligently several hours every day." she admitted.

Elizabeth laughed softly. "I do admire such devotion." she stressed smilingly, raising her brow. "I am ashamed to admit this, but I am much too lazy to force myself to practice every day. It is the main reason why my own playing is seriously lacking."

"Oh, no!" Miss Darcy denied at once in all seriousness. "My brother said your playing was delightful, and that he had rarely heard anyone to play with such a feeling, and my brother never lies."

Elizabeth was a bit taken aback with her companion's words and the unexpected praise for her own playing, which she knew was in best case decent; and for a moment she did not know how to respond. "You mentioned feeling lonely, Miss Darcy." she said at last, hoping to bring a new turn to the conversation. "But can you imagine that one can long for a moment of peace in his own company, which is hardly possible, when like me, one lives with four sisters."

"I have always wanted a sister." Georgiana spoke earnestly, staring straight at Elizabeth, a kind of longing in her expression.

Elizabeth was again quite astonished with her new friend's words, wondering if she was imagining herself, or if the young girl was making certain suggestions.

Smiling awkwardly, Elizabeth found another subject for discussion. "I remember your brother mentioning to me that you enjoy reading ghost stories." She could not really help the blush when she thought in what exact circumstances she had gained this knowledge.

"Oh, yes!" Georgiana clasped her hands together. "But my brother thinks that..."

Her words were interrupted by a strong, commanding male voice calling her name. Even if she could not yet see the man, Elizabeth knew instantly who the owner of the voice was.

In a matter of seconds, Mr. Darcy emerged from the other end of the grove, making Georgiana wave her hand at him and cry. "I am here, Brother!"

The man spotted the girl and started marching towards her, a scowl on his face. Elizabeth felt immediately sorry for the girl. She was sure that Mr. Darcy had not noticed her yet, as she stood right behind his sister, who was built on a larger scale than Elizabeth.

"Georgiana, I have been so worried about you. You informed Fitzwilliam about your intention of taking the walk in the gardens around the house, not miles away from…" Darcy stopped speaking, his eyes widening and then blinking a few times, when he recognized who his sister's companion was.

Georgiana trustingly scooted to his side. "But Brother, I was entirely safe, truly." she looked up at him. "You see, I met Miss Bennet, who has been here for several weeks already, visiting her friend Mrs. Collins, and she knows the grounds around the park very well.

"Miss Bennet." Darcy bowed, his brow furrowed. "I did not expect to see you here."

Elizabeth curtseyed coolly. "Sir."

"Brother, did you not hear Cousin Anne mentioning yesterday that Miss Elizabeth Bennet is currently visiting at Hunsford?"

"No, I did not." Darcy murmured, not tearing his eyes from Elizabeth for even one single moment.

"Mr. Darcy." Elizabeth spoke with calm dignity, not smiling. "Pray, believe me, I was also surprised to hear about your presence at Rosings from Mr. Collins." her expression softened when her eyes moved to Georgiana. "I am afraid, Miss Darcy, it is high time for me to return to the parsonage. I have promised to accompany Mrs. Collins to the village this afternoon." she walked a few steps to the girl, and took her hand, squeezing it gently. "I am most pleased to have made your acquaintance, Miss Darcy." she smiled warmly at the younger girl, without even a second glance at her brother standing beside her. "I shall be walking this path tomorrow morning as well, so I would be very happy if you could join me; of course, if your brother allows it." she nodded towards Darcy, meeting his dark eyes fleetingly.

"I will be here." Miss Darcy ensured, clearly not finding it necessary to ask her brother for permission.

Elizabeth smiled again, and with a final slight nod of her head towards Darcy, moved past the brother and sister, disappearing between the trees.

When Georgiana was quite sure that her new friend was out of earshot, she nudged her brother strongly. "Why did you not propose walking her back to the parsonage?"

"I…" Darcy creased his bushy eyebrows. "How did you meet her… how did you know it was she…?" he was mumbling incomprehensibly.

"It was easy, Brother." Georgiana chatted amiably, all smiles and enthusiasm. "As is said, I learned from Anne that she was visiting and that she liked taking walks every day. Moreover, she was exactly as you described her, a gentleman's daughter, not very tall, of slight build, with dark hair and sparkling eyes."

Darcy stared down at his sister with unseeing eyes, speaking nothing. Georgiana took his arm firmly and directed him back towards the manor. "She has been very nice to me, we spoke at briefly but many different matters, and I felt that she truly wanted to speak with and listen to me, not like Miss Bingley who talks with me just because I am your sister. Miss Bingley only pretends to be my friend to get closer to you." Georgiana added grudgingly.

"Sweetie, I know you do not feel comfortable in Caroline Bingley's company, but I can hardly do anything about it, as her brother is my close friend. We must tolerate her for Charles' sake." Darcy spoke distractedly, as if his thoughts had been on something else.

"Oh, I do understand." Georgiana assured earnestly. "What I meant was that Miss Elizabeth is so different than Miss Bingley in every respect. Still, I am so glad that Mr. Bingley will marry Miss Elizabeth's sister." she glanced up at his brother from behind her dark blond eyelashes. "It gives me hope that there will be the opportunity to see Miss Elizabeth at least from time to time."

Darcy stopped abruptly, but again said nothing.

"Brother, are you quite well?" Georgiana tried to look into his dark eyes, which were stubbornly hidden from her.

"I am well, I am well." he murmured. "Simply, I did not expect her to…" he cleared his throat, shaking his head. "Let us go." he said somehow resignedly, "Otherwise, in no time, Lady Catherine will send a search party looking for us."

Chapter Twelve

As Darcy was approaching the grove, his heart began to beat faster, matching well his overall agitation. [i]Calm down,[/i] he ordered himself inwardly, repeating to himself that she was merely a woman; a slight girl, years his junior, with no real consequence in the world. She should not capture him so much, and even less intimidate him. He still could not understand how it could have happened to him. He had always been in control of himself, of his feelings and emotions, being his very own master. And now, it was enough for her to look at him with those pretty eyes, or even worse, smile, and he seemed to temporarily forget everything which should matter to him.

Most unnerving was that he never knew what particular aspect of her would distract him. Like yesterday, when, as was his custom of late, he had been listening to her conversation with Georgiana. Actually, he had not been really following the subject of their discussion, but had let himself concentrate on Elizabeth's warm, softly accented, musical voice. And suddenly he had found himself wondering how it would have felt if he had her whispering in his ear, some sweet nonsense as they snuggled together in bed late in the evening. Such visions terrified him, but at the same time, kept enchanting him.

There was little point in denying that he was in love with her; so much in love, that he started considering marriage. If only last summer someone had told him that in the near future he would want to marry a young country lass without position and connections, with family in trade, he would have laughed him off. He still could not believe it himself, but it was an undeniable fact.

Since the day he had first set eyes on her again, three weeks ago, she occupied his every thought, and his day was miserable when he lacked the opportunity to see her, to talk to her.

On reaching the grove, he stopped in the shade of a large tree, and allowed himself to simply stare at her. She was sitting on a fallen log, her straw bonnet removed, abandoned next to her feet on the green grass, her eyes closed, her lovely small face titled up to the sun, with the wind gently blowing the curls around her face.

He swallowed, not being able to tear his eyes from her. Perhaps it was his destiny to marry her? He tried to escape her last autumn, trying so hard to forget her for the course of the entire winter. But it was all in vain, their paths crossed again, here in Kent, and she was even more perfect in his eyes than he had remembered. Bingley would surely propose to her sister, so it was inevitable he would meet her again in the future. Georgiana loved her already. His little sister was a different person when in Elizabeth's company. Her shyness was gone, and she actually acted as a young girl her age should.

Was it that Providence was telling his something? After all, who cared whether his wife came from a well connected family or had a large dowry? He did not need more money, and though her position in society was nothing to his, she was a gentleman's daughter, after all. The men from his social circle sometimes married actresses, governesses, or even servants, and in time society eventually accepted the matches. His marriage would cause some stir to be sure, but when his relatives and acquaintance met her, and got to know her, they would understand why he had decided to make her his wife. Suddenly all the reasons for which he had rejected the possibility of marrying Elizabeth Bennet before, seemed to be irrelevant to him.

From the very beginning of their acquaintance, he had felt bonded to her in every way, both physically and mentally. There was some invisible connection between them. He could not really explain how it happened, but nevertheless, he had felt it from the first moment he had laid eyes on her. The way she talked to him, the way she smiled and teased him, it all made her seem designed especially for him. He did not want to regret in ten or twenty years from now that he had let her slip away.

Moreover, he was almost sure she was not indifferent to him either. They had a difficult beginning, entirely due to his own rude comments about her, uttered to Bingley at the Meryton Assembly. However, even then, he had felt she had been affected by him the same as he had been by her. And those few times when they had been in private at Netherfield, his behaviour was not as it should be; when he encountered her in the corridor late at night, or when she had hurt her foot at the ball. It would have been so easy for her then to make others aware of their private moments, endangering her reputation, and at the same time forcing him into marriage. She had not done so, and he could only admire her for that. Despite her mother's vulgar matchmaking schemes, she always conducted herself with self respect and dignity. Those were certainly the features he would have liked to see in his children one day.

Taking a deep breath, Darcy walked energetically out of the trees. Elizabeth turned her head to him, and her eyes widened at the sight of him.

Darcy was by her side in a split of second, wordlessly raising her small hand to his lips. Suddenly, all felt good and right in his life. It was enough to have her hand in his, and all his doubts, worries, apprehensions and fears, were swept away, nonexistent, irrelevant.

"Mr. Darcy." she whispered, her face flushed. "I did not expect to see you here this morning."

Darcy felt her trying to free her hand from his grip, and very reluctantly released her. "My sister sends me to you. She has asked me to tell you that she cannot join you on your walk today."

"Is she well?"

"Yes, she is fine." Darcy assured her, his heart melting at the genuine concern he detected in Elizabeth's expression. "It is just a slight indisposition, I believe."

"Oh." she said with a slight frown, her eyes lowered.

Darcy winced inwardly for delivering to her that white lie. In truth, Georgiana had been more than fine this morning. When he had knocked at the door to her rooms, she had already eaten breakfast and was preparing herself for her daily walk in the company of Miss Bennet. He had said nothing to this, just walked to the window and stared out of it, thinking what would he have given for the opportunity to walk with Elizabeth, side by side, on such a fine spring morning.

Georgiana must have discerned the ability to read his mind, because she had approached him, and snuggling to his side, spoke. "You know, Brother, I think I feel a bit tired this morning. Yes, quite tired indeed, and I even start to feel the beginning of a headache. Perhaps it would be wise to stay home today and have some rest? I only worry that Miss Bennet will be waiting there for me, and she will surely get worried if I do not come on time." She looked up at him innocently. "Perhaps you could go to the grove and inform her that I would not be able to join her today?"

Darcy had looked into Georgiana's laughing eyes, and of course, agreed, struggling to keep his usual stern expression in place. He knew that his sister was perfectly aware that his interest in Miss Bennet was very special, and that all he craved was the opportunity to see her alone, but he still had some pride to behold.

"Mr. Darcy." Elizabeth's voice brought him back to the present moment. To his disappointment, she had put her bonnet back on her head, and was just tying the bow under her chin. "I thank you for taking so much trouble, and coming here to tell met that your sister cannot accompany me today. I hope it is only passing indisposition."

"Oh, I am sure it is." Darcy confirmed immediately.

Elizabeth smiled, curtseyed and began turning away from him, with the obvious intention of walking away.

"Miss Bennet!" Darcy cried, his tone much too agitated for the occasion, even to his ears, causing Elizabeth to look up at him with surprise.

"Could I replace my sister and walk with you this morning?" he asked quickly, in one breath, suddenly afraid she would say no.

However, Elizabeth smiled brightly at him, stepping toward him. "Of course you can, sir. It would be my pleasure."

Darcy wrapped her hand tenderly around his arm, and with a happy feeling in his chest, strode forward.

For a long moment, he had no desire to even speak with her. Having her by his side was enough to make him satisfied.

"You are very quiet, sir." Elizabeth noted, her eyes teasingly sparkling at him. "Sometimes I think that you do like conversing with me."

"That is not the case, I assure you." he said in all seriousness. "I do enjoy your company. Always." he stressed gazing warmly at her, causing her eyes to widen a bit. "I especially enjoy listening to you when you sharpen your wit on the others. Pray, believe me, it was not my intention to neglect you today, by not talking to you. Most of the time, I tend to voice myself only when there is something crucial to say, in my view, at least. Drawing room chit chat is not my strong point, and frankly, I think quite often, it lacks the purpose."

Elizabeth frowned slightly. "Should I understand, sir, that you find I speak too much in general on irrelevant matters? You are aware, that I quite enjoy participating in this idle chit chat to which you refer."

"No!" Darcy contradicted at once, stopping in place. "I always admire the way in which you express your opinions. It was not my intention to offend you." he covered her hand resting on his arm with his own to stress his words. "What I wanted to say was that, I am so pleased to be in your company this morning, that conversation seems unnecessary."

In the course of his speech, Elizabeth's face turned a lovely shade of pink. Darcy's eyes followed the flush spreading to her neck and lower, making her flush even more. Lowering her eyes, she bit her lower lip, as if worried, and resumed their walk.

Darcy kept gazing at her from time to time, worried he had upset her, because she seemed somehow distressed. "May I ask how long do you intend to stay in Kent?"

"About ten days." she answered absentmindedly.

"Only ten days." Darcy whispered to himself.

"Yes. I received letters from home yesterday." she spoke softly. "My father writes that he misses me, and my sister, Jane, adds that she needs me as well. Perhaps you are aware that she has accepted

Mr. Bingley's proposal, and wants to start wedding preparations as soon as may be, even though the date has not yet been settled."

"Yes, Bingley wrote to me that he has been accepted. He seems genuinely pleased with his decision to marry Miss Bennet."

"The same can be said about Jane." Elizabeth said with a smile, her voice more animated. "Her last letter was all enthusiasm, though usually she is so very guarded about showing her feelings."

"I understand your family needs you, but Georgiana will miss your company." Darcy remarked sadly.

"But we shall meet in a few months in Hertfordshire, because I believe you will attend Mr. Bingely's wedding." Elizabeth noted lightly.

"Of course we will." Darcy replied automatically. "Bingley has asked me to be his groomsman."

They walked silently for a while, Darcy gathering his courage to bring the conversation on the topic concerning their, he hoped, future together. But at last, he chose safer ground to begin.

"I would like to thank you for the time you chose to spend with my sister." he spoke sincerely. "Georgiana is very shy, and in general does not trust people easily. I am glad to see her so open with you. I am afraid that my company is often not enough for a young girl like her."

"She loves and admires you so much, Mr. Darcy." Elizabeth said with great conviction.

"But there are things I find awkward to discuss with her." he remarked uneasily. "Sometimes I feel I cannot help her in some matters."

"I agree there are certainly subjects which she would find hard to discuss with you, perhaps, but it is to be expected after all, considering the age difference between, or the simple fact that she is a female." Elizabeth said gently. "And truly, Miss Darcy is an exceptional young woman, in the sense of her mind, reason, accomplishments, manners, temper; in almost every respect I can think of. It is hard to believe she has been raised by an older brother alone, who has so many other responsibilities lying on him. If you would allow, I can exchange the letters with Miss Darcy."

"Thank you." Darcy said, covering her hand with his again. "I would wish her to have a female friend like you with whom she could share her troubles. I know she will be delighted with the idea of keeping a correspondence with you."

They did not talk much more that morning, but simply, as Darcy had suggested, enjoyed each other's company. But there was a new resolution in Darcy when he walked her to the gate of the parsonage. He decided to have her word to marry him before her departure to London.

***

Lady Catherine de Bourgh was seated on her usual place of honour, right in the middle of the drawing room. To her left, sat her daughter, Anne, with her companion Mrs. Jenkins; to her right, her parson, Mr. Collins, with his wife and sister-in-law.

The sound of animated female laughter came from the far end of the room, where the pianoforte was located, drawing her attention in that direction. Lady Catherine narrowed her eyes at the smiling face of the young woman who was currently playing the pianoforte. That Miss Bennet! She engaged others too much with her person. Even now, her nephews and niece abandoned their company, leaving Anne all alone, to listen to Miss Bennet's playing, which was quite poor, to say the least.

Cleary it was enough, that Miss Bennet smiled, and uttered some silly nonsense, to make Colonel Fitzwilliam and Georgiana laugh openly, while Darcy stared at her, spellbound. It was very fortunate indeed, that she was leaving next week. Darcy would be able to concentrate entirely on Anne. Catherine did not even blame her nephew entirely for taking an interest in this girl. It was understandable, as Miss Bennet could be attractive enough, and her company entertaining for gentlemen, with her pretty face, smiling eyes and daring opinions. But as Mr. Collins assured her she was to be married to her father's neighbour before the end of the summer, she was, thankfully, no real threat to her nephew.

Lady Catherine, calmed with that thought, was about to ask Mrs. Collins whether she had applied the medicine which she had recommended to her previously, when the wave of laughter was heard again from the other end of the room. One voice especially dominated the others, it was Darcy, laughing out loud, in a rich, deep baritone, clearly at something which that country chit from Hertfordshire had just said. In all her life, Catherine had never heard him to laugh so, to be so unreserved and unrestrained in company of others.

"Fitzwilliam, Darcy, Georgiana, come here all of you." she ordered sharply in a raised voice, putting an end to the merry chit-chat by the pianoforte. "I want to talk with Miss Bennet."

When her niece and Miss Bennet sat next to Anne, and Colonel Fitzwilliam and Darcy stood by the fireplace, but close enough to participate in the conversation, Catherine turned her attention to the young upstart, speaking pleasantly. "Miss Bennet, I believe that I owe you congratulations. Mr. Collins tells me that you sister has recently become engaged to a very promising young man."

Miss Bennet smiled, nodding her head. "Yes, Lady Catherine, to our neighbour, Mr. Bingley."

"Yes, that is a splendid match for your sister, as I know that Mr. Bingley's fortune is considerable. However, it is a good match for him as well, I believe, as his fortune comes from trade, and your sister is a gentleman's daughter, after all."

"I am sure that both my sister and Mr. Bingley are happy about their decision." Elizabeth remarked diplomatically in a light tone.

"Yes." Lady Catherine regarded her carefully, narrowing her eyes at her. "But I do hear that you are to be married soon, as well, and most advantageously to say the least too."

The sudden silence remained in the room. It was as if all at once, no one in the company dared to even take a deeper breath to break it. "To another neighbour." Lady Catherine continued, immensely pleased to gather such attention. "What is his name? Mr. ... Mr...."

"Mr. Brooke, your ladyship." Mr. Collins said quickly, with a bow of his greasy, balding head.

"Yes, Mr. Brooke, a widower, I hear. A man of great fortune, fifteen thousand a year, well, well." Lady Catherine pursed her lips. "He is a very wealthy man, quite a catch for your family,

Miss Bennet, especially when your estate is entailed to Mr. Collins."

Elizabeth said nothing, her eyes stubbornly lowered to her lap. It was Georgiana who spoke first, her voice unsteady.

"Miss Bennet, you are engaged?" she asked tremblingly, wide eyed.

"No, I…" Elizabeth stammered awkwardly. "Nothing has been settled yet, officially."

"Do you plan a double wedding together with your sister, Miss Bennet?" Lady Catherine asked loudly. "It would be very convenient, and save much work with preparations, not to mention the expense for your mother."

Elizabeth's very quiet voice was heard. "I have not yet thought about it, Lady Catherine."

"Well, Miss Bennet, if your Mr. Brooke and you will be passing by Rosings Park in the future, please do visit me. I would be very happy to meet him." her ladyship offered generously.

"I thank you, Lady Catherine." Elizabeth murmured very quietly again.

Lady Catherine was very pleased with her herself. Miss Bennet, though so animated before, barely spoke to anyone for the rest of the afternoon, and most importantly, stubbornly avoided looking directly at Darcy. Her nephew was also very withdrawn, even more than usual.

Soon Mrs. Collins gave the sign for the party from Hunsford to leave, and Lady Catherine kindly allowed them use of one of her carriages.

***

The next morning, Darcy paced the grove impatiently for more than an hour, unsure whether she would come today, but he had to see her immediately.

"Miss Bennet!" he exclaimed catching her pale mint dress passing across the pasture beneath the grove from the corner of his eye.

She froze, glancing up at him, only to lower her eyes a moment later. "Mr. Darcy." she murmured when he reached her.

"Miss Bennet." Darcy started, slightly out of breath, speaking hastily. "Forgive me, but I must be allowed to be quite forward in asking you." He paused, his eyes concentrated directly on her face. "Are you engaged to Mr. Brooke?"

Elizabeth returned his gaze and spoke in a calm voice, but strangely not resembling her usual one. "As I said to your aunt yesterday, Mr. Darcy, nothing has been settled officially. My engagement has not been announced." she paused. "Not yet, at least."

Darcy let himself relax. "Heavens to be thankful." he breathed, stepping closely to her, so he could feel her warmth and her scent. "But he did propose to you?" he wanted to know.

Elizabeth took a step back from him, straightened herself and spoke coolly, her eyebrow raised as if in a challenge. "Mr. Darcy, it is a private matter concerning only me, Mr. Brooke and my closest family."

Darcy took her hand in both of his, and leaning forward, spoke fervently. "Miss Bennet, it concerns me as well. You cannot imagine how I felt yesterday when I heard about your possible engagement. It makes me sick and terrified when I think that I could lose you so easily, due to my own fears, my stupid pride and indecision." he paused, his breathing laboured. "Miss Bennet," he whispered, placing her small palm on his chest, covering it with his own. "I have…" he trembled, overtaken with emotions. "I have admired you from the earliest moments of our acquaintance. I loved you last autumn, but convinced myself that what I felt was a mere infatuation, that it would go away in time. I ran away from you, taking Bingley with myself. But when Bingley informed me about meeting your sister in town, and his decision to court her, I knew already that forgetting you would not be easy, because I would most likely meet you again at their wedding. And when I came here to visit my Aunt, and saw you that day talking with Georgiana… I already knew I was lost, but I fought still, trying to convince myself that you were not for me, that the difference in our situation in life was too great for a man like me to take a serious consideration in you."

Elizabeth spoke nothing, all range of emotions crossing her face. A few times Darcy felt her attempting to release her palm from his grip, but he did not let her, only reaching for her free hand and placing it upon his chest, next to the other. "Now I think I was just making excuses against our union, because I was terrified of how strongly I have felt for you. And yesterday, when I realized how close I was to losing you to another, I finally saw what fool I was." he took a deep breath, whispering fervently. "Please tell me it is not too late, promise you will become my wife."

She freed her hands and walked away from him, speaking clearly with her back to him. "Mr. Darcy, I cannot promise you anything. I am practically engaged to another."

"You said you were not." Darcy insisted, crossing her way, trying to meet her eyes.

"I said that there was no official announcement of the engagement." she clarified. "However, Mr. Brooke proposed to me, and I accepted. It was my father who insisted on delaying the official announcement until my return from Kent."

"Has he got something against Mr. Brooke?" Darcy asked sharply.

She shook her head. "No, it was rather that he doubted whether I was entirely sure of the decision, and that is why he withdrew his consent for the time being. His explanation was that he wanted to give me the time to consider everything thoroughly again. The trip to Kent seemed to be an excellent opportunity for this."

"Your father is a wise man." Darcy said in a calmer voice. "I would be grateful to him till my last days."

"It does not change the fact I gave my word to Mr. Brooke." she reminded him.

"Do you care for him?" Darcy asked without preamble. "And please do not say it is not my business to ask you so."

"I respect him." Elizabeth spoke smoothly, in a sure voice. "I value his reasoning, and I enjoy his company. He has been very good to me and my family."

"But do you love him?" he insisted.

It took her a moment to respond, but with a shake of her head she said clearly, "No."

"Do you love me?"

"No... Yes..." she hesitated. "I do not know. I mean, I am confused."

Darcy took a deep breath and asked patiently. "Do you think you could come to love me one day?"

Now her answer was clear. "Yes." she said, meeting his eyes.

"Oh, my dearest, loveliest Elizabeth." he murmured, stepping towards her, pulling her decidedly into his arms. Her eyes widened in surprise, and she pushed at his chest in a momentary panic. But he ignored her resistance, hushing her. Leaning towards her face, his lips sought hers persistently, till she turned her face to him, so he could kiss her.

Darcy took his time and care to make the kiss memorable, coaxing her lips gently to open, stroking her cheek, pressing her small body against his large one, kissing her neck, stroking her back, eliciting some small gasps from her. He put his best effort into the job, wanting to make sure she would not wish to be held by another ever again.

When he finished, and lifted his head, looking down at her, her reaction was all that he wanted. She was practically sagging against him, her dark eyes unfocused and misty, staring into his without comprehension, her pretty, delicate lips, swollen.

Very gently, he gathered her to him again, resting her head on his chest, wrapping his arms around her. Only then, did he realize how slight and small she was. Of course he had always been aware that she was not among the tallest, even for a lady, but when she stood by him like that, she barely reached his chest.

"What now?" she spoke first, in a lazy whisper, her words muffled against his coat.

Darcy looked down at her. "I know it would be an unpleasant situation for you, my love, but you will have to inform Mr. Brooke about your change of heart."

"I do not want to hurt him." she said worriedly. "I believe he genuinely cares for me."

He stroked her face. "I can well believe this. I doubt there is a man in the world who would not come to love you." he kissed her lips lightly. "I know you possess a tender heart, but it is better to do it sooner rather than later. Perhaps you wish me to talk to him? I will gladly do this to spare you distress. The blame for this situation is all mine, after all. Had I not abandoned you last autumn, we would probably have been engaged for some time, or perhaps even already married."

Hearing his words, Elizabeth frowned. "I am afraid that you presume far too much, Mr. Darcy. I have not agreed to marry you yet." she said sternly, but with a shadow of smile in her eyes.

"Forgive me." he nuzzled her neck. "I shall wait as long as you need to feel ready to marry me."

Elizabeth's expression clouded, as if she had remembered about something unpleasant, and she spoke in dead seriousness. "Mr. Darcy, there are things we have to talk about and explain before I can accept you. I would like to ask you a few questions." she looked straight into his eyes. "Questions concerning the life you had led before we met."

Darcy held her gaze, clearly surprised with the turn of conversation. "I have no secrets." he spoke evenly. "You can ask me about anything you wish to know."

She seemed to calm with his assertion, and this time of her own will, placed her head on his chest. "I will ask, but perhaps not today." she whispered, her eyes closed. "I will have to go back to the parsonage soon."

"I will walk you back." he ensured. "But first…" he murmured, lifting her against his frame, and cupping her face to kiss her again.

Chapter Thirteen

John Brooke stood by the window in the parlour at Hunsford, his gaze concentrated on the attractive couple standing for a long time at the gate leading to the parsonage.

"Oh, there she is, Mr. Brooke." Mr. Collins spoke from behind his back. "It seems Mr. Darcy, our noble patroness, Lady Catherine's nephew, was so kind to walk her down from her walk."

"Yes, so it seems." Brooke murmured darkly.

"They must have met accidentally somewhere in the park." Mrs. Collins said quickly, glancing with slight alarm at their guest's stormy expression. "Elizabeth will be so pleased to see you. She was not expecting your visit."

"Yes, I can well believe it." Brooke said, his eyes narrowing as he observed Darcy following Elizabeth to the house.

Brooke turned from the window, and rested his gaze on the door till it opened, and Elizabeth entered with Darcy close behind her.

"Mr. Brooke." Elizabeth curtseyed, walking to him. "How very unexpected. I thought I should not see you until next week in London."

Brooke smiled, putting a pleasantly engaging expression on his face. In one long step, he approached Elizabeth closely, taking her hand, and raising it to his lips. "I could hardly stay away from you longer, Miss Bennet. I thought I might convince you and Miss Lucas to return a few days earlier. My carriage is at your disposal." Saying the last words, he looked over Elizabeth at Darcy, who was standing firmly behind her the entire time. Brooke nodded his head slightly, acknowledging the other's man presence, and was rewarded with the same serious bow on Darcy's side.

Elizabeth freed her hand from his, as she stubbornly avoided looking at him. "I am not sure if it is possible, Mr. Brooke." she said quietly, stepping back. "Everything is arranged for us to return at the end of next week. My uncle is to send a male servant to escort us."

Brooke took her hand again, closing it within his and stroking the top of her soft palm with his thumb. "Please consider this, my dear. It would be much more comfortable for you and Mrs. Collins' sister to travel in a private carriage. I, myself, can gladly return on horseback."

Elizabeth closed her eyes briefly, before opening them, and lifting her head to look straight into his eyes. "Mr. Brooke, I would wish to talk with you in private." she said decidedly before turning to her friend. "Charlotte, would you be so kind to leave us alone for some time?"

"Of course." Charlotte agreed instantly. "Mr. Collins, let us take a tea in the dining room." she said, taking her husband's arm and leading him out of the room. "Mr. Darcy, would you care to join us?" She looked pointedly at the tall man when passing by him.

Darcy placed his hand on Elizabeth's arm, and leaning forward whispered. "I will be close by if you need me." Having said that, he gave Brooke one last hard, challenging look, then silently walked out of the room after the Collinses.

The moment the door closed, and they were alone, Brooke approached Elizabeth closely, leaning forward, obviously expecting a kiss. She, however, averted her face quickly and stepped way from him, far enough that he could not reach her.

"What is wrong?" Brooke asked, eyeing her carefully.

"I cannot marry you." she said quickly, and then lowering her head added softly. "Forgive me."

"You cannot marry me." he repeated dryly. "I see. Can you give me some explanation why you have changed your mind?"

Elizabeth took a deep breath before she spoke, this time in a clear, if not a very strong voice. "For the last weeks, I have given much consideration to your proposal, and I came to the conclusion that a union between us is not possible. Though I like and respect you, sir, and additionally hold you in high esteem, I am certain I will never be able to have that kind of affection for you which a wife should have for a husband."

Brooke stepped to her, placing his hands on her shoulders. "Elizabeth, you cannot know that." he tried to convince her in a warm, patient voice. "You are still very young, and all that can change. On my part, I swear I will do everything in my power to make you happy. Perhaps in time, you could learn to love me as I came to love you."

Elizabeth walked to the window and stared out of it.

"I was afraid of this separation between us, and I was right." he continued, coming behind her, feeling her to stiffen when he wrapped his arm around her from behind, pulling her to him. "I will not demand anything for which you are not ready." he whispered into her ear. "You will have all the time you need to get used to me in every respect. You have my word on that."

Elizabeth broke from his embrace and turned to face him. "The marriage between us cannot be." she spoke firmly. " I am so…" she looked up at him pleadingly. "...so sorry that I have to cause you pain, but it is utterly impossible. We would be like two strangers living under the same roof. Believe me, I have seen the results of such a union, and nothing good can come of it. I know I would be very unhappy, and I am also sure that I could never make you happy. It is best for both of us to end it now."

"Be honest with me." he paused, making sure she looked straight into her eyes. "Is there someone else?"

"Yes." she said quietly, and looked away from him.

"Darcy." he guessed.

She only nodded. "When I agreed to marry you, I thought I would probably never meet him again."

"You are sure he will be willing to marry you?"

She nodded again. "He has proposed."

"I see. I am the inconvenient obstacle for you future happiness." He did not try to stop the bitterness in his voice.

The tears brimmed Elizabeth's eyes. "You must believe that I did not want this. I have never wanted to hurt you."

"Do not flatter yourself." he said in such a cold tone that Elizabeth felt cold shivers running down her spine. "And do not think it is the end between us." He cupped her chin between his fingers, making her look directly at him. "I have invested too much of my time and attention into you." With these words, he stormed out of the room, directing himself straight to the entrance, not speaking with anyone on his way.

Left alone, Elizabeth started to cry, tears running freely down her cheeks without any control on her part. Her vision blurred, but she soon felt Charlotte's voice enquiring gently, and then she knew it was Darcy by her side. He enveloped her into his arms, and she let out all the pent up emotions, breaking into more tears, effectively wetting his coat and shirt.

"Hush, sweetheart, he is gone. All is well now." he whispered, kissing the top of her head, rocking her in his arms. "You have been very brave. Now you need to forget about this, and we can be very happy together. Yes?"

She only nodded into his chest, clinging to him, as if afraid to let him go.

***

The next morning, Darcy was attending to the correspondence from Pemberley in the library, when the out of breath, pale as a ghost, Georgiana flew into the room.

"Brother, Elizabeth…" she uttered, trying to catch her breath.

Darcy stood up abruptly from behind the desk. "Something happened to her?" he cried, seeing the expression on his little sister's terrified face.

Georgiana put her hand on her chest to calm her breathing and started speaking. "Brother, it is so horrible. I have just seen Elizabeth being abducted by some man."

Darcy's face went rigid. "What are you speaking of?" he demanded sharply. "That cannot be."

Georgiana shook her head. "It is true, Brother. I was on my way to meet her at our usual spot, and I saw her nearly a quarter mile from myself, on the other end of the road leading to the parsonage.

I was about to call to her, but suddenly a carriage drove past me at great speed. It stopped by Elizabeth, and a dark dressed man came out of it. They talked shortly, and then he simply took her forcibly into his arms and dragged her into the open carriage door. She struggled, and I believe attempted to scream, but soon he pulled her inside, and they drove away. I cried and ran after them, but they soon disappeared by the turn of the road."

Darcy stared at her in tension, before speaking calmly. "Did you see the man?"

"Hardly. But he was big, and as tall as you, quite old. His carriage looked expensive, even luxurious. Oh, Brother, who could do something like this to her, and why?"

"When was it?" he asked, ignoring her question, his face an unreadable mask.

"I am not sure." she frowned in concentration. "I ran here as soon as quickly as I could… so perhaps half an hour ago, or even less."

"Do not worry." Darcy placed a distracted kiss on the top of his sister's head. "I will find her." he said, running from the room, leaving a still shaking Georgiana alone.

***

Elizabeth was tossed not so gently into the carriage. John Brooke climbed after her, and gave the driver the sign to drive on.

She leaped to the other end of the carriage, trying to open the window and scream for help; but before she could open her mouth, the big hand clasped over it, and an iron arm wrapped around her. She struggled against him as long as she could, but in vain. Her captor was simply stronger than herself.

At last, her strength seemed to abandon her, and she ceased her fight. Only then did he let her out of his grip, allowing her to move into the far corner of the carriage.

"Where are you taking me?" she whispered.

"London." he answered calmly, not even bothering to look at her. "We will be married tomorrow morning. I have already acquired the special license. Till our wedding, you shall stay at my townhouse. Your reputation will be entirely ruined, and simply, you will have no other choice but to obediently marry me." he informed her calmly.

"Let me free!" Elizabeth cried with new found energy, but he ignored her.

"I demand to be released!" she cried again desperately.

"I told you yesterday that I invested too much time into you to just let you go. I want to have a gentleman's daughter as my wife, and I will." he informed her. "And remember this well." he paused menacingly. "I always get exactly what I want. You can say that it is a matter of principle for me."

"I will run away!"

"Elizabeth, be reasonable about this." Now he sounded almost gentle. "My promise stands, I will do everything to make you pleased, safe and happy. In no time, you will forget about him."

"I will not!" she denied heatedly. "I will always love him, and I will never marry you. He will come after me."

"I seriously doubt it." he said flatly. "Even if he decides to take any action, it will be too late anyway. Knowing your love for long walks, it will take them several hours, at least, to discover that you are gone. By the time he finds you, though I do seriously doubt whether he cares enough to take the trouble, you will be safely married to me. Now come to me, Elizabeth." he gestured towards her. "I want to show you that our life together does not have to be as bad as you imagine." Having said this, without preamble, he pulled her forcibly into his arms and started roughly kissing her.

"Do not fight me." he murmured, when her body started twisting desperately in his hold, her hands pushing at him. "Be nice, or I will take you even before the wedding." he threatened her. "You do not really want your first time with a man to be on the floor of a running carriage, do you?"

Elizabeth gasped and stilled in horror. He used it, effectively pushing her flat on her back on the seat, covering her small body entirely with his.

"No!" she cried, struggling again, trying to somehow dislodge him from her, and eventually biting hard on his hand, when he tried to cup her face.

Brooke hissed, cursed crudely, and catching her hands together, pinned them easily over her head with just his one hand. "I told you to be nice." he murmured, reaching with his other hand to her chest, opening her spencer and kneading her small breast roughly through the thin material of her cotton dress.

"I hate you!" she spat out with vengeance.

He only laughed. "Really?" his hand abandoned her breasts and moved down her body. "And what will you say now?" he kept smiling cruelly when he gathered the folds of her dress, lifting it high over legs, bundling it around her waist.

Terrified, Elizabeth glanced down to see his hand reaching under the hem of her chemise, his heavy hand resting on the side of her hip.

"How do you like this, Miss Bennet?" he asked crudely, his hand moving lower to the right, just below her navel.

"Please stop." she whispered, tears in her eyes. "I beg you…" she trembled in fear and disgust. "Please, let me go."

His hand kept resting lightly on her most intimate parts, and he seemed to be regarding her carefully. At last he sighed and slowly let her go, climbing away from her, straightening his clothes. "You are right." he said, when she began hastily covering herself, her cheeks burning, her eyes still wide in terror, hands trembling.

"You deserve at least a bed for this." he continued, observing as she curled in the far end of the carriage. "Perhaps you do not want to believe it, but it is not my intention to hurt you unnecessarily."

Elizabeth did not speak again, and only turned herself with her back to him. She was so shaken and out of control, that she could not stop herself from crying, violent sobs shaking her body regularly.

"Stop it." she heard an irritated raised voice, when an especially loud sob escaped her. "I do not want to hear any crying here."

Elizabeth kept herself to her corner, not daring to breathe, hoping not to raise his anger again. She was in utter despair. She knew that if she could not manage to escape before they reached his townhouse, there would be no hope for her. She was not even aware how much time had gone by, when she saw them passing through the village, and spied the inn where she knew they should change horses. As they had moved at a fast pace, the horses needed to be replaced soon.

He seemed to read her thoughts as he spoke. "Another carriage waits us just outside the village. I thought there was no need to waste time at the inn, when I have several carriages at my disposal. Besides, you can understand that I was afraid you would try to gather some attention were we to stop to change the horses at the inn." he glared her. "And it is seems that I was entirely right."

"I would have behaved." she said as calmly as she was able to in her state, glancing up at him.

Brooke raised his brow doubtfully. "Oh, really? Just a little while ago you gave enough proof that you would not cooperate."

She closed her eyes. "I would do anything to prevent you from…" she trembled. "being so rough with me."

Her words must have kindled something within him, because he moved to her, turning her gently to him. She let him cradle her, allowing her head to rest on his chest. "I do not wish you to be afraid of me." He rubbed her back and kissed her hair. "What happened here shall not be repeated as long as you are good to me. I want to treat you as the gentlewoman you are, but you have to behave. I know you are surprised with all this, but all will be well. You will lack nothing as my wife; I promise you. Do you hear me? You will be a real lady as my wife, and we will raise our sons as gentlemen and daughters as true gentlewomen. I will even set aside a considerable sum for the dowries for your yet unmarried sisters, and I will make sure your mother is well cared for after you father's death." He titled her face. "But you must be nice to me." he murmured, stroking her face. "Do you understand?"

She nodded in response, and let him lean closer, trying very hard not to flinch when he kissed her this time very gently.

The carriage came to a halt, breaking their kiss. Brooke smiled at her, and looked out the window. "Come." he gestured to her, opening the door. "Another carriage is already waiting."

The moment he turned to look at her, he saw the door on the other side of the box was wide open, and her white dress was quickly disappearing among the trees in the forest on the other side of the road.

***

Elizabeth ran the fastest she could, not caring that the branches were hitting at her face and hands, scratching at her delicate skin. She did not dare to turn back even once, and kept running, with each passing moment feeling more and more secure that he would not reach her. The wind was blowing in her ears, and she did not even register the heavy footsteps just behind her and a male voice calling her name.

Suddenly the air was knocked out of her, when a strong arm wrapped around her middle, stopping her effectively in place. She screamed and started fighting wildly against the man's firm hold on her. He let her go immediately. Without looking back at him, she leaped forward, but somehow tripped over a protruding root, and fell flat on the ground.

The next moment, she felt him next to her, touching her. "No, do not touch me, leave me alone!" she cried, battling at his hands resting on her. "I will kill myself if you touch me! Do you hear me?! I swear I will kill myself!"

"Elizabeth, calm down." she heard the familiar deep voice. Strong hands were lifting her up, and she was gently cradled to his muscular, male chest; the familiar clean spicy scent overpowering her, his deep, warm voice murmuring gently. "It is me. You are safe."

She lifted her eyes, blinking her tears away. Suddenly, she was clinging to man beside her. "It is you." she choked. "I knew you would come for me. He said that you would not, but I knew you would."

"Of course I would. Always." Darcy whispered, cradling her to him, soothing her. "All is well, my love, all is well. You are safe."

Chapter Fourteen

"You are well?" Darcy enquired, pushing her gently away from him to regard her carefully. His hands touched her face gently, and moved down her body. His lips pressed tightly, his countenance darkened when he noticed the red marks on the delicate skin of her shoulders and neck, accompanied by even more visible ones on her wrists.

"Did he hurt you?" he asked very quietly.

Elizabeth flushed bright red, new tears brimming her eyes. "He tried but…" she swallowed. "He…" she shivered visibly "… touched and manhandled me a bit, but I was spared…" she did not finish, because she started crying again.

Darcy cursed roughly under his breath, and wrapped her tightly into his arms.

When she gradually calmed into his comforting embrace, and her crying ceased, he cupped her face to have her look at him. He spoke softly, "We cannot stay here forever, Elizabeth. We must go back to the road."

Instantly her face went ghostly pale, eyes wide in terror, and she shook her head. "I will not return there."

Darcy put calming hands on her shoulders. "You do not have to be afraid. Colonel Fitzwilliam came with me. That scumbag will not dare to harm you again. He cannot be so stupid as to attack an armed soldier. Besides from what I have noticed, he, himself, is unarmed. Clearly he was not expecting anybody to stop him."

Elizabeth was still reluctant, her expression scared and unsure, but Darcy brought her decidedly to his side, wrapped his arm around her back and started walking. "We must get you to Hunsford as soon as can be. I want the doctor to see you. I do not like those scratches and bruises on your skin."

"I do not need a doctor." Elizabeth said, walking obediently, snuggled close to him the entire time. "How did you manage to find me so soon?" she waned to know, lifting her eyes at him.

"It was Georgiana who alerted me." Darcy stated as he kept walking, clearing their path when necessary. "Thankfully, she witnessed how he abducted you, and she ran to me, telling me everything. In ten minutes, the two best horses in my aunt's stables were ready. Colonel Fitzwilliam suggested that Brooke probably would wish to take you to London, thinking that he was safe in his plan, and that your absence would not be noticed till late afternoon. Our hope was that he would change horses in Bromley. You must imagine how worried I was when it turned out that he had not. I started thinking that perhaps our suspicion about London was incorrect, and that he took you somewhere else, probably to some secluded estate in the country. Thankfully my cousin insisted that we should ride further along the road to London, and he was right, as we came upon his carriage just outside the village. When his carriage came to a halt, I saw you running out of it into the forest. Fitzwilliam took care of Brooke, while I ran after you. I was afraid you would get lost somewhere."

Darcy finished his tale, just as they were close enough to see the road through the trees. Elizabeth attached herself more firmly to Darcy's arm, stepping closer while trying to remain a step behind him.

Brooke and Colonel Fitzwilliam stood in front of the carriage, the second man keeping a sword in one hand and the pistol in the other directed at his companion.

When Elizabeth and Darcy came out of the trees, Brooke gestured towards the lady, calling her in a commanding voice. "Elizabeth, come here."

Instantly she hid herself behind Darcy, her hands clasping at his coat. Darcy turned around to face her, and leaned to whisper something into her ear, calming her.

The next moment, he turned swiftly, and without any kind of warning threw his fist straight into Brooke's nose. "This is for scaring her." Another strong blow was directed into the older man's stomach. "And this for manhandling her."

"You will never again come anywhere near her." Darcy continued calmly, while Brooke was kneeling, half bent on the ground. "And you will pay for this, do not doubt it." he informed him. "Perhaps you are not aware of the customs among higher classes, but kidnapping a gentleman's daughter against her will, taking her without the consent of her father and family is not something commonly accepted."

"I am in my rights." Brooke stammered, raising slowly to his feet. "She is mine, promised to me."

"She is not yours, and never has been." Darcy replied in the same tone. "Mr. Bennet has never given his consent. Elizabeth has agreed to be my wife. If you were the gentleman you pretend to be, you would respect her wishes."

"That is unusual, that you still want her now, after I had her." Brooke said menacingly, narrowing her eyes at the younger man.

"That is not true!" Elizabeth cried in a high pitched voice from behind Darcy's back.

"Shut your mouth you little..." Brooke started speaking, moving behind Darcy's back to reach for her, but he did not finish, because one more time, his face came into close contact with Darcy's fist.

Brooke swayed under the blow, but he did not fall to the ground this time.

"Elizabeth, I give you one last chance to come with me." he muttered after a moment, wiping the blood from his mouth.

"Miss Bennet is not going anywhere with you." Colonel Fitzwilliam said calmly and firmly.

"Is she not? Really?" Brooke laughed unpleasantly. "I see. In this case, Mr. Darcy, I do not feel obliged to keep the secret of your little sister's near elopement last summer."

There was a moment of silence, both Darcy and the colonel looked simultaneously at each other.

"Surprised?" Brooke enquired with obvious satisfaction. "Back in Hertfordshire I became, let us say, well acquainted with Mr. Wickham. He turned out to be very talkative." He smiled, adding, "With the right incentive, of course."

Darcy did not manage to respond to this, because the blade of Colonel Fitzwilliam's sword came just beneath Brooke's throat.

"You must be completely out of your mind." he said evenly. "To fabricate such nonsense about the granddaughter of an earl without any evidence whatsoever, but the word of some servant's son. In your place, I would not even try to spread such gossip. Besides, who do you think Society will believe? Darcy, the respected landowner from one of the oldest families in the country, who has his entire, well connected and respected family behind him, or a Mr. Wickham, the steward's son, who has probably just enough debts to be jailed for them even now? You really believe that spreading such lies would help you to get a place in upper circles of society, to which you clearly aspire?" Colonel Fitzwilliam shook his head. "I do not think so."

Elizabeth peeked at Brooke from behind Darcy, crying fiercely "You are a despicable liar! You are lying now about Miss Darcy! Just the same as when you told me that falsehood about Mr. Darcy, his mistresses and out of wedlock children."

Darcy stared at her in shock. "What?"

Elizabeth nodded. "At Netherfield Ball, he advised me that I should keep my distance from you, saying that you kept mistress in town, and that you had seduced some young girl whose father is in trade, and who had later given birth to your child, but you refused to marry her."

"He is more pathetic that I thought." Colonel Fitzwilliam said to Elizabeth and Darcy as if Brooke was not even there. "He cannot even get himself a woman without fabricating some utter nonsense about his competition."

"True." Darcy said, imitating his cousin's haughty and superior tone. "I should probably call him out for this, but he is not worth the blade of my sword."

"You are perfectly right, Cousin." Colonel Fitzwilliam agreed calmly, still ignoring Brooke's presence. "God knows who his parents were. Perhaps some fishmongers in London?" he twisted his lips in distaste. "That would be a dishonour, both for our family and Miss Bennet as well," he bowed elegantly towards Elizabeth, "to even call him out."

Brooke looked furious, red in the face. "Elizabeth, this is your last chance." he threatened. "Come with me now, and I promise you that there will be no scandal. If you choose to stay with him, the whole of Hertfordshire will know tomorrow about your scandalous behaviour with Mr. Darcy, here in Kent. I will tell everyone that you paid very special attention to him while still pretending to be my betrothed. You will be ruined. You and all your sisters. "

Elizabeth stepped bravely in front of Darcy. "I prefer to ruin my reputation than go anywhere with you." she lifted her chin up. "I am not afraid of you."

"Really?" Brooke eyed her menacingly. "You were not that sure of yourself when I had my hands under your skirts back in the carriage!" he spat out angrily.

Darcy pushed Elizabeth gently aside to have a free way to hit Brooke again several times, this time effectively dropping him to the ground.

Elizabeth stared in shock at her former captor, lying now bleeding on the ground.

"Come, Elizabeth." Darcy blocked the unpleasant view with his chest. "I am sorry you had to witness this."

She nodded, her eyes still wide, but she let herself be gathered to Darcy's side, as they walked to the horses awaiting down the road.

"Should we let him to go?" Darcy asked his cousin when they reached their mounts, observing Brooke's servant helping to lift him off the ground and climb into the carriage.

"We have little choice now, especially with Miss Bennet here with us. I think we should try to avoid any more unnecessary attention. She will soon be a member of our family." The colonel smiled at Elizabeth, who still stood closely by Darcy's side. "And for her own good, we must avoid any more scandal. However, we should think how to make him pay for this." he added seriously.

Darcy looked into his cousin's eyes, agreeing silently before looking down at Elizabeth. "Shall we go?" he smiled, directing her to one of the horses.

She managed a pale smile. "Yes. But…" she looked apprehensively at the black stallion to which Darcy led her to. "I am afraid I do not ride very well."

"You will ride with me." Darcy smiled warmly, and before she knew it his hands were on her slim waist, she was effortlessly lifted on the horse's back. A moment later, Darcy was in the saddle behind her, one of his hands wrapped securely around her middle while his other hand held the horse's reins.

Elizabeth's eyes widened as she glanced down. "It is a very big horse."

Darcy chuckled, bringing her closer to himself. "We will go slowly." he promised, turning the horse.

"Thank you for coming for me." Elizabeth said softy, burying herself more comfortably into his chest.

Darcy's embrace around her only tightened, and he bent his head to place a kiss on the side of her neck, whispering. "Always at your service."

The tender moment was interrupted by the colonel, who stopped his horse, waiting for them to catch up with him.

"I think we should not go through Bromley." he said, "A lot of people stop there. Someone may recognize us, and it is not necessary."

"I agree." Darcy nodded. "We will take the longer way." Darcy leaned to Elizabeth. "Will it not be too tiring for you?" he enquired warmly.

"Not at all." she smiled and settled herself more comfortably against him. "There is only one matter which bothers me." she said seriously.

Both men stared at her with concern, while she turned to Darcy, looking up at him and saying with a smile. "I still do not know your first name."

Colonel Fitzwilliam laughed shortly, regarding Elizabeth for a moment with obvious fondness in his blue eyes, before he kicked his horse's side, riding forward to give the couple some privacy.

***

When they returned to the parsonage, it was already very late afternoon, nearly evening. Darcy, himself, carried his precious burden upstairs to her room. Elizabeth was grateful for that, as her bottom and lower back hurt from the activity to which she was unused.

At first Darcy strongly insisted that the doctor should be called. However, when Elizabeth protested, and Mrs. Collins supported her, saying that she was perfectly able to take care of a few scratches, as she had many times helped her mother to cure such cuts when her brothers had still been boys, he reluctantly conceded.

When Mrs. Collins left them alone in order to see to Elizabeth's bath, Darcy sat on the edge of the narrow bed on which she reclined, taking her hand.

"I do not want to leave you alone after the ordeal you have been through today. Still," he sighed. "It would be improper for me to stay with you."

"I know." she moved, wincing slightly.

It alerted Darcy instantly. "Are you in pain?"

"Yes." she acknowledged reluctantly.

"Where?" he put his hands on her, wanting to examine her, but she slapped them.

"It is nothing serious…" she settled herself more comfortably, putting a small pillow under her back, which brought her some relief.

Darcy was staring at her, a genuine concern written on his face.

She rolled her eyes. "My back parts are sore." she admitted shyly, but seeing his amused reaction to her words, she frowned at him. "Do not dare to laugh at me. I have no idea how one can find anything pleasing in horse riding."

He kept smiling at her. "I will be happy to instruct you to ride properly one day at Pemberley."

"No, thank you." Elizabeth scowled at him.

Darcy chuckled, shook his head, and before she could protest, moved swiftly, settling himself on the head of the bed, pulling her to him, so that her back was against his chest. "Let me." he said, as he pushed her slightly forward, his hand moving down her back to massage the area at the base of her spine.

She was startled at first, but soon, a rather unladylike groan escaped her. "It feels good." she murmured, blushing furiously, while his warm hand kept rubbing the small of her back. "Thank you."

He bent to kiss the nape of her neck, his arm supporting her from the front.

"William…" she paused, "But you believe me… you do believe me, please say that you do."

He frowned, his hand on her back stopping its movement. "About?"

She sighed and shivered. "That he did not ruin me…"

"Yes." his hand resumed its stroking, "But I do understand that he tried..."

"Yes." she turned into his arms and looked up at him, two big tears rolling down her cheeks. "And it was true what he said before you started to hit him again…"

"Shush…" Darcy cradled her to him again, kissing her hair. "You do not have to tell me about it."

"No, I want to…" she whispered, her face hid on his arm. "In the carriage, he pushed me down on the seat, laid on me, and started touching me where… I always thought only my husband one day would have right to… But I begged him to stop, and he did. He let me go. Then the carriage stopped and I managed to run away…"

Darcy kept rocking her.

"You want me still, after what I told you?" she asked when he said nothing for a longer moment.

He pushed her from him, cupping her face, making her look at him. "I love you."

"Yes, but every gentleman expects his wife to be untouched."

"But you are untouched, you protected yourself." he spoke, looking steadily into her eyes. "I can only admire your spirit and courage. We must be thankful that nothing worse happened than his daring to put his dirty hands on you. You will see, after our wedding, in time you will forget about this. I will make sure that you will know and remember only my touch on you. And what happened today will be just a bad dream."

She seemed to hesitate for a moment before she asked, "But you would not want me any longer if he had…" she did not finish.

"I cannot imagine not wanting you, no matter what might have happened. Believe me, I have tried." He let out a heavy sigh, "But I will not lie to you. It would probably have been difficult for me to come to terms with it. I presume I would have killed him, and any man who would have forced himself on you or Georgiana. I barely stopped myself today and last summer."

Elizabeth eyes widened. "Last summer?" she gaped at him. "Does it mean that what he said about Georgiana and Mr. Wickham was true?"

"Yes. Fortunately my sister trusted me with her secret before the planned elopement actually took place."

"How horrible! Poor Georgiana! And Mr. Wickham he seems so…" she looked for the right word. "…so agreeable, so trustworthy."

"Oh, yes, he certainly does. One thing George Wickham can certainly do well is recommend himself to strangers."

Elizabeth was shaking her head, as if trying to comprehend what she had been told, when she looked up abruptly at Darcy. "Does it mean that what Brooke told me about you is the truth as well?"

Darcy raised his brow. "About my supposed illicit affairs?"

Elizabeth nodded slowly, her eyes wide.

Darcy laughed. "No, no mistress and no out of wedlock children. Though I do hope to have at least one or two little ones running around through Pemberley in the years to come." he grinned at her. "Still, I do intend to acquire them in a most legitimate way…" he paused, leaning towards her, and murmuring in low voice, his large, warm hand resting heavily on the top of her thigh. "through the marriage bed."

Elizabeth lowered her head, blushing bright red, and produced a small embarrassed smile. "Stop that." she whispered.

"Stop what?" he enquired innocently, his hand moving very slowly up her body.

Her blush increased. "You know what." she stopped his hand just below the ribbon decorating her dress under her bosom.

"Oh, I think I will not, because I do see that my teasing is vastly improving your spirits." he said warmly, combing the curls which escaped the pins away from her face.

Elizabeth rested her head on his shoulder. "I was very fortunate. I cannot believe I once trusted him."

"I should have perceived he would try something." he whispered, squeezing her to him, "I will never let you out of my sight." he added, before pushing her away from him, speaking seriously, "Elizabeth we must marry as soon as can be."

"But I must talk to Papa, to explain everything to him." she protested. "I am sure that he will understand and give us his consent, in time of course. He never seemed to like Mr. Brooke, still he barely knows you, so he will likely be apprehensive at the beginning…"

"Sweetheart," Darcy interrupted her gently. "There might not be time for that, for returning to Longbourn and courting you properly. We cannot be sure what Brooke will do now. He will probably try to use all his influence to ruin your good name, your reputation. And as he is well respected in Meryton, people know and trust him."

Elizabeth frowned, biting her lip worriedly.

"He may make himself a victim," Darcy continued. "He can tell everyone that you eloped with me, or even worse, that we have no intention to seal our union. What I mean is that we must return to Longbourn already married."

"But my parents, my sisters…" she tried to protest.

"Trust me, it is for the best that we marry immediately." Darcy's voice was firm now. "I understand that you have some relatives in London."

She nodded.

"Perhaps you could stay with them till I secure the special license?"

"Oh, yes, I am sure they will agree."

"What is their name?" he wanted to know.

"Mr. and Mrs. Gardiner." she said quietly, and then lifted her chin up as if in a challenge. "They live in Cheapside."

Darcy regarded her for a moment. "You said Gardiner?" he asked sharply.

Elizabeth nodded, surprised with his tone. "Yes, Gardiner. Uncle Edward is my mother's brother." she explained, and when he still looked at her as if he did not comprehend, she added. "Gardiner is my mother's maiden name."

"Edward Gardiner? Are you certain?" he asked unbelievably.

"William, I do remember my uncle's name."

"And he is in trade, yes?"

"Yes. His house is close to his warehouses. We visit them ever year, my sister Jane and me. I like them very much, especially my aunt. I am sure they will have nothing against me staying with them for a few days in this situation. My aunt even once suggested I should be careful with Mr. Brooke. She said that he was well known for his ruthlessness in business. I know they will understand our haste once we explain everything to them."

Darcy kept staring at her with unseeing eyes, as if he had not heard her, a heavy frown on his forehead.

"Is something wrong?" Elizabeth asked, touching his hand.

He shook his head. "No… No." he shrugged his arm, "That is not possible." he murmured more to himself than to Elizabeth. "Gardiner is a common name."

There was a knock on the door, and Mrs. Collins entered. "The bath is ready."

Elizabeth smiled at her. "Thank you."

"Mr. Darcy." Charlotte glanced pointedly at the clock on the mantelpiece. "It is quite late, and my friend is tired."

Darcy bowed. "Yes, of course Mrs. Collins. I only ask for a moment to bid goodnight to Miss Bennet, and I will be going."

Charlotte nodded, smiled and walked out of the room.

Darcy cupped Elizabeth's face. "If you are able, we will travel to London tomorrow morning."

"I am."

"Good. You will stay with your relatives till I secure the special license. Then we shall be married and return to Longbourn." he kissed her lips gently. "Sleep well, sweetheart. And do not worry about a thing. I love you."

Darcy was at the door when he turned to her again. "Elizabeth, what is you aunt's maiden name?"

Elizabeth met his eyes curiously, answering slowly. "I do not know. I was a little girl when she married my uncle. I never thought to ask her that."

"I see." he looked as if he wanted to ask her more, but he only smiled the last time, and walked out of the room.

When he left the room, Elizabeth shook her head, whispering to herself. "No, that cannot be possible, can it?"

***

Darcy entered the manor, Georgiana waiting for him in the great hall together with his cousin.

"How is she?" she asked, running to him

Darcy smiled tiredly at his little sister. "She is fine. We are going to London tomorrow. Please tell your maid to have your things packed and prepared to leave in the morning."

"Is she coming with us?"

"Yes."

Georgiana clapped her hands happily, and after bidding goodnight to her guardians, ran lightly upstairs.

"I could not convince her to go to bed." Colonel Fitzwilliam walked to Darcy. "She informed me she would wait till your return. Her sweet disposition can be misleading in times, as she can be very stubborn when she sets her mind on something."

Darcy smiled proudly. "Yes, a true Darcy."

Colonel's expression sobered. "How is Miss Bennet?"

"Better. She is slowly retuning to her own impertinent self." Darcy acknowledged dryly.

The colonel chuckled. "You know, Darcy, it amazes me the way Miss Bennet…" he hesitated, "let me just say, influences you. Good God, man!" he cried, "She wrapped you around her little finger, and you even do not seem to mind."

Darcy shrugged. "Because I do not mind."

Lady Catherine walked in, interrupting the cousins' conversation. "Fitzwilliam tells me that you recovered Miss Bennet." she said to Darcy.

"Yes, we did." Darcy confirmed.

Her ladyship narrowed her eyes at him. "Oh, and how is she?"

"Unharmed."

"I am glad to hear it, but truly, Darcy I cannot understand why both of you rushed so quickly to her rescue. She is promised to that man, after all."

"She has never been promised to him." Darcy said, barely controlling irritation in his voice.

"Brooke took her against her will." Colonel Fitzwilliam supported him quickly.

Lady Catherine regarded her nephews carefully before she spoke. "I do agree that the idea of elopement, when there are no obstacles to the marriage, is very inappropriate, and for sure, Miss Bennet would wish to have the usual wedding celebrations, but what was done was done. You should have not intervened into the private affairs of Mr. Brooke. You made the whole situation a lot worse for Miss Bennet as well. What will she do now, after being involved in such a scandal? He may not wish to marry her now at all."

Darcy chose not to comment on this. "Aunt, we return to London tomorrow." he informed her only.

"So soon?"

"Yes. I have some very urgent business in town."

"It cannot be that urgent." Lady Catherine noted, her tone displeased.

"Good night, Aunt." Darcy bowed. "Sleep well."

The colonel bid his goodnight as well, and both cousins headed toward the staircase.

"Darcy, I intend to take Anne to London in the beginning of May." Lady Catherine said when her nephews were already on the staircase steps. "Do you plan to stay in London till summer?"

"I cannot say now, Aunt. My plans are not fixed. But, of course, you and Anne are always most welcome in my home." he bowed respectfully.

"I see, Darcy, that you have learned to deal with Lady Catherine." Colonel Fitzwilliam whispered when they were out of their aunt's earshot.

"I am a grown man." Darcy spoke, stopping in front of his room. "I shall have my own family soon. It is high time she stopped treating me like a little boy who she can order around." he said firmly but then his expression softened, "Good night, Richard. Thank you for everything. I am in your debt, cousin."

Colonel Fitzwilliam smiled. "If that is so, I reserve myself to be the godfather to your firstborn."

"We shall be honoured." Darcy assured his cousin, and the men embraced briefly, before stepping into their rooms.

Chapter Fifteen

Elizabeth opened her heavy eyelids and frowned. She stared at the fire dying in the unfamiliar, elaborately decorated, marble mantelpiece. It had to be quite an early hour in the morning, as the grey light was seeping into the room through the crack in the heavy, dark, velvet curtains. Her eyes moved higher, and she saw the dark brown wall coverings. Her frown deepened. *What a gloomy room,* she thought. *Where was she?*

Then a soft sigh above her ear engaged her attention, and the understanding of her current situation dawned on her. She turned her head slightly to see Mr. Darcy snuggled to her back, his heavy arm draped loosely over her middle. Very gently, so as not to wake him, she turned on her back, and gazed at him.

That he looked so young, was her first thought; young and vulnerable. His brown hair was mussed, and dark stubble covered his cheeks and chin. Last night, she had not really had the opportunity to take a good look at him in his less formal state. She decided to take her time now. *What long eyelashes he has; like a lady.* Her eyes moved lower. *Nice neck too,* she thought. The top ties of his nightshirt were open, and her gaze rested on the top planes of his broad chest. Reaching forth her hand, she patted gently, the pelt of curly chest hair peeking out the opening of his shirt. Who could have thought him to be so hairy? She glanced at his arm, still draped over her middle. The sleeve was rolled up, and there was hair on it too. It almost reached his knuckles. She wondered briefly about other places where he grew hair.

She glanced down at her hand, where a beautiful ring decorated her middle finger; his mother's ring, as he had said to her. Good gracious, she was actually married to Mr. Darcy. Who could have thought? A little over a week ago, she thought herself to be practically engaged to a completely different man. She shrugged inwardly when she thought about Mr. Brooke. Thankfully they had not heard a word from him since that horrible day in Kent, when he had tried to kidnap her.

Her musings stopped when she felt her husband moving beside her. She stilled herself.

"Elizabeth?" he murmured thickly in a sleepy voice. "You are awake." His eyelids were only half open.

"I have just woken up, and I felt confused about my whereabouts when I saw the unfamiliar room." she whispered softly.

He smiled, already closing his eyes. "Go back to sleep." he gathered her tightly into his arms, her back to his chest. "It is too early to get up." he yawned. "Especially in London."

She tried to obey him, but she could not fall asleep. With every minute, she felt more and more pressure on her bladder, which was quite usual in her case early in the morning. After some ten minutes of deliberation, she turned her head again and saw that he was sound asleep.

Gathering her courage, she began moving away from him. She was almost freed from his embrace, when she was effortlessly pinned back to his chest. "Don't go." he murmured.

"William, I must." she tried to unsuccessfully move his hand away from her waist. "Please, let me go."

"You did mention being an early raiser, but I did not expect…" he started sleepily, but she interrupted him.

"I simply need to refresh myself."

"Oh." he shifted on his back. "The chamber pot is in my dressing room." he pointed to the door on his side of the bed, and closed his eyes again.

Elizabeth flushed bright red, not knowing where to hide her eyes. How could he be so indelicate, and so… crude? She was deeply convinced that a gentleman should not refer to such body functions in the presence of his bride, or any lady whatsoever. It was highly mortifying and embarrassing.

She found her pretty robe, abandoned on a chair last evening, and put it on over her own nightgown and William's shirt she wore. Then she padded to the dressing room.

He had insisted she wear one of his long linen shirts over her nightgown. It reached to her knees, and covered well her upper body in a kind of large, shapeless tent. When she had entered his room last night, wearing the gown given to her especially for the occasion by her Aunt Madeline, he had first simply stared at her for a good deal of time. Then he had disappeared for a moment, returning with one of his shirts, asking her to put it on. He had explained that he would not be able to keep his resolution not to make love to her, with her wearing completely transparent attire, under which he could see everything.

Her wedding night had been surprising in many ways. There had been no opportunity previously to talk about the exact arrangements of their future life; all had happened so quickly. The marriage had been arranged in barely three days, with the help of the Gardiners. Consequently, she and William had very little privacy since the moment he'd delivered her to her uncle's home till the day when their wedding had taken place.

She had expected that her husband would wish to consummate their union on their wedding night. She had not been exactly sure how she felt about it. The idea of being intimate with any man did not seem to be especially appealing to her. It was enough for her to return her thoughts to what that man tried to do to her in the carriage, and she felt sick all over again. She trusted William, of course. She enjoyed his touch, and felt safe in his arms, but she was not sure how she would have reacted if he had wanted to be with her the way a husband and wife should be. So far, he had never initiated anything more than kissing, cuddling her to him, and stroking her back and arms.

When last night, he had brought her his shirt, asking to put it on, she had been more than confused. Then he sat in a comfortable chair in front of the fireplace and pulled her onto his lap. She had to admit that she had felt very much relieved when he had told her that he had no intention of consummating their union either this night, or any time soon. She felt strongly for him and enjoyed his presence by her side, but it all had happened so quickly. She was grateful he had given her time to adjust.

He did not intend to be intimate with her, but clearly, he expected for them to sleep in one bed. There was not much choice for her to sleep elsewhere. She had expected that in such a grand townhouse, there should be two master bedrooms, preferably connected with one another, but she was wrong. She had been informed that the once Mistress' bedroom had been turned years ago into the private family room, as her husband's parents had always shared the Master's bedroom. Elizabeth had always thought that the partners in aristocratic marriages slept separately; her parents did, though her father was just a country gentleman.

After they had talked, William had carried her to bed and tucked her in, joining her soon after. She first lay stiffly, being afraid to make even the slightest move, but William pulled her unceremoniously into his arms, kissed her thoroughly, and then simply fell asleep. It had taken her a bit longer to do the same.

Elizabeth finished her business in his dressing room, taking her time to wash her face. For a moment, she looked out of the window at the small garden behind the house. She even brushed her hair with his comb. She hoped he would not mind it.

On returning to the bedroom, she found herself not sleepy at all. She took a turn around the room. There was not much furniture there, only the most necessary pieces. In the place of honour, above the mantelpiece, hung the large painting of a young woman. There was little doubt after whom Mr. Darcy had inherited his pretty looks. He had his mother's dark, soulful eyes, her colouring, and her smile.

She quietly returned to the bed and slipped under the covers. She closed her eyes, and minutes later, she managed to doze off.

***

Darcy woke up a few hours later. At first, his eyes rested with confusion on the small female body nestled beside him, but soon his face broke into an affectionate grin. His wife was sprawled on her back, almost drowned in his shirt. Her hair was in disarray, spread on the pillow and down her arms. Supporting himself on his elbow, he simply stared at her adoringly.

She was lovely, and she was all his. He did not remember ever having felt so unconditionally happy. There were still many unresolved matters concerning their rushed marriage that they had to face together, but it did not spoil his deep contentment because of the union with Elizabeth. Tomorrow they would go to Longbourn to learn how much damage Brooke had already managed to have done there. All he really wanted was to conclude all their affairs here and take his family home to Pemberley; but that would probably not happen soon. Elizabeth would want to stay until Bingley's wedding to her sister, to help with the preparations.

His wife murmured something and rolled to her side, trying to find a new comfortable position for herself, and in the process, kicking the covers off her lower body. Instantly his eyes glued to her gauzy nightgown, which had ridden up above her knees. She had smooth, slender legs, and the prettiest little feet he had ever seen. He stared hungrily at her uncovered lower body before decidedly drawing the covers back over her.

He was deeply convinced that his decision to wait for the consummation of their marriage was the only right one. To tell the truth, this young girl, sleeping now so peacefully next to him, barely knew him. They had been denied the customary period of courting and wooing. Consequently, she had no time or opportunity to mentally prepare herself for her new role as his wife. In more usual circumstances, he would have introduced her gradually into the physical side of the marriage during their engagement. First some kisses, then gentle touching of her breasts through her gown. And only then, reaching under her skirts too pleasure her more thoroughly. Had he had time for all of this, he would have not hesitated to consummate their union on their wedding night.

But their situation was different. She needed her time, not only to get to know him better, but to also forget what that bastard, Brooke, had tried to do to her. He wanted Elizabeth to trust him implicitly in every aspect. At the same time, he was convinced that forcing her too soon into the intimacy that she might have not been ready for, was definitely not the best way to achieve that goal. Moreover, he anticipated that she would need a thorough preparation before the actual intercourse could take place. She was petite and delicate, and he was sure that all parts of her were small. He dreaded the thought of hurting her more than it was absolutely necessary.

"William?" her sleepy voice brought his attention.

He smiled warmly at her. "Good morning, my love. Have you slept well?"

She stretched and yawned. "Yes, thank you." she smiled back. "And you?"

He grinned. "Like a babe."

She kept smiling at him rather shyly. He reached his hand to smooth her tousled hair. "I am afraid I cannot stay with you today. I have business with my solicitor to attend. I want to be prepared when I talk with your father tomorrow."

"I understand. Actually, I have plans too."

"Can I guess?" he asked knowingly. "A shopping excursion with my sister?"

Elizabeth nodded. "Yes... she was very determined that we should visit some shops before our trip to Hertfordshire, so that when we return, at least a few of the new gowns could be ready."

"I support her on this. You will need many new gowns, especially some woolen ones. The winters in the north can be long and harsh. Georgiana is right. It is for the best to order several dresses today so you will have them ready as soon as possible."

"Yes, William... but..." she hesitated, "I am aware that I will need new gowns as a married woman, but still perhaps... It is customary that the bride's family pays for such expenditures before the wedding, so perhaps my Papa could this time..."

"No." Darcy announced flatly.

"Oh." she said, and bit her lower lip.

Darcy sat up in the bed, supporting his back against the headboard. Next he drew her to him, tucking her into his arms, propping his chin on the top of her head. "All was so rushed, and there was not time to discuss the matter of your pin money. And to tell the truth, I wanted to talk with your father about this first. But you do not have to worry about it when you go shopping today. I can assure you that Georgiana will instruct you very well where to send the bills for your purchases." his eyes twinkled in amusement. "Additionally, I will give you a sum today, so you could feel comfortable visiting the coffeehouse, or buying ribbons or other trinkets, whatever you like."

"No, it is not necessary." Elizabeth assured him quickly. "I still have most of the ten pounds Papa gave me for my trip to Kent."

"Lizzy, it may not be enough." his voice was patient. "I do not want you to feel uncomfortable, not knowing whether you can afford something or not. London is not Meryton. You must know how much more expensive things are here."

"Yes, I know." she acknowledged in a small voice.

"It is natural for me to give you money and support you." he said gently. "You are entitled to it." he stressed.

She sighed. "I do not feel entitled to it." she murmured very quietly under her breath.

"Please, do not say that." He kissed her hair. "It hurts me to hear it."

She turned into his arms to face him, and snuggled even more closely into him. "Just hold me, William." she asked, and he complied.

They stayed in each other arms for some time, before Elizabeth pulled out of his embrace, looking up at him. "Aunt Madeline will come with us. We are to pick her at half past ten."

Darcy smiled. "Good."

Elizabeth shook her head in wonder. "I still cannot believe that you are actually related, that you are cousins."

"Yes, she would have been Miss Darcy, had my uncle took his responsibility as any man in his situation should, and married her mother."

"I did not tell you so, but I think that it was wonderful of your father that he felt responsible for his brother's orphaned baby girl, especially an illegitimate one." she said sincerely.

Darcy shrugged. "It was the only decent thing to do then. I would do exactly the same in his place."

Elizabeth gazed at him in an open admiration. "I am sure you would."

Darcy stroked her hair absently. "I understand that my uncle was always, let us just say, troublesome to the family. You see, Madeline is not the only illegitimate child he fathered."

Elizabeth's curiosity was piqued and her cat-like eyes stared at him in wonder.

"You cannot guess?" Darcy asked. "You have met him in Herefordshire."

"Him?" Elizabeth frowned. Then her eyes shone in sudden understanding, "You mean Mr. Wickham?"

Darcy nodded.

"Does he know?"

"No, it was all kept secret. I did not know myself till the time my father became sick."

"Were there no rumours?" Elizabeth wondered.

"No. I do not know the details, as I was not even born when the arrangements were made for George's mother to marry Mr. Wickham, but obviously my father managed to discreetly put the whole affair to rest. It helped that George is the spitting image of his late mother. I remember her to be very pretty. From what my father told me, it was an extremely unpleasant affair. While my infamous uncle nearly seduced Madeline's mother, when it came to Wickham's mother, the situation was much direr. George's mother was a maid at Pemberley, and it all happened against her will, while she was still very young. I do not even want to think what would have happened if Wickham had ever learned the truth. As for Madeline, I suppose everyone in Lambton and Pemberley knew who her father was."

"Because of her resemblance to your family?" Elizabeth guessed.

"Yes. At Pemberley I will show you the portrait of my paternal grandmother. Georgiana and Madeline took their looks after her."

"And you after your mother?" Elizabeth guessed, glancing at the painting of the dark haired beauty over the fireplace.

"Yes, though I have my father's disposition. But I think it is enough of family tales for one morning." he pushed her gently away from him. "I am sure that your maid is already waiting for you."

Elizabeth smiled and scrambled out of the huge bed. Innocently, she removed his shirt in front of him and put it neatly over the nearby chair. Darcy had once again the opportunity to admire her shapely, light form in the nearly transparent gown; but not for long, because she quickly donned her robe. Giving him one last smile, she disappeared behind the door leading to the sitting room.

***

Late that afternoon, Darcy entered the townhouse. The day had been exhausting, but he had managed to finalize all that he had previously planned. Now he deserved some nice quiet time with his ladies.

"Where are my wife and sister?" he asked the servant who opened the door for him. "Have they returned?"

"Yes, Mrs. Darcy and Miss Darcy returned over an hour ago." The servant took his hat and the papers that he had brought from the solicitor. "They are in the drawing room now, entertaining Lady Catherine de Bourgh."

Darcy's heart squeezed in involuntarily panic. He nearly ran to the room indicated by the servant. Already, from the corridor, he heare his aunt's raised voice, followed by Elizabeth's, whose tone was more sharp than usual.

"…I will ask you to leave, Lady Catherine." he heard his wife's voice

"How dare you?!" his aunt shrieked. "This is my sister's house, and you are nothing more than some common harlot, good enough only for one thing…"

He did not wait any longer, but opened the door with a loud bang. Elizabeth stood straight as an arrow in front of his aunt, her chin high. Georgiana stood just behind her, pale, trembling and tear stricken.

"Aunt!" he spat out, "You will apologize to my wife. Now."

"Darcy, here you are." Lady Catherine walked dismissively past Elizabeth to him. "What sort of jest is this? I hear you married this little country nothing." she glanced sideways with barely concealed disgust at Elizabeth.

Darcy walked to Elizabeth, taking her cold hand in his warm one. "Aunt, before we speak, you must apologize to Mrs. Darcy."

"I will do no such thing." her ladyship cried haughtily. "In my eyes, there is no Mrs. Darcy here."

"In that case, I am forced to ask you to leave my house." Darcy announced calmly.

Her ladyship gasped. "Have you lost your mind?"

Darcy rang for the servant. "Lady Catherine is leaving." he said when the servant appeared a short moment later. "See her to the door."

Lady Catherine stood unmoving for a moment, her furious eyes shifting interchangeably from Darcy to Elizabeth. "It is not the end." she muttered through clenched teeth. "I will know how to act now." and with the rustle of heavy silk skirts, she walked out of the room.

***

"Again, I am so sorry you had to go through that." Darcy said softly, cradling Elizabeth to him, when they were snuggled together in bed that evening.

"It is not your fault." she whispered, cuddling closer to him.

"I should have informed my aunt myself." Darcy said guiltily. "I knew perfectly well what her likely reaction would be."

"Do not beat yourself about this." her eyes met his, her expression earnest, "The only matter which worries me, is that she might have been right; that I am a disgrace to you and to your family."

"Elizabeth, never say so, or I will be very angry." He shook her gently, to emphasize his words. "Lady Catherine is nothing to me. If anyone behaves disgracefully and brings shame to us, it is only she. You and Georgiana are my world, my family. I do not care for the others. My aunt is furious because she always wanted me to marry Anne."

"You never considered that?"

"You mean marrying Anne?" Darcy stared at her incredibly. "It was never my desire I suppose that I do care for her in a way, but only as for a relative. But at the same time, I must admit that I tend to forget about her existence completely, unless she stands right in front of me. Moreover, until I met you, the idea of marriage had not appealed to me at all."

"But you must have met many pleasant and interesting young ladies before coming to Hertfordshire." she reasoned.

Darcy shrugged. "Perhaps, but I had not noticed them. They did not affect me the way you always have." He chuckled. "Do you remember when you came on foot to Netherfield to nurse your sister?"

"Yes."

"I was so terrified of you then."

"Terrified of me?" Elizabeth gazed at him suspiciously. "Do you jest with me?"

Darcy started laughing quietly. "No, not at all."

She frowned. "But I barely spoke to you then."

"It did not matter. Your sheer presence was quite enough to put me into a state of utter disorientation. I did not know what was happening to me. I felt myself losing my usual self control whenever you were close. I did not know how to handle you and the feelings I started rapidly developing for you. I well knew how to deal with the Caroline Bingleys of the world, but not how to act with a little outspoken lady, who snarled at me at every opportunity, and teased me mercilessly, making a total fool out of me in front of other people."

Elizabeth's frown deepened. "I did not nothing of the kind."

"You are right." he agreed happily. "I had been the fool before, and you simply uncovered that side of me."

Elizabeth rolled her eyes. "You do exaggerate."

"As for today, you were wonderful." Darcy squeezed her to him. "I am so proud of you. You handled yourself admirably. You had the courage to do something I should have done years ago. You stood up to my aunt, while I preferred to let her continue to delude herself for the sake of my own convenience and peace of mind."

"I was abominably rude to her." Elizabeth pointed out reasonably.

"I would say you were much too polite; but let us not talk about this…" he whispered, shifting her on her back, his lips coming on hers.

Elizabeth returned the kiss trustingly, her arms wrapping around his shoulders. Still kissing her, he let his hand glide down her body. She must have liked it, because she pressed herself more closely to him. He made sure to keep the touching innocent, more comforting than arousing. Moving on his back he pulled her over him.

"Am I not too heavy for you?" she asked with concern.

He chuckled. "You weigh less than nothing."

"Mama always despaired over me being so slight." she whispered with a sigh into his neck. "She made me eat twice as much as my sisters, and still I never could put on much weight. She kept saying that no gentleman would want me with such a boyish figure."

"Your mother was obviously very wrong. Moreover, you certainly do not look like a boy." he said, and to emphasize his words, his hand moved lower and gently squeezed her rounded bottom.

"I am apprehensive about tomorrow." she said, her fingers playing with the opening of his nightshirt. "So far, Papa has not answered to the message Uncle Gardiner sent to him, informing him of our wedding."

Darcy squeezed her to him. "We do not know what possible lies Brooke has tried to spread in Meryton." he kissed the top of her head. "But please, love, do not worry yourself over this now. I will be by your side at all times."

She sighed. "I know."

Shifting her on her side, he tucked her in the crook of his arm "Now, close your eyes. We need our rest before tomorrow."

Chapter Sixteen

The next day, the Darcys had an early breakfast in a small dining room. Darcy's concerned eyes stared at his wife for the entire course of the meal. She was very quiet, pale, and only nibbled at her food. He was perfectly aware that she felt apprehensive about their trip to Hertfordshire, and meeting her family and relatives. This morning, after they had woken up, she had lain silently, cuddled against him for a long time, as if being afraid to face the day. Suddenly, he almost regretted that he had not killed that bastard Brooke when he had the chance. It would have put a definite end to her misery caused by that man.

She must have felt his eyes on her, because she lifted her gaze to him, managing a small smile. He smiled back, reaching across the table to squeeze her small, cold hand.

The door opened, and slightly out of breath, Georgiana stood in it.

"I am sorry. I overslept." she said, sitting beside Elizabeth.

"You could sleep longer today." Darcy noted calmly.

Georgiana shook her blonde head. "I wanted to say a goodbye to you before your departure."

"It is very thoughtful of you." Elizabeth smiled at the younger girl, but her tone was still uncharacteristically listless.

"I wish I could go with you." Georgiana said longingly. "I cannot wait to meet Lizzy's sisters."

Darcy and Elizabeth's eyes met. They both knew that bringing Georgiana to Hertfordshire was out of question when the militia was still stationed there.

"I would like that too, Georgiana." Elizabeth spoke gently. "But I do think that for now it is for the best that only your brother and I pay this first visit. I cannot be sure how my family will react to the news that I married, without their consent, a man with whom they are barely acquainted."

"I know that all will be well, Lizzy." Georgiana assured her

"You could have never found a better husband than my brother." she added with great conviction.

"Georgiana." Darcy shook his head reproachfully, but there was a smile in the corner of his mouth.

Elizabeth bit her lower lip, attempting to hide her smile, but her sparkling eyes betrayed her amusement. "Georgiana, I can assure you that I am deeply convinced of your brother's worthiness as a marriage prospect. Still, I am afraid that my family may not be aware of the fact yet. I think that they simply need some time."

The conversation ended, because their attention was brought by the raised voiced coming from the back of the house.

The next moment, the door opened with a bang, and Thomas Bennet entered, followed by the agitated servant.

"Papa?" Elizabeth mouthed, her eyes wide. "You have come!" she fled straight into her father's arms.

Mr. Bennet first hugged his daughter tightly, then pushed her at the arm's length as if examining her, checking if she was well.

"Lizzy, child." Mr. Bennet stared down at his daughter, his hands on her shoulders. "Are you well? You are not harmed?"

"I am very well, Papa." Elizabeth smiled through her tears. "I am so happy to see you."

"Thank you, God." Mr. Bennet whispered, hugging her to him again. "What a horrible story is that?" he asked. "Is it true what the Gardiners told me? What that scum Brooke tried to do to you?"

"Yes, Papa." Elizabeth admitted. "But I am fine. He had no chance to really hurt me."

"Come, child." Mr. Bennet gathered her to him, only fleetingly looking at Darcy. "I am taking you home."

"But Papa." Elizabeth gently stepped away from her father. She walked to Darcy, and stood next to him. "I cannot go with you. I married Mr. Darcy two days ago. Have you not received the message from Uncle Gardiner?"

"I have received it." Mr. Bennet confirmed gravely and then cried angrily. "I could hardly believe it! My daughter leaves my home to visit her friend in Kent, and the next thing I hear is that she is married to a man we barely know. When you mother heard about it, she put herself to bed. And this time I am not the least bit surprised that she did that. I would have come earlier if not for her illness caused by the news."

"Sir, I assure you that the wedding was necessary in the situation in which we found ourselves." Darcy spoke in a firm, but still respectful voice.

Mr. Bennet stepped to him. "Is that so? Will you tell me the same nonsense about the supposed rumours that Brooke was to spread in Hertfordshire? I have already heard all of that from my brother-in-law."

"It is the truth, sir." Darcy insisted. "Brooke threatened to ruin Elizabeth's reputation."

Mr. Bennet walked closer to the younger man, speaking decidedly. "John Brooke has not been seen in Hertfordshire for the last three weeks. All I know is that you abused my daughter's trust, taking her away without the consent of her family, forcing her into this marriage!"

Elizabeth caught her father's arm. "Papa, it is not like that!" she protested. "Nobody forced me into anything. You must have heard that it was Mr. Darcy and his cousin, Colonel Fitzwilliam, who rescued me from Brooke."

Mr. Bennet looked down at his daughter. "Yes, Lizzy, I was acquainted with that tale yesterday when I arrived at the Gardiners' and demanded they tell me where you were. I must admit, daughter, that it all seems very strange to me. I am not sure whether I can trust their word, with Madeline so closely related to the family of this man." He gave Darcy a menacing look.

"Does it mean that Aunt Madeline told you who her real father was?" Elizabeth asked.

"She did not have to tell me that." Mr. Bennet snorted. "I knew from the very beginning who her real father was. The thing I cannot understand is how you involved yourself into all of this." He gestured in the general direction of Darcy. "What happened,

Lizzy? You have always acted so respectfully, so maturely. It is so unlike you to involve yourself into such a sordid affair."

Elizabeth blinked away the tears gathering in her eyes. "Papa…" she whispered.

"Sir, it is not her fault." Darcy interjected angrily, seeing Elizabeth's distress caused by her father's harsh words.

Mr. Bennet, however, ignored the younger man. "Lizzy." He looked searchingly into his daughter's face. "Tell me one thing." He paused. "Did he force you into this marriage?"

"He did not." Elizabeth shook her head. "I swear, Papa."

Mr. Bennet leaned forward and asked in lowered voice, "Was the marriage consummated?"

Elizabeth's face instantly flushed in embarrassment. "Papa…"

"Lizzy." Mr. Bennet persisted.

"Yes, it was." Darcy said, stepping before Elizabeth. "Sir, I beg you to come with me to my study. I would prefer not to talk about such matters in the presence of my sister."

"You bastard." Mr. Bennet moved to Darcy abruptly, his hands curled in fists. "How do you dare to touch her?"

"Georgiana, be so kind as to take Elizabeth to the music room." Darcy ordered.

Elizabeth did not move, looking from her father to her husband.

Darcy stared pointedly at his sister, who stood in the other end of the room, her eyes wide, mouth agape. "Georgiana, I asked you to take your sister to the music room."

At last, Georgiana moved, and walked to the other woman. She took Elizabeth's arm and pulled her out of the room.

In the music room, Georgiana started playing, but Elizabeth did not to pay attention. She paced the length of the room nervously, clenching her hands together.

Georgiana stood from the pianoforte. "Your father seemed to be very displeased." she said tentatively.

"He barely knows your brother." Elizabeth whispered, nibbling at her fingernails.

"I am sure that all will be well when they know each other better." Georgiana spoke softly.

Elizabeth nodded, not looking at her. "I hope so."

Another half an hour passed before the door opened and the two gentlemen entered the music room.

Elizabeth stood up immediately, her big eyes widened even more

She glanced from one man to the other in an attempt to decipher their mood and attitude.

There was a long moment of silence before her father walked forward and hugged her to him. "Lizzy, forgive me my outburst earlier." he kissed the top of her head.

"I do understand, Papa." she murmured into his coat. "Just please do not be displeased with me." she pleaded, her dark eyes lifted at him. "That is the one thing I cannot bear."

"I am not displeased with you, child." Mr. Bennet stroked her hair. "I do believe you that you thought… that you were convinced that the marriage to Mr. Darcy was the only choice. Still, I cannot pretend that I am happy with this union. It does not matter now, however. It is too late too change anything." He looked at his son-in-law for a short moment with an open hostility in his eyes. "I have invited your husband, and your new sister, to Longbourn for a prolonged stay. I think it would be for the best for you to come in a few days, perhaps by the end of this week. I need some time to prepare your mother for your visit; not to mention our relatives and neighbours."

"I understand." Elizabeth nodded. "Will you stay for tea, Papa?" she asked with hope.

"No, thank you." Mr. Bennet refused stiffly. "I plan to return home yet today."

Elizabeth caught his hand. "Papa, please stay. You could, perhaps, have dinner with us? You could go to Hertfordshire tomorrow."

"No, Lizzy." Mr. Bennet said, with his eyes focused not at his daughter, but on her husband. "I do not think it is possible."

Mr. Bennet bowed formally and left the room.

***

Elizabeth lay curled on the bed in the Master bedroom, staring miserably out of the window.

"Elizabeth." Darcy sat beside her. "Dinner will be served soon."

"I am not hungry." she whispered, not looking at him.

"You have barely spoken a word to me since your father left."

She did not comment.

He stroked her face. "Sweetheart, please speak to me."

She turned to him and sat up. "I had not expected Papa to react like that." she said at last.

Darcy stroked her back soothingly. "In time, I know he will come to terms with our marriage."

Elizabeth shook her head sadly. "I am not so sure about that. He trusted me, and I feel that I betrayed his trust. I got myself involved in some horrible affair, first with one man, then with the other. I acted shamefully. I know how highly he thought of me. He is disappointed; and has every right to be."

Darcy pressed his lips together, swallowing his irritation. It was not a pleasant thing to hear that she referred to him as the other man.

He stroked her arm. "You judge yourself too harshly."

She sighed, closing her eyes. "I simply wish that I had never met John Brooke; or at least that I would have been wiser and more prudent in my dealings with him. Then all of this would not have happened."

There was a moment of silence before Darcy spoke very quietly. "Our marriage included."

She looked to the side and whispered. "At least in different circumstances."

"We cannot change what happened." He cupped her face to make her look at him. "We must make the best of it now."

"Why did you say to Papa that we…? You know…" She averted her gaze again. "You said to him that the marriage was consummated."

Darcy frowned. "Cannot you guess? Surely he would have probably insisted on an annulment, had he known the truth."

She met his eyes shortly, and then looked down, biting her lower lip.

"You would agree, would you not?" he asked incredibly.

"Brooke has disappeared… and…" she hesitated.

He narrowed his eyes at her. "So it was the only reason you agreed to marry me?" he demanded. "Just to rescue your reputation?"

"No, William, of course not." she spoke, looking up at him. "But I think that Papa is right. We should not have acted so hastily." she acknowledged softly.

"I cannot believe that." He stood up and began pacing the room

"One word from him, and you turn into some little girl who cannot make a move without his approval."

Elizabeth stood up as well. "He is my father. His opinion is important to me." she stressed.

"I do not understand." Darcy walked to her. "You stood up to my aunt yesterday, and today you could not do the same when it came to your father."

"How can you not understand it?" she cried. "It is an entirely different situation. I do not care what your aunt thinks of me. It does touch me deeply though, what my father thinks of me. You cannot expect that I will ignore his opinion about me."

"Even if he is wrong about our marriage?"

"I am not sure he is so wrong." she spoke calmly. "He has every right to be concerned. He does not know you. He has seen you perhaps three times in his life, and talked with you once."

Darcy stared at her, his entire face tense. He gave the impression he had wanted to say something more, but stopped himself.

"Just imagine that something like this would happen to Georgiana." Elizabeth continued. "How would you react if she went away for a few weeks, then you hear that some man…" she stopped, and covered her lips with her hand, realizing what she had said. "William, I am so sorry." She caught his hand in both of hers. "It was not my intention to bring up what happened in Ramsgate… please believe me." She stepped closer to him. "It was thoughtless of me."

Darcy freed her hand and said formally. "I will tell Georgiana that you will not join us for dinner." he bowed and left the room.

Georgiana Darcy did not dare to ask her brother to elaborate about the reasons why Elizabeth stayed upstairs. It was enough to look at Darcy's face, to know he was in no mood for small talk. She knew her brother well enough to stay silent.

Darcy stayed in the library long into the evening that day. It was past midnight when he put his cigar down and decided to go to bed. His bedroom was dark when he entered. It was illuminated only by the dying fire in the mantelpiece.

He let out an involuntarily sigh of relief on seeing Elizabeth's small form sleeping on one side of the bed. He disrobed himself quickly, and in just his shirt, climbed into the bed. He lay for some time on his side, staring at her slumbering form. He made a move as if he had wanted to reach for her and pull her into his arms, but he hesitated. Eventually he rolled to the other side, to the far end of the bed and closed his eyes.

***

"So, Lizzy, please tell me what exactly happened when your father visited you yesterday." Mrs. Gardiner asked. The aunt and niece took an early afternoon walk in the park close to Gracechurch Street.

"Oh, Aunt, it was horrible." Elizabeth stopped walking and hid her face into her hands. "Papa was so worried and angry about what happened in Kent. But the worst was that he seemed to be so disappointed with me."

Madeline rubbed her niece's back. "It had to be difficult for you." she remarked compassionately.

"And what is even worse, later I quarreled with William." Elizabeth resumed her walk. "We have not spoken a word to each other since yesterday afternoon. When I woke up, the bedroom was empty. He was already absent when I walked downstairs. I feel so miserable about it."

"All couples quarrel from to time." Madeline noted diplomatically

"It does not mean that they do not love each other." she stressed

"It does not indicate that it is a bad marriage, on the contrary, I would say."

"I think he hates me now." Elizabeth whispered.

Madeline laughed, shaking her head. "He does not. Believe me."

"But I was so cruel to him." Elizabeth insisted. "I reminded him of some matter which I know very well that it is very painful to him. I should not have."

"We often say things we do not mean, especially in anger."

"He was not without fault as well." Elizabeth cried defiantly after a moment. "He spoke as if he had expected me to choose between him and Papa, and admit that he was right and Papa was wrong."

"Perhaps he is jealous of your father." Madeline pointed out reasonably. "He wants to be the most important person in your life."

Elizabeth frowned. "That is so selfish."

"Perhaps." the older woman agreed gently. "But it may be possible that he acts like that because he is not sure about your feelings for him."

Elizabeth shrugged. "I am not so sure myself how I feel about him." she sighed. "I know I am in love with him. I have been from the very beginning, since the evening I met him." she gritted her teeth. "Ahhh.... He can be so infuriating sometimes!"

Madeline stopped and caught her niece's hand. "Darling, you put too much pressure on yourself." she reasoned. "All will be well. You both simply need time to get to know each other better. Tell me one thing." She looked searchingly into Elizabeth's face. "Do you want this marriage to be a success?"

"Of course." Elizabeth answered without hesitation.

"Well, if that is so, you must learn to talk to him, and yes, even quarrel with him. I think that he is accustomed to everyone following his lead and listening to him. Still, it does not mean that you are not entitled to your own opinion, even if it does not match his. As for you, my dear, I am afraid that you must accept some traits of his character, even if you do not find them overly attractive. He is a good man, and I do believe that you have a chance to build something worthy together. Do not repeat your parents' mistakes. Tell me, do your parents quarrel?"

Elizabeth shook her head.

"Does it make them happy?"

She shook her head again.

"You see." Madeline started walking. "One more thing, Lizzy. I know how important your father is to you; but now your first loyalty should be to your husband. He is your family now."

Elizabeth sighed heavily. "I know that. But it is hard to change your attitudes in the course of a couple of days."

"Do not worry. It will come naturally with time." Madeline assured her. "In a few years, when you bear several of his children, he will be your entire world. You shall see."

***

Elizabeth knocked softly at the door to her husband's study. Nobody answered, so she knocked again, harder.

"Enter." Darcy's voice was heard.

She took a deep breath and entered.

"William…" she started hesitantly. He was sitting behind his desk, looking imposing and distant.

She lowered her eyes, but heard him moving out of his place.

"Me too." he whispered into her ear.

With relief, she wrapped her hands around his neck. "I hate disagreeing with you." she admitted.

Darcy hugged her tightly and picked her up so her feet dangled in the air. "God how I love you." he murmured.

He put her gently on the floor and walked to the door, locking it.

Elizabeth gave him a curious look, her eyebrows raised. "You want to talk?" she asked innocently.

"Yes. Later." he said, taking her hand into his and leading both of them to the sofa. He sat down, and in one swift movement pulled her on his lap.

"What are you…" she started speaking, but was not given the opportunity to finish because her lips were closed with his.

She relaxed under the sweet pressure of his kiss and returned the embrace. However, very soon, she became aware of his hand tugging insistently at the small buttons at the back of her dress. She closed her eyes and dipped her head into his neck, letting him push the top of her dress to her waist. The next moment, she felt that he freed her from the stays, which were thrown dismissively on the floor.

"Open your eyes." Darcy ordered softly.

She did, and watched as he lowered his head slowly. His mouth closed around one wide pink nipple and started to suckle.

Her eyes rolled to the back of her head. "Oh, William… oh…" she whispered throatily, her small hands clenching on his shoulders. "It feels so… so nice."

Darcy smiled. "You are so pretty." he murmured quietly before turning his attention to the other small breast.

Elizabeth closed her eyes and started to breathe unevenly, letting out small, short gasps. When he ceased the attentions to her breasts, she cried in raw disappointment. "No!" she opened her eyes. "Why have you stopped?" she demanded.

He laughed. "I am a little too overdressed for this." he noted with amusement, pushing her gently off his lap. "Let me at least remove my coat before we resume."

His expression indicated utter surprise when she all but jumped at him, small hands tugging impatiently at his clothes, as if trying to remove all of his outfit at once.

Darcy chuckled. "Easy." he pushed her gently away from him. "I think we will achieve better results if I do it by myself." He stood up and started undressing, first removing his coat and next untying the complicated knots on his neck cloth.

Elizabeth watched him with curious, wide eyes. When she caught the first glimpse of his naked neck, she reached for his hand energetically, making him sit next to her again. Then she unceremoniously climbed back on his lap, astride, and started kissing his neck.

Darcy relaxed for a moment under the assault with a blissful smile gracing his countenance, indicating that at this moment, he considered himself the luckiest of men. As Elizabeth seemed to have successfully attached herself to his neck, his hands were free, and soon wandered under the layers of skirts and petticoats.

He began stroking her smooth, bare bottom when she gradually switched from nibbling at his jaw to kissing his mouth. Very slowly, his right hand moved from one firm globe to the cleft between them.

"Ah…" Elizabeth's voice caught into her throat and her eyes popped out when his long index finger touch her already moist feminine flesh.

His eyes were focused on her flushed face as he began stroking her. His efforts proved to be successful, and soon a loud moan escaped her.

"Be quiet." his free hand clasped over her mouth. "Hide your face in my neck if you must."

She did as she was told, and stayed relatively silent, her moans muffled against his shoulder. Darcy continued his touching, combined with soothing stroking of her naked back.

It did not take long before she first stiffened, then trembled, and eventually relaxed, slumping in his arms.

They did not speak for a while. Darcy cradled her to him, kissing her hair from time to time. It was Elizabeth who voiced herself first.

"You are very accomplished." she murmured.

Darcy chuckled, and very gently pushed her off him, helping her to stand on her own still rather wobbly feet. He bent and picked up her stays, wordlessly helping her into them.

"I am afraid you must hurry, my love." he said, pushing Elizabeth's hands into the short sleeves of her dress. "I have not had the opportunity to tell you that as I was distracted by other matters," he cleared his throat, winking at her. "But my cousin, Colonel Fitzwilliam, invited himself for a dinner tonight when I met him this morning."

Elizabeth seemed not to comprehend, and kept staring at him numbly with a gentle smile on her swollen lips.

"It means that he should be here any moment." Darcy added.

This sobered her. She lifted her hands to her flushed face. "I must look a fright!" she exclaimed, feeling her cheeks being still hot.

Darcy shook his head with smile. "You look lovely, as if you just crawled out of my bed."

"That is not funny." she cried, checking with her hands the state of her crumpled gown and dishevelled curls. "What will he think of me? I must change this dress and ask the maid to redo my hair."

Darcy brought her to him for the last short kiss before unlocking the door and pushing her gently out of his study.

Despite Elizabeth's efforts to make herself presentable, Colonel Fitzwilliam had no trouble to vividly imagine what his cousin and his wife had done earlier in the afternoon. Mrs. Darcy's hair might have been freshly coiffed, and her elegant, white gown perfectly ironed, but her swollen lips and the red marks on her delicate neck spoke for themselves. Moreover, Darcy arrogantly pushed up his chest with every glance at his wife. It was also quite enough for her to catch a glimpse of his hand resting on the tablecloth, and a lovely, intense blush spread charmingly from the top of her forehead down to the lace decorating her dress.

Chapter Seventeen

"It was a very pleasant evening." Elizabeth said, when they were slowly ascending the stairs.

Colonel Fitzwilliam had bid his goodnight and left their company about an hour ago. Soon after, Georgiana excused herself as well, and went upstairs to her rooms. Darcy and Elizabeth had sat alone in the music room for some time yet. He had asked her to play for him, but she had been too distracted to do that properly. Her fingers stumbled over the keys far too many times. It was hard to concentrate when her husband stared at her like that. He sat on the sofa opposite her, and she could literally feel his gaze on her skin. She had managed to finish the song, and proposed to end the evening and retire.

"Yes, it was." Darcy agreed. She trembled when his arm wrapped around her waist. She looked around consciously, to make sure no servant was around to see them.

"Your cousin is very good company," she noted.

Darcy brought her closer and kissed the top of her head as they walked towards their rooms. "He can be very intimidating when he wants."

Elizabeth gave him an unbelieving look.

"He can really be." Darcy tried to convince her with a smile. He opened the door for her and ushered her inside. "Trust me on this. It is a part of his training as a Fitzwilliam, I believe."

"It is so difficult to imagine," Elizabeth said slowly as she walked after Darcy through the private sitting room to their bedroom. "He has always been so amiable when in company."

"In your company," Darcy corrected. "He likes you. He cared enough to make an effort."

He closed the bedroom door after them with a quiet click and walked to the four poster bed. He sat on the edge of it; his eyes focused on her. Elizabeth stood unsurely in the middle of the chamber. After a moment, she began to slowly remove her hairpins with absent fingers.

"You need your own vanity in here," Darcy remarked when she put the hairpins on the smooth surface of a small, richly incrusted writing desk, "I should have thought about it earlier," he murmured as he stood up and walked to her, "We will go tomorrow and order some nice piece for you. Perhaps to Sheraton's?"

Elizabeth's eyes widened involuntarily hearing the name of one of the most fashionable furniture makers in the town. Lady Lucas had a small cabinet from his shop, and it was widely admired by the entire neighbourhood. She was even afraid to think how much it would cost to have a vanity made by Sheraton.

Darcy reached for her and pulled her closer to the bed. His hands arranged her long hair around her shoulders.

"I love you hair."

She smiled in acknowledgment for the compliment.

He brought her to him completely, so she stood between his legs. His large hands wrapped around her slender wrists. He lifted her hands to his mouth and kissed them.

"I have not seen my maid anywhere." she whispered.

Darcy looked straight into her eyes. "I have informed my valet we would not need their assistance this evening."

She held his gaze for a moment before she very gently removed her hands from his. Without breaking eye contact, her hands went to the back of her dress. Soon the fine material of her best evening gown pooled at her feet. She bent, picked it up, smoothed it and placed it neatly on the chair.

She turned with her back to him. "Help me?" she pointed with her eyes to her stays.

Darcy moved her hair to one side, and his lips sucked at her neck. His fingers were quickly busy unhooking the clasps of her corset. Soon the restricting garment was taken off her.

She felt his nimble fingers at her waist, and in no time her petticoats joined the rest of her clothing on the heap on the nearby chair.

She let out a surprised gasp when he effortlessly lifted her into his arms, walked a few steps to the bed and deposited her on it gently.

Elizabeth sat dazed on the still-drawn bed covers for a moment, but her attention was promptly engaged by the sight of her hastily undressing husband.

When his upper body was all bare, she forced herself to avert her eyes. She concentrated on removing her own shoes and stockings. All she had on herself was a short chemise, reaching only to the middle of her thigh. She felt his eyes on her back as she turned to pull the bed covers and move under them.

Her eyes widened to the size of saucers, she was sure, when she laid back, and her eyes caught the sight of her naked husband standing next to the bed.

She did not have a chance to take a longer look at his manly parts, because all too quickly, he joined her under the covers.

"Oh, sweetheart," he murmured thickly and pinned her to the bed with his weight.

At first Elizabeth supported her hands protectively on his arms as he kissed her neck. She felt a bit overwhelmed with his ferocity and passionate response. Slowly she relaxed enough to enjoy his attentions. Her hands went to his cheeks and she brought his face to hers for a kiss.

Their lips danced for a moment, but soon Darcy moved lower, and started to tug at the rest of her clothing. Her chemise was disposed swiftly, and from the corner of her eye, she saw it flying over their heads to land on the floor beside the bed.

His head again dipped lower, and the next thing she felt was the sensation of his warm, moist lips closing around the tip of her breast. She moaned, pushed her chest forward and her hand went into his curls.

His kisses and suckling on her tender peaks brought her pleasure she had neither known nor imagined, but soon she noticed a pattern in his administration. He would begin a new form of touch or caress, and then seemed to wait for her response to determine the success of his efforts. She realized that he was learning her and what she liked.

Darcy kissed back the path from the tip of her breast to her mouth, and brought her tightly to him so they lay sideways.

His tongued slid gently into her mouth, and while his left hand kept her close to him, the right one moved down between their bodies.

She gasped when he touched her like he had in his study earlier that day. Again this sweet pressure began to rapidly build inside her. It was similar to what she had felt sometimes before her marriage while having a bath, and cleaning her private parts. She had discovered quite early in her life that rubbing in a certain way a rough washcloth against the flesh between her legs could bring the most delightful sensations. She was a bit ashamed of it, and had never shared her secret with anyone, even Jane. However, she was sure that she would never again need to do that any more, because her husband's ministrations felt incomparably better than her own feeble attempts.

In no time, she surrendered herself to the sweetest pleasure, and went limp into his arms. On coming to herself, she felt her fingers having been wrapped around something thick, firm and hot. She squeezed it without a second thought, eliciting the immediate groan from William.

She looked down and pulled her hand back immediately, but William caught her by the wrist and put her hand again on his manhood.

Elizabeth hesitated, not knowing what to do, and looked up at him. He shifted onto his back and closed his eyes. She hesitated for a moment longer, and then gently petted this part of him. It moved up. She felt like giggling, but she contained herself. She did not want to offend and humiliate him. Her fingers wrapped around his manhood, and she began stroking it. He had to like it, because his hips began to move up and he groaned a few times.

Soon she learned that what he liked the most was pulling at the thing from the base rather than squeezing it. He took her by surprise when he removed her hand decidedly and pushed her on her back. He threw the covers away and kneeled in front of her.

Elizabeth swallowed. He looked huge and imposing between her legs. His gaze focused entirely on her private place.

He started touching her again with his fingers before he took his manhood in his hand and directed the tip so it touched her flesh. He rubbed against her for a while. Elizabeth felt that once again, the sweet pressure was building inside her. Just as she was about to surrender to it, he stopped.

Elizabeth's eyes opened. He moved her thighs futher apart and combed away the clipped curls she had down there.

He took a deep breath, and she felt as he pressed his manhood against her. Her body accommodated him, and the tip pushed inside her. The sensation was as if she was stretched a bit, but it did not feel bad at all.

His powerful frame moved forward, and he covered her carefully with his body, his weight supported on one arm.

He started a slow, lazy kiss, and as his tongue invaded her mouth, his manhood pushed inside her.

She cried in pain, but it was muffled with his mouth. She tore her lips from his and averted her face to the side.

"Have I hurt you?" he panted over her.

She did not answer at first. She wanted to calm her breathing and do something to make the pain go away.

"Elizabeth," he cradled her face so she had to look at him, "Am I hurting you that much?" he sounded terrified.

She shook her head, "It is just uncomfortable."

She was lying to him, but she did not want to disappoint him. To tell the truth, what she wanted most was for him to finish with it and get off her.

She managed a tiny smile. "I am fine."

He groaned like he was in pain too, and dropped more heavily onto her. He started moving slowly and carefully, his face buried into her neck. The pain was gone now, but still it was very uncomfortable and felt impossibly tight.

Before long, his movements became faster, and he seemed to become lost in his desire. His eyes were closed, the sweat dripped from his back and brow, and he kept panting her name into her ear as he surged into her again and again.

It did not take long before he dropped on her and stopped any kind of movement. His manhood was still in her, but even she could feel it shrinking.

After a moment, Elizabeth tried to shift under him because he was heavy.

"Forgive me." he murmured and slipped carefully out of her, moving on his back.

Elizabeth pulled the covers over both of then and shifted on her side. She felt terribly sore between her legs, and her lower back was tense.

He lay next to her, staring at the canopy. He did not look at her.

She snuggled closer to him. He did not respond. She moved closer again and dipped her face into his neck.

"What is wrong?" she looked up at him.

He sighed and then pulled her tightly to himself. "I am so sorry, sweetheart," he whispered as he kissed her hair, "I will make up it to you… next time."

"Shush," she interrupted him, her finger on his lips, "Nothing wrong happened," she whispered back.

He shifted her on her back, and loomed over her. "Are you all right?"

She cupped his face. "William, do not do it," she pleaded, "Do not agonize yourself. You did nothing wrong," her eyes sparkled, "And as your aunt wisely pointed out, all we need to do is to practice more," she grinned at him.

"My Lizzy," he croaked. He pulled her on him. His hand smoothed her hair and he kissed the top of her head repeatedly.

"Yours," she whispered, "Only yours."

***

William woke up the next morning and jerked up instantly when he realized that the bed was empty.

"Elizabeth?" he cried. "Elizabeth! Where are you?"

He thought there were sounds coming from his dressing room. He pulled on his breeches and stormed into the small room.

Elizabeth was in the bathtub with soap in her hair. Her maid was in the process of pouring hot water over her head. It was enough for him to look at the servant, and the woman left instantly.

He kneeled down by the edge of the tub.

"How are you?" he cupped her face.

She smiled a big, bright smile. "I am very well, thank you."

His serious eyes searched hers. "Are you?"

She placed a peck on his cheek. "Yes, I am."

He smiled, but still unsurely. "Have you finished your bath?"

She shook her head. "Not exactly. You saw the maid was about to rinse my hair when you scared her away."

"I will help you with that," he offered,

"But first I need to…" he walked behind the partition in the corner of the room.

Elizabeth blushed to the roots of her hair. She cleared her throat, "You want to assist in washing my hair?" she asked loudly, hoping to deafen the sounds he was making.

"Why not?" he came back, carelessly buttoning the lap of his breeches.

He reached for the bucket. "Lean forward." he said, and when she did, he started pouring water over her head.

"Thank you." she began to wring the rest of the water from her long, thick hair and she did not notice him removing his breeches.

"William!" she let a small squeak when he climbed into the tub behind her.

He ignored her protest and pulled her to him, with her back to his chest.

"Comfortable?" he asked, wrapping his arms around her.

"Yes." she sighed, as she closed her eyes and let herself relax against his strong frame. Darcy reached for the washcloth, lathered it and started to wash her arms and chest.

They were silent for a while. When he reached below the surface of the water to wash her belly, she sighed and turned around to face him. She took the washcloth from him and started to rub his chest with it.

His eyes focused on her delicate breasts. He touched them gently.

"I still feel terrible about our quarrel the day my father visited," she said quietly as she wetted his hair with the washcloth and started to soap it, "It was not my intention to mention what happened to Georgiana."

"I know," he kissed her mouth, and at the same time stroked her breasts repeatedly, "And I know as well how important your father is to you."

"I cannot bear when he is so displeased with me," she whispered

"William," she tried to remove his hands from her chest, "Do not… tease me," she pleaded, "You do not know what happens to me when you touch me like that." He dove into the water to wash the soap off his hair. When he re-emerged, he climbed out of the tub and helped her out as well.

"Are you cold?" he asked as he enveloped her into a large sheet.

She shook her head.

Darcy handed her the dressing gown which the maid had prepared for her earlier, and started drying himself. He did not care to dress, and was still naked when he picked her up into his arms.

Elizabeth let out a soft gasp. "Are we returning to bed?"

"Have you got anything against it?"

"No…" she hesitated, "But I think that we should rather get dressed, and go downstairs to have breakfast."

He put her on the bed. "We can eat breakfast here this one time. Once we arrive at Pemberley I will need to get up very early. There will be no opportunity for such luxuries as lounging in the morning together. It is our honeymoon, after all."

He joined her on the bed and brought her to him. "You mentioned earlier that we need to practice."

Elizabeth raised her eyebrow. "You want to practice now?"

"Mhhh," he murmured, his hand moving to the ties on her dressing gown, "God, Lizzy I want you all the time," he groaned into her throat.

He took an endless amount of time to prepare her. She panted in his arms, pressing herself to him in abandon.

"Come," he shifted on his back and pulled her on top of him.

Her eyes widened, "Like that?"

"You may like it better," he said as he helped her to settle in, "Let us try it this way. You shall be the one in control."

Elizabeth leaned forward and started a long kiss. Darcy concentrated on stroking her back, and her bottom, from time to time reaching to palm her small breasts, pulling gently at the wide nipples with his fingers.

Elizabeth closed her eyes, rubbing herself against him. She enjoyed the feeling of the thick hair at his groin tickling her, giving her pleasant shivers.

"Elizabeth, please…" Darcy croaked as he lifted his pelvis up in silent plea.

She threw her hair over her back and took his manhood carefully into her right hand. It took her a moment to put the tip inside her. She lowered herself very slowly on the throbbing member, which elicited a throaty groan from its owner.

"Are you well?" she asked him with concern.

He gave a short laugh, "Yes," he placed his hands on her hips, but gently, not trying to control her in any way.

Elizabeth started to move up and down. She did not take him fully in herself yet, but with each movement she felt he reached deeper in her. As she leaned forward, she felt the shot of pressure running from between her legs to her breasts. In this position she found a new pressure on that certain spot he had caressed so devotedly every time when loving her. She moaned quietly which brought Darcy's immediate attention.

"Is it good?" he asked, his hand reached to cup her face.

"Mhm…" she moaned again in a low voice. She closed her eyes and bit her lower lip.

"Thank you, God." he grunted. In one swift movement, he shifted and pinned her to the bed, covering her with his body.

"Aghr…William!" she squeaked, "I was to be the one in control," she slapped him on the chest.

"Sweetheart, please," he murmured, spreading kisses her all over her face, "Do you want to be the end of me?" he panted as he surged deeper into her.

She sighed in resignation and wrapped her arms and legs around him. He chose a steady rhythm, which made the pleasure build gradually between her thighs. He began groaning harshly, and she guessed that he was on the edge of surrendering to his own fulfillment, because his back turned all sweaty.

She closed her eyes and relaxed, focusing on the tension building in her.

"Ahh…" she started panting soon, the pleasure overflowing her. Her nails dug into his arms and the loud moan escaped through her tightly clenched teeth.

It had to be a signal for him, because after a few decisive pushes, he groaned harshly and dropped onto her.

"William," she nudged him after a long moment.

"So sorry, darling," he rolled off her and at the same time pulled her with him.

She yawned, closed her eyes and snuggled even closer to his side.

"I think we need another bath," she murmured, "But perhaps a separate one this time, since we shall want to eventually leave this room today."

His hand lazily stroked her delicate back. "All day in bed… It sounds very promising."

"You know we cannot," she reasoned, "What would Georgiana think?"

He sighed, "Just give me a few minutes to recover," he said. "You exhausted me."

She puffed. "Me?"

"Yes, who would have thought that?" he ran his hand over her bottom, "Such a little nothing like you."

She still pouted, but he ignored her, saying. "How could I ever have even considered living my life without you?" he squeezed her to him so it almost hurt her, "I will never let you go."

Chapter Eighteen

A young, elegant woman knocked at the door of one the newer built houses in the residential part of London. Several moments passed and a tall, handsome butler opened the door.

"Yes, Madam." he asked with a bow. "Can I help you?"

"Good afternoon, John." the woman smiled at him, showing dimples in her creamy cheeks.

The butler frowned and stared down at the woman. Then his eyes widened in recognition.

"Becky?" he whispered.

"You did not recognize me, did you?" she asked as she turned her head to the side.

"No…" the servant shook his head. "What are you doing here dressed like that?" his frown deepened. "That gown… you look like a lady."

The smile gradually vanished from her face. "I came here to see Master."

"He is not at home." he answered automatically.

"Please John, I know that he is here." she insisted. "I need to see him."

"I have strict orders not to allow anyone…"

"He will see me." she interrupted him. "Tell him that his mistress came to talk to him." she looked straight into his face.

John stared at her for long moment; a whole range of emotions crossed his face.

He bowed his head, moved aside and silently let her in.

"I often wondered what happened with you." he said when they reached one of the rooms at the back of the house. "You disappeared so suddenly. I was worried that something happened to you."

She looked up at him. "You are disappointed."

"I would never thought that you…" he shook his head. "I thought you were a decent girl."

"I had my reasons."

He gave a pointed look at her expensive outfit. "Certainly."

"You know nothing about me and why I did that."

He shrugged, "You sold yourself." he said flatly.

"Yes, I did." she acknowledged, her voice calm, "And for a very good price, I assure you."

John knocked at the study's door, bowed his head and walked away from her.

She followed him with her eyes. Then she put her hand on the doorknob and entered.

"I said that no one is to interrupt me." the voice from the back of the room came.

"It is me." she said as she walked into the darkened room.

Brooke lounged in the comfortable chair.

"You?" he looked up at her with a heavy frown, "What are you doing here?"

"How can you sit like that all day long?" she asked and walked to the window. "It's so gloomy here." she opened the drapes and then the window.

Brooke was silent.

She sat on the sofa next to him and gave him a searching look.

"I have not invited you." he straightened in his seat. "I thought our matters were finished." he muttered.

"Yes, they are." she agreed quietly, "I decided to sell the house I got from you. I came to ask you to buy it from me. It would make everything much easier for me."

"You plan to leave London?" he asked.

She nodded. "Yes. I want to buy a nice cottage and perhaps some land in the country so I could live there with my siblings."

"Ah, yes your brother and sister." he stood up and walked to the window. "How are they?"

She followed him with her eyes. "Sally was sick, but she is well now. I saw her last week."

"Really?" he stared down at her. "How old is she now?"

"Almost five years old." she answered.

"And your brother… I remember him to be a bit older?"

"Yes, Henry is twelve now. He learns how to be a carpenter."

"A carpenter?" He frowned. "I thought you wanted to send him to school. You said he was very smart. I thought you wanted him to be a lawyer... to learn some profession."

Becky shook her head. "I am not sure I can afford that. My capital is sizeable, but it must last for many years to support all three of us. I must be very careful with it."

He moved closer and sat next to her. For a long moment, he stared at her pretty profile.

"Sending your brother to school is still possible… who knows perhaps even to university." he murmured, his hand reached to stroke her face.

She glanced at him sharply.

Brooke covered her hand with his. "I am willing to resume our arrangement."

She averted her face and snatched her hand away. "No. I have enough money."

There was a long moment of silence before Broke spoke again. "I could not understand why you never brought your siblings to live with you in your home, and kept them in the country the entire time."

"I did not want them to witness their sister whoring herself." she said very quietly.

"For their sake." he pointed out.

She let out a sigh and looked up at him. "Could you buy the house from me?"

"I can do that."

She lifted herself. "Thank you." she looked at his face. "Who did that to you?" her hand reached to touch his bruised cheek.

"My… fiancée's lover."

"You mean to say her husband." she said tentatively, and seeing his surprised expression, explained. "I do read newspapers. There was an announcement that in a quiet ceremony Miss Elizabeth Bennet of Longbourn was married Mr. Fitzwilliam Darcy of Pemberley, Derbyshire."

He frowned. "How do you know who she was?"

Becky shook her head. "You really know little of me. My sister stays with my aunt, who is a servant at Mrs. Phillips' house in Meryton."'

"You knew from the very beginning."

"Yes. You may not believe me, but I am sorry about what happened to you. You always treated me with honesty. You always paid and never deceived me."

"Yes, I paid you…" he walked to the window. "This time I wanted… I wanted her to really like me… to care for me… I courted her, and I respected her, treated her like a lady… I was ready to give her everything, but she left me. It was enough for that spoilt boy to nod at her, and she ran to him, forgot about me."

Becky walked to him and put a hand on his arm. "I am sorry. I do believe that your intentions towards her were honourable."

Brooke shook his head, and turned with his back to her. "I will die alone, without a wife and children, without anyone."

"You cannot say that. You are still young." she reasoned. "I am sure that you will find a woman who…"

He turned abruptly to her. "You?"

She gaped at him. "What?"

"Will you marry me?"

Becky shook her head. "You cannot be serious."

He placed his hands on her shoulders. "I am serious."

"I was your mistress, you paid me to be with you."

He shrugged. "I do not see the difference between this and a woman who would marry me only for my money."

"You want to marry a lady, not a maid who became a whore."

"Do not say that about yourself. I know very well that I was the only man in your life. And you did it for your brother and sister." He took her hands and brought them together on his chest. "I will sell Purvis Lodge. We can move somewhere in the country as you always wanted; somewhere where no one will know us. I can send your brother to school, and your sister will be healthier leaving in the country."

Her eyes searched his face. "You are serious."

"Was I ever not?" he whispered, "I will take care of you…"

She freed herself from his embrace and walked away a few steps. "I do not know."

"Why? No decent man would take you now."

She lowered her head. "I know that."

"Do you not want to have children on your own?"

"Yes… but… I compromised myself with the thought that I would never have a husband and my own children when I agreed to our arrangement."

Brooke walked to her, took her hand and pulled her to the sofa.

"When we were together I always was careful so there would not be a child." he explained, when they sat together, "I wanted to have children, only with my lawfully wedded wife. But now all will change. You will have your own home, children… I promise that you will lack nothing. You will be respectable. If you want to, we can even leave England… I bought a lot of land in America..."

She bit her lip as she listened to him.

"It is not as easy as you think." she said at last. "Part of me resents you because of what happened between us and what you did to me." she admitted. "I am not sure whether I would ever be able to overcome these feelings and learn be a good wife for you."

"Think about it. Consider it very well." He lifted her hand to his lips. "I will not leave home until I heal completely. Can I pay you a visit next week?"

There was a moment of hesitation before she answered. "Yes, you can."

***

Elizabeth looked apprehensively out of window as the carriage was approaching the village of Longbourn. She did not know what to expect. She was more worried for William and Georgiana's sake than for her own. She believed that her father would be polite enough, if not overly enthusiastic, but she could not perceive her mother's reaction.

Georgiana had been so eager to go with them that William eventually allowed it. They had heard that the regiment had left Meryton a few days ago. William had, of course, been forced to tell his sister that Wickham had been in Hertfordshire for the entire winter. They thought it was better for Georgiana to know in advance about it, rather than to hear the man's name unexpectedly during conversation. Despite the news about Wickham, Georgiana could not wait to meet her new sisters.

When they drove into the lane leading directly to the manor, Elizabeth moved closer to window. She saw Kitty running out of the house. Soon all her family walked outside; her father, too, but he was the very last.

The carriage stopped and the servant opened the door. Darcy got out first and handed his wife down.

"Lizzy!" she heard the high pitched voice, and before she knew it, she was in Jane's arms.

She returned the embrace, rather taken aback by her elder sister's outburst. It was so unlike the usually poised and composed Jane to be so animated. She cried and laughed as they hugged.

Soon Mary, Kitty and Lydia surrounded her too, and each of them embraced and kissed her. They all spoke all at once, which convinced her that she was really back at home.

Her sisters were shoved away, and Elizabeth, for a change, was enveloped in her mother's fierce embrace.

"Lizzy, my child." Mrs. Bennet cupped her cheek. "I am so happy to see you safe and sound."

Elizabeth blinked a few times as she stared at her mother. Mrs. Bennet acted so sincere, as if she had really cared what had happened with her second daughter for the last weeks.

"Thank you, Mama." she whispered.

Mrs. Bennet smiled at her and patted her cheek. Then she turned her gaze to Darcy who stood together with Georgiana a few steps away from the Bennets who gathered around Elizabeth. The siblings stared with round eyes at the loud laughing group consisting of the five Bennet sisters and their mother. Mr. Bingley, who was also present, stood firmly rooted by his friend.

"Mr. Darcy." Mrs. Bennet announced when she walked to the tall man.

Darcy bowed in acknowledgment.

The matron opened her arms widely in an almost theatrical gesture and spoke slowly and very loudly.

"Welcome my dearest son-in-law." She stepped forward, lifted on her toes and placed affectionate kisses on both of the man's cheeks.

Darcy did not say anything, just stared at Mrs. Bennet, who now moved to his sister.

"Miss Darcy!" she exclaimed. "We are so happy to welcome you in our home. My girls have desired to meet you for such a long time. What a fine young lady you are." she said in still unnaturally raised voice.

"Thank you, ma'am." Georgiana whispered.

Mrs. Bennet smiled at her and took Darcy's arm. She looked into the direction of the road and spoke even louder.

"Let us walk into the house. We are so happy that Lizzy caught such a match as you, Mr. Darcy." She looked around. "She could not have done better for herself." she added, and dragged Darcy inside the house.

Darcy stopped and bowed his head when they passed by Mr. Bennet, who barely acknowledged his son-in-law's gesture.

Very pale, Elizabeth touched Jane's arm. "Jane…?" she whispered. "Why is Mama acting like this?"

Jane leaned to her and whispered back quickly. "She had convinced herself that all the neighbourhood has been hidden in the bushes since the early morning, curious about you and Mr. Darcy. I think that she has decided to demonstrate in her own way that we support your marriage."

"Oh, no…"

Jane squeezed her arm. "It is not that bad, sister. She put herself to bed when the news about your elopement and marriage reached us. However, now she seems to be more than content with the fact of your marriage. Aunt Phillips told her that she had heard that Mr.

Darcy was in truth even wealthier than Mr. Brooke ever had been, and that his uncle was a Duke."

"Oh, no…" Elizabeth moaned again.

Jane lowered her voice. "I would be more worried about Papa. I think he has not come to terms with your marriage yet."

Georgiana walked shyly to them, which put an end to their conversation.

Elizabeth smiled at the girl. "Georgiana, I want you to meet my sisters." she gestured to the row of ladies. "This is Jane, my elder sister, and these are Mary, Kitty and Lydia, who is the closest to your age."

Georgiana smiled the tiniest of smiles and curtseyed. "It is a pleasure to make your acquaintance."

Bennet sisters curtseyed as well and smiled at her. There was a moment of silence, before Lydia stepped forward and impulsively reached for Georgiana's hand.

"We are so happy to meet you! Since last autumn, we have heard so much about you from Mr. Bingley's sister. We will have such fun together." Lydia chatted. "Do you like dancing? Do you want to sleep in our room, together with Kitty and me? You must go with us to Meryton to visit our Aunt Phillips tomorrow. She cannot wait to meet you."

"I…" Georgiana found it clearly hard to formulate the answer under Lydia's verbal assault.

But Lydia did not wait for the answer. "She is so curious about you. When we heard that Lizzy married your brother, we asked Maria Lucas to tell us something about you, but as always, she could not say anything truly interesting. She is our closest neighbour, and she says she met you."

"Yes, I was introduced to Miss Lucas in Kent, Miss Lydia." Georgiana managed to cut into Lydia's monologue.

Lydia waved her hand. "Oh, nothing of that. We must address each other by first names as we all are sisters now. What a beautiful dress you have; and your bonnet! So elegant! Is it the latest fashion in London..."

Lydia pulled Georgiana towards the house, asking more questions. Mary and Kitty followed close behind.

Only then did Mr. Bennet walk to Elizabeth and Jane.

"How is my girl?" Mr. Bennet smiled at his second daughter.

"I am well, Papa." Elizabeth beamed at him in obvious relief.

Mr. Bennet offered his arm to Elizabeth, while Mr. Bingley offered his to Jane, and all of them walked into the house.

***

Longbourn was a comfortable, modern house, with spacious and airy rooms both downstairs and upstairs, quite adequate for the family of seven people. However, there was only one official guest room, so it was always a problem to have a larger number of guests. Mrs. Bennet had initially planned to install Miss Darcy in the guest room. Then Jane would move to Mary's room, so Mr. Darcy and Elizabeth could sleep in the room usually occupied by the two eldest Bennet girls.

However, during dinner it was announced that Georgiana was invited by Lydia and Kitty to sleep with them. The girls thought it to be a great idea to move a spare bed from Mary's room into theirs. Mrs. Bennet protested, arguing there would be no room for three beds in one room. Then Mary expressed in a slightly offended voice that she would have been very pleased to invite Miss Darcy to stay in her room, but of course, nobody had even considered that.

Eventually it was agreed that Miss Darcy would sleep with Mary, while the Darcys would occupy the guest room.

The evening ended early, as Jane suggested that their guests must be tired after the journey. Mrs. Bennet supported her, and soon Elizabeth and Darcy found themselves alone in their bedroom.

"At last." Darcy breathed as he turned the key in the door.

"Yes." Elizabeth let out a relieved sigh. "It has not been that bad. I think that Mama is pleased."

"I was even surprised by your mother's… enthusiasm." Darcy noted dryly.

Elizabeth glanced at him with frown. "I think that she meant well." she said quietly.

Darcy did not say anything to that, but Elizabeth noticed that he shrugged his shoulders.

"I am worried about Papa, though." she said, as she walked into a dressing room. "He barely spoke to any of us throughout the entire evening."

Darcy followed her. "I have agreed with him that we will speak about the settlement for you and our children tomorrow after breakfast."

She shook her head. "He is still displeased. I know that."

"I think that he accepted the facts."

Elizabeth took her nightgown out of her trunk. "Perhaps, but I would wish the he would be happy with our marriage the same as Mama and my sisters are."

Darcy stepped closer to her, "Do not think about this today." he murmured into her ear. "Let us go to bed."

"It is still early." she averted the kiss. "Besides, I promised Jane I would talk with her and give the younger girls the presents I bought for them in London."

Darcy pouted. "Can it not wait till tomorrow?"

"I promised, William." Elizabeth said as she reached to the back buttons of her dress and started unbuttoning it.

Silently, Darcy turned her around and helped her first out of her dress, and then the stays. When she was just in her petticoats, she hesitated.

"Could you turn around, please?" she asked weakly.

Darcy only smiled and shook his head. "I cannot understand how you can still be shy with me."

"It is different when we are in bed…" she said as she slowly removed all her clothes in front of him, leaving just her chemise and stockings. "William, please, I need some privacy now." she said, walking behind the partition. "I want to refresh myself."

Darcy sighed, but left the dressing room.

He was lying on the bed when she entered the bedroom twenty minutes later, already dressed in her nightclothes, the heavy mess of her hair let free down her back. She had her arms full of numerous smaller and bigger parcels.

Darcy only shook his head and opened the door for her. Soon he heard the loud squeaks at the other end of the hall. It was clear that the youngest Bennet girls enjoyed their presents.

His valet came, asking whether Mistress would need her maid. Darcy said no, but asked him to prepare his own nightclothes and bring more hot water so he could wash himself.

Over an hour later, he was in bed, already in his nightclothes, but there was no sign of Elizabeth coming back. He waited another half an hour before he put on his breeches and walked into the hall. The house was silent.

He could not remember which room belonged to Jane. He walked from door and door and listened under them. He felt stupid doing that, but it was better than storming into Mr. Bennet's, or even worse, Mrs. Bennet's room.

At last he heard Elizabeth's quiet voice. He knocked softly. The blush crept on his face when Jane, dressed only in a gauzy nightgown opened the door.

"I am looking for Elizabeth." he murmured, averting his embarrassed eyes from Jane's well developed bosom.

"What are you doing here?" Elizabeth's much smaller form appeared next to her sister's.

"I have waited and waited for you." he whispered in exasperation, keeping his eyes stubbornly above Jane's head.

"I thought you had fallen asleep a long time ago." Elizabeth whispered.

"You know I cannot fall asleep without you by my…" he started but stopped, remembering they had a witness.

"Are you coming with me or not?" he whispered furiously, giving only a fleeting glance to the both sisters. Jane looked as if she was on the verge of bursting out in laughter.

He gritted his teeth and looked to the side.

"Go Lizzy," Jane whispered. "We will talk tomorrow."

They were approaching their room, when they heard someone's steps on the staircase.

"It's Papa." Elizabeth whispered.

Darcy grabbed her hand and pushed her into a dark corner, pinning her with his body to the wall.

They held their breath till Mr. Bennet safely disappeared inside his bedroom.

Back in the guest room, Darcy undressed quickly. He did not bother to put his nightgown and slipped under the covers.

When Elizabeth crawled into the bed a moment later, she went into his arms willingly, but when his hand reached under her nightgown, she stopped his hand.

"William, no." she said in a clear voice.

Darcy tried to roll on her. "Lizzy, I need you." he murmured into her lips as his big hand curled around her hip.

"William, not here." she protested. "My mother's bedroom is next to this room, and my father's opposite the hall."

He rubbed himself against her body. "The walls are thick."

She pushed at his chest. "William, no."

"What is wrong?" he mumbled.

"This is my parents' house, and I do not think we have enough of privacy to do this here."

"You say I cannot touch my own wife for the next three weeks of our visit here?" he asked incredulously.

"Well… I do not know… but certainly not tonight. Perhaps we will find some way later. Besides, we have done it this morning." she pointed out rationally.

Darcy stared at her incomprehensibly. "Lizzy…"

She only huffed at him in frustration. "I am worried about my father and everything, and you can think only about one thing." she whispered furiously and turned on her side with her back to him.

That was the first night for Fitzwilliam Darcy under his in-laws' roof.

Chapter Nineteen

Mr. Bennet sat with his now even more extended family in the parlour, taking an early afternoon tea. The room was much too crowded for his taste, as not only his wife and all his daughters were present, but also their guests, Darcy and his sister, and Mr. Bingley, who since his engagement to Jane had seemed to occupy Longbourn daily.

Mr. Bennet realized then that in the years to come, there would be even less peace and quiet in the household. With the older girls married, the grandchildren would unavoidably come, and likely sooner, rather than later. His eyes stopped on his son-in-law. Mr. Bennet sighed inwardly and frowned at the younger man. Darcy sat next to Elizabeth, who talked animatedly with Jane and the well behaved and polite Miss Darcy. Elizabeth did not pay much attention to her husband, very much engrossed in the conversation with the women. The older man observed as Darcy shifted a little closer to Elizabeth, his serious eyes focused on her profile. He looked hungry, as if he had wanted to touch her very badly.

Mr. Bennet cast his eyes on his newspaper, a strange sadness enveloping him. Lizzy was gone from him. What was worse, as much as he was set to resent the man who had taken her away so abruptly and without his consent, he was forced to admit there was not much that he could hold against Darcy as a person.

This serious, brooding, even unsocial young man was not only besotted with his favourite daughter; he seemed to love her deeply and ardently. He was patient and understanding with her, even when Elizabeth tended to frequently forget about his presence, occupied with her sisters and friends. Elizabeth, though clearly infatuated with her husband, seemed not yet to fully match his devotion for her.

Darcy bore all the silliness of Mrs. Bennet, who fawned over him constantly. He bore the impropriety of the youngest Bennets admirably too; although there were moments when a trace of disapproval crossed his face, especially at Lydia's antics.

Mr. Bennet felt that this young man stood above him in many ways, perhaps not intellectually, but certainly Darcy took his responsibilities towards his family far more seriously than he ever had. Darcy would have never allowed any of his children to grow wild and uninhibited as he had done.

The older man tried to convince himself that he should be pleased for his daughter, that she was not married to an idiot like Collins or a creepy, suspicious type like Brooke. Still, he felt sad and defeated. Lizzy would not visit him any more in the library every day to talk with him and discuss the books they read. Derbyshire was so far away. They would see her no more than once a year.

Mr. Bennet raised himself slowly from his chair. "Mr. Darcy," he said in a quiet voice. "Perhaps you would like to join me in the library?"

There was an immediate silence in the room, and all eyes focused on him for a moment.

Darcy stood up. "Yes, sir." he nodded seriously and kissed Elizabeth's hand before turning to the door to follow him.

In the library, Mr. Bennet gestured his guest to the armchair opposite the one he usually occupied himself, and walked away to prepare drinks.

"Here you are." He walked back and handed the younger man the glass of port.

"Thank you." Darcy took the drink.

"I invite you to come here whenever you wish."

The younger man stared at him, trying to read him.

"It is the only place in a house full of women where a man can keep his sanity." he clarified. "I think we will not bother one another."

"Thank you, sir." There was a trace of smile on the young man's serious face. "I do appreciate that."

"Well, well..." Mr. Bennet murmured and returned his attention to his newspaper.

Some time must have passed before there was a soft knock at the door.

"Papa...." Elizabeth's curious eyes peered in.

Mr. Bennet smiled. "Come in, child."

"I have been worried..." Elizabeth looked hesitantly from her father to her husband. "I was concerned... You have been in here alone for quite a long time."

She stood uncertainly in the middle of the room. Darcy put aside the book which he had beed reading and walked to her.

"I see that you came to collect your husband." Mr. Bennet looked up at them. "Well, off you go." He waved at the couple.

***

Darcy was surprised when his wife pulled him out of the library, and without a word of explanation tugged at his hand and led him to the back of the house. They went down the stairs to the cellars where the kitchens were located. She ushered him into a small room behind the pantry. Judging by its very modest furnishing, it had used to be the servant's room.

She turned the key into the door.

"Elizabeth, why..."

She placed his finger on his lips and pulled him to the small bed which took most of the space in the room.

She pushed him on the bed and stood in front of him. "I want to apologize to you." she announced.

He shook his head. "I am not angry at you."

She sighed and peered at him from behind her long eyelashes. "I neglected you, and I was unkind."

He pulled her to him on his lap and kissed her temple.

Elizabeth nestled against his chest. "You have been so patient with me. I do not deserve you."

"Do not say such nonsense. Neither of us is perfect, but we are together, and there is no artifice between us. I detest the pretence and deception. I much prefer your snarling at me and your moodiness than to have a marriage like some of my acquaintances. At least you are honest. I would not survive with a wife who smiles compliantly to my face, but laughs at me behind my back, and who shares my bed only because she finds it to be her duty in exchange for the pin money and the position I can give her. " His embrace around her tightened and he sighed. "I just wish we were already at Pemberley." he murmured into her hair.

"What is it like there?" she asked after a moment.

Darcy smiled. "You will love it. I know you will. I would prefer to stay the whole year there, but I know you will want to come here often, missing your family."

"Let us not talk about this now." she reached for the buttons of his waistcoat. "No one will hear us here." she whispered into his ear, giving him shivers. "No one ever comes over here. Jane will tell the others that you have a headache and that you need a refreshing walk before dinner. We have at least an hour."

Darcy looked at her with surprise painted on his handsome face. From the moment she had brought him here, it had not crossed his mind that it was for that very reason.

"Are you recovered from your indisposition?" he asked in a soft voice against her neck, referring to the monthly bleeding that started just the second day of their stay at Longbourn.

In the years to come, he would learn that it was wise not to entirely believe what his wife would say to him a day or two before this time of the month. She tended to see everything in the darkest colours during those days.

She blushed. "You have noticed." she whispered.

He nodded. "I noticed the blood on the sheets that morning before your maid managed to change them." he admitted. At first, before he had realized what must have happened, he had been truly terrified when he saw the stains. They were large, and much darker in colour than the ones he had noticed after their first time together.

"It ended two days ago." she said, still avoiding his eyes.

For a moment he wanted to tease her about her shyness around him, but contained himself. It was all still very new to her, sharing such intimate things with a man.

Darcy took a quick look around the room. It was hardly a place where he wanted to make love to his wife. It was situated partially below the ground, and there was only one window with a view over the lawn and a flowerbeds. The bed was small and very ancient, though there was fresh looking clean sheet on it. The furniture itself looked very fragile; he was afraid that it would simply crack under their weight. He could not wait for their first night in the Master bedroom at Pemberley, where they would have all the comfort and privacy they deserved. He wanted to have more than an hour with her. *Two more weeks,* he reminded himself. They were to leave just after Jane and Bingley's wedding.

"I need you so, darling." he pushed the short sleeves of her simple cotton dress down her arms, his right hand moved to the small buttons at the back of her gown.

When he opened her dress completely and pushed it down to her waist, she rose from his lap and removed the gown carefully. She laid it over the old threadbare sofa, which stood in the corner. Soon her petticoats followed and she remained in just a short chemise and stockings. She wore no stays that day.

Darcy's eyes were on her as she walked past him to the bed and stretched herself comfortably on it, one leg bent, which left him the clear view of the dark sweet place between her thighs.

Her dark, huge eyes fixed on his face and then moved slowly down his body.

He did not remember having undressed so quickly in his entire life. His clothes, one by one, were thrown over her dress.

"Remove your stockings." he ordered hoarsely in his old haughty voice. He loved to caress her bare feet.

Elizabeth raised one eyebrow, smiled, and began to slowly remove the thin, silky things, her eyes focused on him all the time.

Darcy already bared to his waist, tugged on the opening of his breeches. He sat back on the chair and tried to remove his tall riding boots. During their stay at Longbourn, he went on rides every day to relive some of the tension from his body and mind.

"Leave them." Elizabeth said as she opened her legs slightly wider, her arms thrown above her head. "It will take a lot of time to remove them without the help of your valet, and nearly as long to put them back."

Darcy nodded with his mouth half open as he stared at her.

"I am not sure whether this old bed will bear it." she laughed when he dropped heavily on her a moment later.

He did not waste any time talking. From her face, his lips moved down to her neck, and after pushing back the straps of her chemise, to her bosom. He felt her small hand tugging his breeches down. He helped her, and pushed them down around his knees before he returned his attention to her breasts. He kissed them for a long moment, just the way she liked it, concentrating on the soft undersides.

Darcy lifted himself from her and knelt between her legs. He took one pretty foot into his hand and brought it to his lips.

She giggled.

He kissed the smooth, pink sole.

She giggled again and tried to retrieve her foot from his grasp.

He did not let it go, and blew a noisy raspberry into the soft pads of her toes, which evoked a new wave of prolonged giggling on her part.

Darcy kissed the path from her foot down her leg, ending on the warm, smooth inside of her thigh.

"William." he heard her unsure voice and felt a gentle tug on his hair. "You are not…"

He interrupted her. "Lizzy, let me this time." he murmured as he kissed the top of the mound, just above the line of her curls.

"William," she tugged at his hair again, this time stronger. "I…am not sure."

He looked up into her uncertain, embarrassed eyes. "Just this one time." he murmured. "I will stop if you do not enjoy it. I promise."

She bit her lower lip. "Perhaps another time… when I am clean after my bath…"

"You are always perfect, and very clean." he said earnestly before he lowered his head between their thighs.

Elizabeth sighed deeply, but did not try to stop him any more.

Darcy felt her body to be tense at first, but then she gradually relaxed. He knew himself to be on the right path when her bottom moved uncontrollably a few times and her breath caught in her throat.

He smiled to himself. She usually kept very quiet when he made love to her, or at least she tried to stay silent. He found great pleasure and satisfaction when he managed to make her produce some louder gasp or even a moan. He wanted to laugh out loud with joy at such moments.

He moved up from her, pushed the chemise up a bit and took a good look at her flushed, swollen flesh.

He took himself in one hand, and pushed himself easily into her. She was still very tight, but it was easier for him to enter her than those first few times in London.

He started moving inside her, mindful to bring her as much pleasure as he was able to. All too soon, he felt the need to finish. In his earlier encounters with women, he had been able to control himself longer. However, with Elizabeth he felt too overwhelmed with the experience of making love to her, and was usually so excited by the time he got into her, that it was over much too soon. This time, as well, he was not entirely sure whether she had her pleasure, though she seemed to be close enough.

They lay together for some time afterwards. She was curled by his side, her leg draped over his midsection, her eyes closed.

"We must be going back soon." she whispered lazily, not opening her eyes.

"No." he pulled her tighter to him.

"We must, otherwise Mama will send a search party to find her favourite son-in-law."

"You wanted to say her only son-in-law so far." he reminded dryly.

Elizabeth lifted on her elbow to look into his face. "She is nice to you in her own way. The cook prepares all your favourites every day."

"Yes, I know." he smoothed her hair. "The food is good." he agreed.

"And Papa seems to like you now."

"I think that like is too strong a word. I took you from him, and he cannot forgive me this. I can understand that. I agree though, that he seems to accept me in a way."

"Come. We must dress." she lifted from him and reached for her stockings. "We have to look our very best when we leave this room. Nobody should suspect anything amiss."

Darcy sighed, but did as he was told. They helped each other to put their clothes back on, checking each other's appearance before they left the room.

When they came back to the sitting room, it turned out that during their absence Aunt Phillips had visited shortly. Clearly, she could not wait till the next day to share with the Bennets the news she had heard earlier that day from her husband. Mr. Brooke did not intend to return to Meryton in the future. All the servants from Purvis Lodge were released, and the estate was to be sold.

Elizabeth and Darcy were silent, and did not voice their opinion. Mrs. Bennet returned to the subject numerous times, trying to guess what stood behind this sudden decision of Elizabeth's former admirer. By the end of dinner, she came to the conclusion that it was because Mr. Brooke was heartbroken because of Elizabeth's marriage to another, so he decided to leave the place forever, not to remind himself about the pain of rejection.

Only after the Darcys retired to the privacy of their bedroom, did they talk about what they had learned about Brooke and his plans.

"Do you think he is gone forever?" Elizabeth asked as she snuggled trustingly into her husband's body in bed.

"I do hope so." he said, combing his fingers absently through her hair. "But I do not trust him."

"I am glad that he is gone, and I do not have to see him." she murmured.

He kissed the top of her head. "I am here, you have nothing to fear."

"I know." she whispered before closing her eyes.

Darcy woke a few hours later at the loud banging upon the door. Elizabeth slept soundly in his arms, thus far undisturbed by the noise.

"I am coming." he cried loud enough to be heard.

Gently, he moved from his wife, and lit the candle on the bedside. Then he quickly pulled on his robe and walked to the door.

On opening it, he saw his father-in-law in his nightclothes, and another figure standing in the shadows behind him.

"What is the matter?" he asked in whisper.

The other man moved forward, and Darcy instantly recognized one of his footmen from Pemberley.

"Master." the tired looking servant with dirt on his face bowed. "I came as soon as I could. There was a fire."

"At Pemberley?" Darcy's eyes widened. "Where exactly? How did it happen?"

"It started in the stables. I do not know the reason. When I was leaving, they still could not put it down. We were afraid it would spread to the manor..."

Darcy was about to ask more questions when Elizabeth's soft voice was heard. "William? Has something happened?"

He turned back to look at his wife, who sat wide awake in the bed, the bed covers clutched in her hands up to her chin.

"It is all right, darling. Go back to sleep." he whispered, momentarily changing his voice from harsh and demanding to soft and gentle.

When he turned to the intruders, his father-in-law looked at him with strange expression on his face, which he had no patience to read now. The footman looked to the side; he knew better than to attend Master's personal life.

"I will take your man to the kitchens. He must be tired and hungry." Mr. Bennet said, already walking away from the door, indicating the servant to follow him.

Darcy nodded. "Give me ten minutes." he said as he closed the door.

***

Elizabeth looked out of the window of the running carriage. She could not stop admiring how different the countryside looked the further north they travelled. Gone were the gentle hills and flat planes she had been used to all her life. Here the nature was so much more wild and unrestrained.

"We are almost there." Georgiana said, twisting her slim gloved fingers. "The grounds should start soon." she sighed. "I only pray that the house survived."

Elizabeth reached for her hand and gave it a squeeze.

William had left Longbourn at first light the same night the servant from Pemberley had come. When they had said their goodbyes that morning, he had assured her that she and Georgiana should stay in Longbourn till Jane and Bingley's wedding, and that he would send servants and a carriage for them at that time.

She knew better. Though she could do little to help with rebuilding the estate after the fire, the Mistress' place was there. Her mother had proclaimed herself ill and gone to bed when she heard that Elizabeth was adamant about joining her husband as soon as it was possible, before her eldest sister's wedding.

Mr. Bennet had supported his second daughter's decision though, and Mr. Bingley had graciously offered to escort both ladies to Derbyshire in one of his carriages. First, he had to understandably give his word of honour to his future mother-in-law that he would indeed return for his own wedding in two weeks.

They drove into the park, which was peaceful, beautiful and very well kept. There was no sign of any kind of disorder or damage.

Elizabeth thought that the park would never end when Georgiana exclaimed. "Stop the carriage."

As soon as they came to a halt, Georgiana, without any kind of assistance, opened the door and jumped out of it on the road.

Elizabeth followed her soon.

The manor was magnificent, situated on the edge of a large lake. Only after a moment did Elizabeth notice that the left corner of it was partially destroyed. There was no roof, and there were dark holes instead of windows.

Georgiana stared at the house, and the tears ran down her cheeks.

Elizabeth walked to her and wrapped an arm around the girl's shoulders. "It will be built up soon, and become ever more beautiful than before."

"I know." Georgiana sniffed. "It is only so hard to look at it in such a state."

They walked slowly back to the carriage, and Mr. Bingley handed them in.

When they arrived at the front of the main house, nobody was waiting for them. They walked inside the house, and Georgiana rushed through the assembly of rooms to the part of the house which suffered during the fire. Elizabeth followed her, her eyes widened at the beauty and refined elegance of the interiors.

Finally Georgiana pushed at the last door, and they walked into the burnt rooms.

There were people everywhere, occupied with cleaning the area from the soot and black dust. No furniture could be seen, no glass in the windows, no curtains, and no ceiling or roof. The bright sun was looking into the place. The only proof that it was once a room was the rest of the yellowish wallpapers on the burnt walls.

Georgiana left her side and ran to one of the workers, in whom only after a moment, Elizabeth recognized her own husband. He looked tired, and was dirty from work, no less than the other men.

"Brother!" Georgiana tried to touch him but he stopped her.

"What are you doing here?" he looked over Georgiana's head at his wife.

"Mr. Bingley has brought us." the girl explained.

Elizabeth walked to them. "I am so sorry." she said as she looked with concern at him.

Darcy made a move as if he wanted to touch her but only smiled at her. "It is not so bad. All of the paintings and some of the furniture were rescued." he looked at his sister. "Including your pianoforte."

"It must have been a beautiful room." Elizabeth noted sadly.

"And it will be again." Darcy assured firmly. "Next week the architect from London will come to see to the rebuilding. The new ceiling and the roof must be laid. Then we need to put in the floors and windows anew."

"How can we help?" Elizabeth asked shyly.

His eyes smiled at her. "You can start to think what fabrics and colours to choose for the walls and curtains. This is the first room you will design all by yourself, Mrs. Darcy."

"Good God, Darcy." Mr. Bingley's voice was heard as he stepped inside. "It does not look good. I trust that nobody was killed."

Darcy shook his friend's hand. "Thank you, God, not."

"Has something else suffered?"

Darcy sighed. "The stables are completely burned down." he acknowledged sadly. "Some animals died in the flames, some escaped. We have not found two mares yet. They had to run in the woods."

Bingley shook his head. "Such fine horses."

"Thankfully most of them survived." Darcy said as he put a hand on Bingley's shoulder. "I must thank you for bringing my family, my friend."

Bingley produced a toothy smile. "I had no other choice. Your lovely wife was very much determined to go, the same as your sister. My Jane would be beside herself with worry if they travelled all alone."

"Thank you." Darcy repeated seriously.

Bingley shrugged. "We are brothers now. You would do the same for me if something happened to Jane and myself. And speaking of my lovely bride, I must go back tomorrow morning to be on time for the wedding."

Darcy frowned. "The wedding is in ten days. You must be tired after the journey. Stay a day or two."

Bingley shook his head. "No, I had better go tomorrow." He leaned forward and added quietly. "I promised Mrs. Bennet not to delay my return."

Darcy looked at his friend with understanding. "I see." He cleared his throat. "My dears, you must be tired and hungry." he looked upon his wife and sister. "We shall find Mrs. Reynolds to take care of you."

The company left the burnt part of the house, walking back to the main hall, Mr. Bingley and Georgiana first, Elizabeth and Darcy a few steps behind.

At one moment, Elizabeth took a decided hold of her husband's hand and pulled him inside one of the smaller rooms. Before he managed to say something, she raised herself on her toes, threw her hands around his neck and clung to him.

"Easy, sweetie." Gently, he tried to remove her from him. "I am all dirty and sweaty."

"I do not care." she caught his lips in a kiss. "I missed you." she whispered into his lips.

"I missed you too." he picked her up and twirled her around, not minding any more she would get dirty. "I am so glad you are here." he put her down and gazed into her fine eyes. "You cannot imagine how much it means to me."

Epilogue

Nine years later

Darcy looked dully out of the window of the rolling carriage. They were returning to Pemberley from their three week long stay in Hertfordshire. He was tired. Each visit to Longbourn was an ordeal for him; not so much because of the company he found there – over the years he somehow had got accustomed to his wife's family. Simply, he did not ever like leaving Pemberley for a few weeks, no matter where, nor the reason.

The warm, soft form of his wife stirred slightly beside him, and he felt the gentle push under his palm, which rested on Elizabeth's swollen belly.

He gathered her closer to him, guessing from the slight frown of her finely drawn eyebrows that she was uncomfortable with the baby rolling inside her now.

Travelling across the country with a wife seven months along in her confinement was the last thing he wished for, but when the news had come from Longbourn over a month before, saying that Mr. Bennet had developed a serious bronchitis with the threat of pneumonia, Elizabeth demanded to go to see him, despite her condition. The Bingleys could not go because Jane was in confinement, giving birth to their fourth child.

Darcy had tried to persuade Elizabeth to change her mind about the trip, but she had been adamant. She pointed out that all she felt well and was very fit, which was the truth. Despite her petite frame, she had carried their first child well, and the birth itself of the big infant lasted only two hours. This, her second pregnancy, seemed to resemble the previous one, six years ago, very much. Taking everything into consideration, Darcy had come to the conclusion that the journey to the south would be less strenuous for her, than if she had been forced to worry herself about her father at Pemberley.

His eyes moved from Elizabeth's extended belly to his son, Henry, sleeping peacefully on the opposite seat. His face clouded. Not for the first time, he wondered whether it was his fault that in nearly ten years of marriage she had conceived only twice. All the other Bennet sisters had given birth in the first year of their marriages, three of them, as their mother counted, exactly nine months after taking their wedding vows; but it had taken them almost three years to conceive, his pride and joy, their son.

Darcy looked with love and devotion at his child. The boy had his build and tall, lean figure. Elizabeth swore that he walked, stood the same as him and gestured exactly like him. He seemed to have his disposition as well, and was usually very thoughtful when he eventually spoke. There was a time when Elizabeth had been worried that he had not spoken enough for his age.

As for the boy's face, he was the picture of his mother, with her beautiful eyes and engaging smile.

Darcy shared his wife's bed every night for the sheer comfort of having her by his side, and made love to her much more often than most husbands did after nearly a decade of marriage. Still, for many years there was no sign at all that Elizabeth could have been with a baby again. Her monthly indisposition had come uninterrupted for over five years till last Christmas, when she had announced that he would be a father one more time.

Understandably, he was overjoyed with the news, but again started to consider whether he was the one responsible for the fact that his wife had been with child only twice in the course of nine years.

Kitty, who physically most reminded him most of Elizabeth, having the same small, slim body type gave birth regularly every year since her marriage a few years ago.

His parents had had only two children, and his father had only one sibling too. He, himself, had been born a few years after his parents' marriage, and it had taken them over ten years to conceive Georgiana. Still, he never remembered his mother to be ill before Georgiana's birth, so it was probably not a case that she had suffered from a miscarriage. He remembered that despite the fact she had been nearly forty when carrying his sister, all had gone well when the time had come, and she had recovered quickly after the birth. It had been a lump in her breast which had killed her a few years later, when Georgiana had still been a toddler.

Darcy kissed the top of Elizabeth's head. It was a time to face the truth and admit to himself that it had to be his fault that they had begotten only two children. He had never shared this fear with Elizabeth. He felt inadequate in a way that he could not give his beloved wife more children.

"Papa." his son's sleepy voice brought his attention.

"Shush." he brought a finger to his mouth. "Your mother is sleeping."

The boy moved from his seat and sat on his father's other side.

Darcy brought the boy tightly to him, and kissed his curly head.

"How soon the baby will come?" the child asked in whisper, staring over him at his mother.

Henry, of course, knew that he would have a brother or sister soon. They had not explained this to him, but he seemed to understand that the baby was in his mother's swollen belly. The boy had encountered them a few times when his father spoke to Elizabeth's midsection, feeling the baby's kicks. Darcy did not intend to feed his son with the tales that the new baby would come from the cabbage patch or be brought by a stork. The boy was smart and observant for his age, and spent much time around sheep and horses, often accompanying him on the trips around the estate. He knew exactly from whence the young calf came. He had even once or twice witnessed a birth of a horse.

"Before the end of the summer." Darcy answered his question.

Henry looked up at him. "I would wish for a brother."

"Why not a sister?"

"There are my cousins, Uncle and Aunt Bingley's daughters." Henry explained.

"They have a little boy now too."

Henry sighed. "Still, there are too many girls."

Darcy smiled at him. "Well, we can only wait and see whether the baby will be a boy or a girl."

The child looked at his mother. "Mama's tired."

"Yes. She was worried about Grandfather Bennet because he was ill."

Henry smiled. "I like Grandpa Bennet. He tells me stories and talks to me."

Darcy smiled too. His father-in-law, for the lack of a better word, adored his eldest grandson. He visited Pemberley at least once a year for prolonged stays, spending full days with Henry, walking with him, reading him books and telling him about the world around. Darcy always thought that the older man had never fully forgiven him taking his favourite daughter away from him, no matter how irrational it was. Still, he could not wish for better guidance and company for his son than Elizabeth's father.

Elizabeth stirred beside him and opened her eyes.

"Have I slept long?" she asked sleepily.

"About an hour." Darcy answered.

Henry moved from his father's side to sit beside his mother. With all the talk about the new baby in the family, the boy started to be very possessive about Elizabeth's attention. Darcy remembered that he, himself, had been jealous about Georgiana when she had been born, at least at the beginning.

"Have you slept too, darling?" Elizabeth gathered the boy to herself.

"Yes, Mama." the boy murmured, and snuggled closer to his mother, his little face turned to her side. Henry closed his eyes and seemed to inhale Elizabeth's scent.

They drove for another half hour before they stopped for the change of horses and taking some refreshment.

Darcy walked his family into the best inn in the village, where they often stopped by on their way from the south. The owner's wife recognized them instantly, and invited Elizabeth and Henry into a more quiet, private room away from common travellers. Darcy could return to the carriage to talk with the driver.

"Can I have some cake, Mama?" Henry asked.

Elizabeth sat the boy on the chair, removed his hat and unbuttoned his coat to make him more comfortable.

"Are you not too hot, darling?"

Henry shook his head.

Elizabeth looked at him with concern. He looked pale. She touched his forehead, but it was cool. "Yes, you can have a cake, but first you need to eat something hot, perhaps some soup." she answered his question as she, herself, sat heavily on the chair.

"Yes, Mama." the boy conceded, and leaned against the chair.

Darcy returned, and they were halfway through their meal when the door opened and the owner's wife let another guest inside. Elizabeth looked curiously at the newcomers. It was a strikingly beautiful, very elegant woman, close to her own age, or perhaps a year or two older. She was in the company of two small children, and a young lady who looked to be no more than fifteen years old.

The woman was heavy with child too. Elizabeth guessed that she was ever farther in her confinement than she. Looking tired, she moved slowly to the table on the other end of the small room. As she sat heavily on the chair, her eyes met Elizabeth's; she smiled and nodded in recognition, her hand on her large belly.

Elizabeth smiled back, and a quiet understanding passed between two women.

Elizabeth could not stop herself from observing the newcomers from the corner of her eye. She felt somehow drawn to those people, and she did not know why. The younger children, the boy slightly older and the girl a few years younger than Henry, were very well behaved and quiet when they ate their meal. Soon Elizabeth realized that the young girl was not the woman's daughter, but her sister. The woman's husband was expected to join them any minute.

"Can we go, darling?" William asked in lowered voice as he leaned over to her.

She smiled at his kind face. "Yes, we can. Please, take Henry and go to the carriage. I need a few minutes more to refresh myself."

When her husband and son left, she directed herself to the small side room where, as she remembered from their previous trips, she could wash her face and hands.

On returning, she noticed that the father of the family came. The girl sat on his lap, and the boy clung to his side.

Elizabeth was about to pass by them to the door, when the man raised his head and their eyes met.

A soft gasp escaped from her suddenly dry throat. She stood rooted in place, and could not move; she just stared into his face with wide eyes. Her heart banged in her chest.

John Brooke stood up with his daughter cradled in his arms. He looked at Elizabeth for a long moment before he took a step forward and bowed his head in front of her.

She did not return the greeting. She did not know how, but she managed to tear her gaze from him and move her legs. She did not realize that she ran, till she was stopped by William outside the inn.

"Elizabeth, what is the matter?" he cried, his voice frightened.

"Lizzy, look at me!" he shook her gently.

Elizabeth managed to focus her eyes on him, and later on Henry, whose little hand was tucked into her skirts, his worried face turned up to her.

"I saw him…" she breathed.

Darcy frowned. "Who?"

"That family, that woman and children we saw… it is his family… his wife."

"Elizabeth, but who, whose wife?"

"John Brooke."

Darcy's expression changed in a split second. "Did he talk to you?" he demanded firmly. "Did he try to do something to you?"

She shook her head. "No, nothing like that. He recognized me, but did not try to speak… he stood up and greeted me… I do not know… I ran away."

Darcy crushed her to him and kissed her forehead, not paying attention to the fact that they stood in the middle of the courtyard in front of the busy inn.

"Let us go, Elizabeth." he pulled her towards their awaiting carriage. "There is nothing here for us."

The End

Made in the USA
Lexington, KY
25 March 2010